To Larysa [handwritten]

CW00481496

Driven Into

Exile

with very best wishes [handwritten]

Maria Dziedzan

Maria Dziedzan [signature]

LTP

LINDEN TREE PRESS

Published by Createspace
Copyright © Maria Dziedzan 2017
(ISBN: 978-1542526456)

To all displaced persons everywhere

Chapter 1
England 1990

The mournful strains of the Ukrainian hymn for the dead circled and rose into the bare sycamore trees. The branches dripped melting frost onto the heads of the mourners in the watery January sunlight.

'Vichnaya pamyat, vichnaya pamyat…'

They felt 'Eternal memory' catch in their throats as the melody required them to reach for a higher note, but many in the crowd could not do so. They had either loved the deceased woman or were aware of their own mortality. Old women dabbed their eyes with embroidered handkerchiefs and old men pulled out large white squares. The priest in his black cassock and red stole dipped the gold-handled brush into a bowl of holy water to bless the open grave under the mourners' voices.

As the song died away, he looked across the hole in the clay to the family, a man in his seventies and three younger women. They had agreed there would be a eulogy and he waited for them to gather themselves. He glanced at the husband of the dead woman, but then noticed Nadiya, the youngest of the three daughters, reach into her handbag for a sheet of paper. Clearing her throat, she began in a piping voice:

'Dear family and dear members of our community. Our mother, Natalya, was the light of our lives…'

As her sister continued to speak, the eldest daughter, Lyuba, let her eyes fall on the coffin. Who had their mother been? After her sudden death, Lyuba had tried to absorb the blow of her loss but it had since been compounded by a second shock. Her stomach fluttered with dread as she thought of the incriminating

7

photograph hidden in her handbag.

'May her memory be eternal,' she heard Nadiya saying now over the cold grave. But whose memory? Which woman was her mother, Lyuba wondered: the one lying in the polished coffin, or the young beauty in the sepia photograph?

As Nadiya completed the eulogy, their father stepped forward, took a handful of dirt from beside the grave and sprinkled it over his wife's coffin below. He made the sign of the cross and moved away to make room for his daughters. Lyuba went first but, as she scattered the dry earth onto her mother's grave, she felt a sudden wave of anger. Who are you, she wanted to cry aloud.

Vera went next. '*Mamochko,*' she muttered, more to herself than in any hope of a reply and a release from the nightmare which had begun a week ago. She felt for Lyuba's hand as they moved aside for Nadiya to bend from the knees in her elegant black coat and scatter the earth in a flash of red nail varnish. She raised her lovely eyes to her older sisters and, as so often in childhood, said, 'Wait for me,' as she tiptoed across the ground in her stiletto heels. The three drew away from the grave to be followed by their husbands and children.

Finally the other mourners, friends, neighbours and fellow exiles filed past to pay their respects. They moved forward slowly among the headstones, creating an orderly line of those who dreaded being buried in exile. Their mother country was now little more than a faraway land of mythical beauty, one where unsettling secrets had been left behind with their youth.

***

In the days which followed, all three sisters turned with relief to the routine of work, hoping it would soothe the grief which kept ambushing them at unexpected moments. But Lyuba also had a roiling anxiety in the pit of her stomach as if she were a child whose misdemeanour would find her out. She would sneak into the bedroom she shared with her husband Adrian and take the photograph of her mother from her handbag. She wished she could undo the moment she had found it.

***

'It would be nice to have some photos of Mama to decorate the room for the wake,' Nadiya had said, the week before the funeral.

Lyuba had agreed. 'Will you help me choose them?'

'I'd love to but I can't get away from work. You choose them, Lyuba. I know you'll make a good choice.'

Indeed.

Lyuba had then asked her middle sister, Vera, to help.

'I'm on nights this week and then we've got to register the death and arrange the funeral. Can you manage it on your own?'

'Don't worry… I'll do it.'

And she had. Her father, Taras, had been on his way out to the frozen garden while Lyuba amassed a pile of possible photographs.

'I need an early one of you and Mama.'

He had paused and nodded towards the studio photograph on the sideboard. 'Why not that one?'

'Yes, it's a good one but I don't like this old frame.'

'Well just take the photograph,' he'd said as he had shuffled out of the door.

Lyuba reached for the photograph which had illustrated her life. In it Mama was seated in an armchair, her hair pressed into neat waves, a half-smile on her lips. *Tato* was beside her on the arm of the chair in his best suit and tie, leaning in, his face alight with love. Lyuba turned the old frame over, undid the tacks and lifted the back off. A smaller photograph lay behind the larger

9

visible one. Lyuba frowned but didn't read the handwritten words on the back. Instead she turned the photograph over. It was another posed studio portrait. Two figures looked out at the viewer from the photographer's backdrop of a painted wood. They were partly turned towards one another so that, behind the fall of his jacket and the skirt of her dress, they might have been holding hands.

Lyuba's heart had pounded so loudly she could hear the reverberations thudding through her head. The woman in the photograph was her mother,…but the face of the man was not her father's.

She looked up. Her father was walking away from her down the pale garden. She turned the photograph over. In faded ink it bore the legend:

Buchach 1943
Remember me always, my dearest wife, Natalka, as I will always remember you.
Roman

Lyuba looked at the image again. It was Mama. There was no mistaking her, although Lyuba knew she had never seen her mother look so in love. She shook her head. How could this be?

She rose to follow Taras into the garden but watching his bowed figure, she knew she could not ask for an explanation. Besides, he might not know of this first husband hidden behind the second. In 1943 Natalya would have been sixteen and still living in Ukraine. So what had happened to Roman? Or to Mama for that matter?

As her father had returned to the house, Lyuba stuffed the photograph into her handbag where it had sat like an undigested secret in her aching chest through the funeral and the weeks since…

So who was he? Why had Mama never mentioned him? There he stood in his dark suit with his embroidered shirt, a handsome serious man with his love by his side. Lyuba found it easier to stare at him than at the image of her young mother, her fair hair drawn back from her forehead in two plaits.

Mama?

But there was no answer.

Lyuba had tried to tell Vera. They rang one another almost daily.

'How are you?' Lyuba would ask.

'I'm alright. What about you?'

'I keep thinking I've seen the cat but when I turn around there's no one there. I think it's Mama.'

'I doubt it. You're just overwrought. Don't work yourself too hard.'

'You should talk. I'll bet none of your patients has noticed any change in you.'

'Of course not. I wouldn't expect them to. I'm there to make sure they get well not be burdened by my troubles.'

'Well, I haven't broken down in class yet.'

'I should think not. Your students would hate it. Just give it space when your time's your own.'

'I do.'

'It'll pass. We're grieving and it hurts but it's only early days yet.'

Lyuba felt torn between the comfort of her sister's advice and a desire to shatter what she saw as Vera's complacency. But she couldn't bring herself to share the knowledge of the photograph over the phone.

'I don't suppose Nadiya's rung you,' said Vera.

'No. I expect she's too busy.'

'I think I'll give her a ring. She might need a break from her perfect exterior.'

'She certainly won't be bursting into tears at work.'
'No, but she might be at home.'

***

The girls had waited for several weeks after their mother's death to clear her clothes from their parents' bedroom. Their father had not been able to face the finality of the ordeal, but the day came when Taras said he was ready for them to tidy away her things. They went obediently to work. They had dreaded this moment, the handling of her private possessions and the finality of empty drawers.

There should have been three daughters to face the task together, but their youngest sister, Nadiya, had once again been unable to get away from her job. Apparently. Lyuba and Vera had raised their eyebrows at one another when their father said she had rung him to make her apologies.

'Didn't risk ringing either of us,' said Lyuba as she and Vera went up the stairs to their parents' bedroom.

Vera shrugged. 'What did you expect? Anyway, we'll manage.'

They entered their parents' sanctuary where their mother, Natalya, had been able to retire for some privacy, and the girls, although now grown women, could not repress a little smile at each other as they tiptoed into this 'holy of holies'.

They began with the wardrobe. They sorted through the outfits of the woman they had known into piles to be given away or recycled. All the beloved, embarrassing items of clothing were subjected to a moment's scrutiny before being folded onto one or other of the growing piles, the scent of their mother so present and yet never so absent. Her embroidered blouses were inspected and they set aside her second favourite orange on black for Nadiya. Mama had been buried in her favourite, the black on white. They shared the Ukrainian headscarves and put some aside for their sister and their own daughters, Valeria and Lydia.

Neither of them felt Mama's murmur in the room, nor had they since they had viewed her dead body in the hospital, so peaceful, the lines of worry and loss fallen away. They sorted almost light-heartedly.

'Oh, this hat,' Lyuba popped it on, patting the unflattering soft round cushion of a crocheted chenille hat.

'Not as bad as this one,' said Vera, putting on a firm flying saucer covered in taupe chiffon.

Their mother's insistence on a hat for church had accompanied them throughout their childhood, although recently the hats had been chosen for their ability to keep an old lady's head warm.

They turned to their mother's linen cupboard on the landing.

'Let's give this a good sort out while we're about it,' said Vera. 'We could recycle some of the really old things and perhaps share some of Mama's embroidered pieces.'

Once again the piles grew but the sisters' work slowed as they examined their mother's sewing. There were embroidered cushion covers, table cloths and the inevitable pile of *rushnyki*. These long pieces of fringed linen were embroidered with heavy borders at each end to be draped over the family's icons.

Vera reached into the farthest corner of the shelf for the last one. 'This is an old one,' she said, opening out the yellowing piece of fabric.

'It is. The weave's much coarser than these others,' said Lyuba. She ran her hand over the cloth.

'What is it?' asked Vera.

'I've never seen this one before.'

'No, neither have I.'

There was a pause. 'Am I missing something here?' asked

13

Vera.

'Perhaps. Wait a moment,' said Lyuba. She went downstairs and returned clutching her handbag to her chest.

'What…' began Vera.

Lyuba opened her bag and thrust the photograph at her sister. She watched as Vera took in the implications of the image and its message just as she had done.

Eventually Vera asked, 'Where did you find this?'

'Hidden in the frame of Mama and *Tato*'s photo. The one on the sideboard.'

'Hidden? Why?'

Tato's deep voice startled them both.

'What was hidden?'

They leapt back startled.

'Nothing, *Tatu*. Just an old photo.'

'Let me see.' Their father advanced, hand outstretched.

Lyuba and Vera exchanged a helpless glance.

'What is it?' Taras repeated. 'Let me see.'

Vera reluctantly held the photograph out.

He took it in his gnarled and stiffened fingers, glanced at it and sighed.

The girls watched their father's face intently but still he did not speak.

'And there's this *rushnyk*,' said Lyuba, prompting him to admit ignorance, or to offer an explanation.

'You don't understand, girls,' he said at last. 'It was the war.'

'What was?' urged Vera. When he did not answer, she asked him directly. 'Did you know about this, *Tatu*?'

He looked at his daughters. 'Yes, I knew. Do you think your mother would not have told me? She told me in the camp before we got married.'

They waited to see if he would say more, unwilling to nudge him into painful territory. Lyuba noticed he had not shaved that morning and how white the bristles of his beard were.

'Yes,' he said again. 'That was the war.'

'So who was he?' Vera insisted.

'A boy who came to her village. He was in the resistance, the Ukrainian Insurgent Army. They had to marry secretly. She could have been shot or deported otherwise.'

'Was that when Mama left home?'

'Yes. She didn't know how much other people knew and so she 'volunteered' to go with the slave labourers.'

'But wouldn't that have put her in more danger?'

'Not really. No one could accuse her people of harbouring a traitor if she'd gone to work for the Germans. The Nazis might have shot her family or even the whole village if they were certain someone had been helping the partisans.'

'So she left her husband and her family?'

'All in one day.'

'One day?'

'Poor Mama!' Now as the girls leaned in to look again at the woman in the photograph there was a sense of wonder at the unknown life she had led, before she had entered their family mythology.

'And *Natalka*?' asked Vera.

'What do you mean?' asked her father.

'Well, you…and everyone, always called her Natalya.'

'Yes, we did.'

There was a moment's silence as they absorbed the implications of this and then Lyuba opened the *rushnyk* she was holding. 'Did she embroider this for her wedding?'

'Yes. She carried that with her all through the war.'

'So why didn't she use it here?'

He shrugged. 'It was her first life. This was her second.'

The girls stared at him.

Taras seemed to be pulled out of his dreams of the past.

15

'This was a different life.'

'But not one she would have chosen?'

'Nobody here,' he said, meaning the diaspora, 'nobody would have chosen what happened to them. Everybody wanted to stay at home.'

They were silent for a moment. Taras looked out from his own loss and saw his daughters' uncertainty. 'You were named for her sisters. There wasn't a day when she didn't think of them. But she loved you too. You know how much she cared for you.'

'Yes, *Tatu*, but it's a shock,' said Lyuba, almost apologetically.

'Of course it's a shock. You think you understand where we came from and how we had to live, but you don't know how it really was. Your Mama was sixteen when she left home…'

Chapter 2
Western Ukraine 1943

The path beside the river begins to rise, and apart from saving our breath for the climb, we can't continue our talk for the roaring of the water. It comes down in a great silvery surge, pouring itself out of the mountain above into the dappled light coming through May's green leaves. On a day like this I can't believe I'm on a serious mission to carry propaganda leaflets. Roman and I should be out for a stroll. I look up towards him among the trees and although he has his back to me I know the expression he'll be wearing. His determined face. He's going with his *kurin,* his unit, to blow up German supply lines letting me share part of their journey with them. Vasyl and the rest of the men are behind me, and I don't care that Vasyl disapproves of my being here. He thinks I might distract Roman. Not much hope of that. I hear a cuckoo on my right among the trees, its two notes counterpoised against the rushing water.

We climb until I need to stop to catch my breath, then Roman turns. He waves as if to say, come on, we're almost at the top, and he grins, deepening the dimple in his chin. His cap is pushed back and his dark curls flop over his forehead. My breath catches in my throat for love of him, surrounded as he is by the green and gold of the wood.

A shot rings out… and he appears to dive onto the stony path. What's he doing? Has he tripped? Is he taking cover? Surely we can't be seen. Before I can move forward to ask him I find myself being pulled roughly to the ground.

Vasyl lies half on top of me, his hand clamped over my mouth. He hisses in my ear, 'Keep quiet!'

When I try to ask him what's happening, he just tightens his fingers over my lips. The others have rushed past and I hear more shots as they disappear over the brow of the hill among the trees.

We're being fired upon. Roman! He'll need my help. I try to push Vasyl off me to get up and go to him.

'Stay here,' he grunts and gets up to run towards Roman. He's bent double. I get up. I can do that, too. But Vasyl turns, pointing his finger as if he'd like to shoot me. 'Stay there,' he mouths. Reaching Roman he bends to touch his neck. He gives the slightest shake of his head and turns to follow the others through the trees. I watch him running from the cover of one trunk to another.

I wait until I can't see him then creep forward as quietly as I can. I reach Roman and lean over. I can smell his still-warm scent. I don't think he's breathing, so I touch his neck beneath his jaw. I can't feel a pulse so I try the other side. His neck is bristly despite that morning's shave and I manage to half turn him over. There's a blossom of blood on his chest and his head falls back heavily against my arm. I cradle him to me and kiss his dear face, his open eyes, his lips. Roman…Roman…Roman…I rock him to try to stop the pain.

But I'm dragged away. Vasyl's furious. 'Get up! Get up, you fool!' and he's dragging me again.

I almost sprawl to the ground, he's pulling so hard. 'Get off me!'

'Come on! You'll get us both killed.'

He pulls my arm and we run downhill through the trees. I have to fight to keep my balance, but as soon as I feel his grip loosen I tear myself away and start back uphill again. Grabbing my legs he pulls me down, pushing my face into the fallen leaves. I manage to scream Roman's name.

'Roman's dead!' He holds me down so I can barely breathe.

He repeats, 'Roman's dead.'

He can't be… He turned to me… He was smiling… 'He's not!' I say.

'He is. And so will we be if we don't get away.'

'We can't leave him.'

'We have to. Come on.'

'What about the others?'

'They're dead, too.'

'What? All of them?'

'All of them. Now, for God's sake, come on.'

He gets up and pulls me with him. I have no choice but to follow as we run downhill. I'm stupidly afraid of falling or tripping and I run until we're at the bottom of the path we took only an hour or so ago. He drags me into a green cave among the hazelnuts. We both try to catch our breath.

I don't want him to have enough breath to speak and when it looks as though he has, I turn away.

'Roman's dead, Natalya. So are the rest of the *kurin*.'

I shake my head and try to speak. 'No…' but it comes out as a moan.

'They knew we were coming,' he says as if he's working it out. 'They were expecting us.'

I look at him, not knowing what that's got to do with my tears. 'What?'

'A *syksot*, Natalya. We were betrayed.'

'But who?'

'Anybody. For the right price.'

'No. No one would betray Roman. He was loved.'

He nods as if I'm a child. 'Yes, he was loved. By some of the villagers. The patriots.'

I gape at him. Which of our neighbours would have given him up?

'You're in danger, too, Natalya.'

19

'Me? No one knows what I do.'

'Don't be so sure. You keep odd hours. It's easy to notice things in a village.'

'No. I'm always careful.'

He shakes his head. 'No one is invisible.'

I am. I know I am.

But he won't let me hold onto my illusion. 'Think about it, Natalya. Why would a German unit be waiting on this hillside? Look around you. Why weren't they over there?' He points to another mountain. 'Or over there?'

I shrug. I know I'm being childish, but I can't give Roman up yet.

'Come on,' he says.

'I'm not leaving Roman.'

'Natalya, Roman's dead.'

What he says next gives me pause.

'I promised Roman I'd make sure you were safe if anything happened to him and that's what I'm doing now.'

'How can you make me safe? You said we'd been betrayed.'

'I'm taking you home. You're going to Germany with the next batch of labourers.'

'You're crazy!'

'No, I'm not. You know perfectly well what the Germans do to traitors.'

'I'm not a traitor.'

'Natalya, we're at war. What have you got in your bag?'

I pull my canvas satchel round, but keep my hand over it. 'Just a few leaflets.'

'Propaganda. That alone would get you and your family shot. You may have been seen joining us in these woods.'

I try to say something but my breath is snagged on the rock of my family being shot. I manage to say, 'Mama? My sisters?'

'Yes, Natalya,' he draws out the syllables as if I'm stupid.

'Your mother, Lyuba and Vera…the whole village if they've a mind to.'

'No…' I can't get my breath.

'Yes. You have to go to Germany, then you'll seem like one of theirs.'

How can I go? I don't know where those workers go or what they do. How can I just leave everyone…and Roman…still lying on that hillside. I'm about to tell Vasyl I'm going nowhere but he says, 'Alright. In a minute we're going to set off and while we walk I want you to think this over. Roman knew we could all be killed. It's not going to be easy with the Nazis. They want Ukraine for the same reasons as the Bolsheviks – a breadbasket with slaves to farm it. Roman knew your situation could become dangerous. He asked me to try to get you out of this mess if I could. That's what I'm doing. You're going to be in the next shipment of slave labourers to Germany. Do you know when they're going?'

I hear myself say, 'Tomorrow.'

'You'll be going, too.' He turns away to set off.

'Wait,' I call out. 'I can't leave Mama…'

'You have to. At least you'll get a chance to say goodbye. Lots of people don't.'

'But…'

'We'll be back in your village by nightfall. You'll have time with your mother and sisters. You'll have time to gather your things. In the morning, you'll go.'

'I won't be on the list.'

'I'll sort that out tonight before I leave the village.'

I try to think of some other reason why I can't go but he shakes his head. 'Natalya, I didn't think you were so naïve. Where have you been these last months? Did you think we were playing games?' He sets off at a smart pace.

I'm ashamed and embarrassed so I follow him. He's right.

I've been living in my own world of Roman's smiles, our secret meetings and the biggest secret, our partisan wedding. I have so much explaining to do to Mama when I get home.

When we reach the edge of the woods Vasyl stops. 'Go to the village green in the morning ready to travel to Germany. I'll have sorted everything out for you.' He points to my canvas satchel. 'I'd better have those.'

'Alright,' I say handing the whole thing over.

'Go with God,' he says.

I know he thinks we'll never meet again, but I manage to mumble, 'You, too,' and I set off across the field alone.

***

Our house lies in a hollow at the far end of the meadow full of flowers which have already closed their petals for the night as the sun pours the last of its pink light across the grass. My heart aches for the beauty of it. Who knows when I'll see it again? But I pull myself together as I reach home and check everything is as it should be and go indoors.

Mama's still tidying the warm kitchen and the girls are sewing beside the lamp. Mama looks across at me. But there's no fooling her. The first thing she says is 'What happened to you?' How does she know? She comes towards me and I can't help myself. I'm sobbing and she's holding me and soothing me like she used to when I was little. But I haven't just fallen over and bumped myself this time. I've lost my husband and I'm about to lose my home.

For what seems like a long time I keep crying. I can't stop. But when I do Lyubka passes Mama a cool cloth to wipe my face like a baby. I've been doing this all afternoon. Behaving like a child. I'm going to need to grow up soon.

Mama says, 'When did you last eat?'

I try to hold the tears back again. I can't say before Roman died so I just shake my head. She gets up to warm me a bowl of *borshch,* and little Verochka undoes my jacket and helps me out of it.

Mama's wisdom works. After I've eaten she sits opposite me, waiting. I glance at Lyubka and Verochka, wondering if they should hear what I have to say, but Mama reads my mind again.

'It's alright. They need to know the dangers if they're to be safe.'

I shake my head. 'None of us is safe.'

'I know that. As safe as we can be.'

Where to start? 'I was going to deliver some leaflets. It's better if I don't tell you where to.'

Mama nods, encouraging me to go on.

'I was going to go part of the way with Roman and his *kurin.*' I turn to Lyubka and Verochka. 'He was shot.' I can't go on for a moment and Mama's 'My little daughter' almost undoes me. But I tell them, 'He was killed.'

The girls begin to cry. I hold Mama's hand and I don't know who's hanging on tighter, she to me, or me to her.

'They all were, except one. He brought me back.'

'Natalya,' Mama breathes.

'We were married, Mama. Roman was my husband.' I can't say anymore because I'm crying again.

She's staring at me. 'Married?'

I manage to blubber, 'It was a secret.'

Verochka bursts out, 'Why didn't you tell us?'

'Because she could have been shot as a traitor,' says Lyubka.

'Natalya?' asks Mama.

'In the mountains, Mama, with the chaplain to the partisans.' Then I say, 'I'm sorry.' She understands I'm apologising for not having told her, and not for marrying Roman.

She's ahead of me though. 'Are you…?' as she glances at my

abdomen.

'I don't think so.'

She sighs with relief. One less problem to deal with.

'It was a trap, Mama. Someone knows…knew… we were going that way.'

I can see her thinking this through.

'They may know I've been acting as a courier for our boys in the forest.'

She looks resigned now. I've only confirmed what she suspected. She's holding herself stiff and I know she's waiting for the next blow. She knows it's not over yet.

'I have to leave,' I say. 'Tomorrow.'

They all look shocked at that.

'Tomorrow?' repeats Lyubka.

'Where are you going?' asks Verochka.

'To Germany.'

Mama looks as if this is what she'd expected me to say but the girls start to bawl.

'Hush, children,' says Mama. 'Lyubka! Verochka! We don't know who's listening. You have to be grown up. Natalya is in danger, but so are we.'

They look at her wide-eyed.

'If Roman was betrayed,' she goes on, 'then Natalya may have been betrayed, too. That means we could all be shot.'

There's a gasp as a memory flashes across both girls' faces of what seemed like dozens of booted and helmeted Nazis pointing their rifles at two women and a man in the middle of the street in Buchach on an ordinary market day. They had their arms raised and the German lieutenant just nodded to his troops to fire on the civilians. The rumour was they'd been helping the partisans, but who really knew? The Germans shoot whoever they want to shoot. That day, the bodies had been left lying in the street for all to see.

I can see the girls are going to start crying again, so I say, 'It'll be alright. If I go to Germany no one can call me, or us, traitors. You and Mama will be safe. You'll be left alone. I'll write to you and come back when I can…' I trail off.

We all pretend I'll be able to come back. We've seen so many young people from our village go but not one has come back yet. We make ourselves busy, packing for my journey and, just in case, warm clothes for the winter. I go into our bedroom, to my side of the bed, and pull out from beneath my pillow the *rushnyk* I'd embroidered for the home Roman and I might share some day. Tucked in its folds is the expensive photograph he'd insisted we have taken.

'You're not having a proper village wedding, at least let's do this. We'll have something to remember the day by.'

As if I'd ever forget it.

But I'm glad now that I have this photo of him. He's serious in it, but I can still see the dimple in his chin. For a second I see his face, split in a broad grin, his eyes twinkling…then all I can feel is the weight of his head against my arm when I held him on the path.

'What's that you've got there?' asks Lyubka, coming into the room we've shared all of our lives.

I pass her the photograph. I can see she's taken with the romance of it. She doesn't see a bloodied body on a stony mountain path. 'Natalya, it's lovely,' she says. 'Can I show them?'

I nod and she hurries out into the kitchen to share it with Mama and Verochka. I hug the *rushnyk* to me. It won't ever hang over an icon in our house as I'd imagined when I was stitching it. But I can't leave it behind.

I go into the kitchen where the three of them are huddled over the photo. Mama looks at me. 'At least you'll have the memories,' but I see her grief. She can't decide whether I'm a girl or a woman, and the woman in her can't help but tell me she knows how it feels to be a widow. She covers the moment with characteristic pragmatism. 'You'll need this,' she says, handing me a clean white sack for my things.

'Come,' she says. 'Let's say our prayers, then we should try to get some sleep.'

We kneel before the icon and Mama leads us in our devotions as we pray for our safety and for the souls of our dead, *Tato* and Roman. She gets to her feet with a struggle and I make a mental note to tell Lyubka and Verochka to look after her. Grief makes you old.

We pretend to go to bed calmly, but even though we try to lie quietly, we can't help turning over from time to time as our thoughts banish sleep.

I do sleep for a while and wake with the glimmer of pre-dawn light. The girls are both asleep and I creep out into the kitchen where Mama still sleeps in the bed she used to share with *Tato*, behind the stove. But she's up so we sit at the table drinking tea together. She takes my hand as she used to when I was little and I know she's trying to hold back a world of advice.

I smile at her. 'It's alright, Mama.'

'Just be careful,' she says, 'and let us know how you are whenever you can.'

'I will,' I say.

'You've learned to keep your secrets,' she says. 'You know you mustn't trust anybody. Don't tell them anything.'

I know she's afraid that in my girlish loneliness I might long to confide the story of my partisan husband to a new friend, but I remind her, 'Did you know?'

She shakes her head.

'No one else will either.'

'Good,' she says leaning forward to kiss me on my forehead. She gets up and brings to the table the parcel of food she's been preparing for me to take.

'No, Mama, I can't take all that. You and the girls will need to eat too.'

'We will. We have food here and I know we'll have more. Take this.'

She's giving me food to armour me against the world and to make herself feel better, so I take it. As I'm packing it in my bundle the girls get up and it's all bustle till we leave the cottage for the departure at the village green.

I try not to let Mama and the girls see me taking my last looks around the kitchen with its bunches of herbs above the shiny tiled stove and the bench against the wall where the three of us sat while *Tato* ruled the table and Mama laboured to feed us. I go out into the yard and try not to remember *Tato*'s dead body the morning the Russians shot him. We let the hens out as we go towards the lane. The marguerites shine in the hedgerows.

My stomach is churning as we join our neighbours climbing up towards the centre of the village where we can see a hubbub of families like ours and, scattered among them, the grey uniforms with their hated insignia. I avoid making eye-contact with any of the people I've grown up with and go to stand in the queue of women. They're waiting quietly for the bespectacled German clerk to check them off a list. Standing behind him in a flat cap and jacket is the *starosta's* secretary. He gives me the briefest of nods and we both take our eyes elsewhere.

As each young woman reaches the German clerk, they go through the same ritual of '*Heil Hitler!*' followed by 'Name?' and then they're ticked off the list and gestured towards the waiting wagons. When I get closer I see the list is in alphabetical order and I wonder whether Vasyl managed to get my name typed into the right place. My heart's thumping as it's my turn to look down on the clerk who holds our fate in his hands.

'Palmarenko, Natalya Ivanovna,' I say.

He looks under 'P'. I'm not there. My mouth goes dry wondering if Vasyl gave my married name, but the clerk looks straight at the end of the list where there are half a dozen handwritten names. I'm there. Under my maiden name. He ticks me off and I get the nod and I'm through. I'm so relieved to be sent into exile, I almost smile at him. But I gather myself and turn to say my last goodbyes to Mama and my sisters.

Lyubka and Verochka are watching me anxiously, although Mama is showing her calm face. I know that look. She has shown it to us in public all our lives, but it still means, Where's my child? Is my child safe?

For now, Mama. For now.

I hug the girls. I tell little Verochka, who's only eleven, 'Listen to Mama and Lyubka'. Then to Lyubka, who's thirteen, I say 'Take care of them. I'll send what I can.' She knows what I mean. She's the eldest now and, although Mama is still healthy, Lyubka's the next in command in our shrinking family.

She sticks her chin out, and for once I don't want to slap her for doing so. She says, 'I will. And you take care among these…'

I hug her close to me, reminding her in a whisper of what Mama is always saying, 'Not outside the house.'

Then I turn to Mama. I don't want to do this, dearest mother of mine, but she makes it easy.

'God bless you, my dear daughter.' She kisses me on the forehead. None of the fierce hugs and dry sobs that we had at dawn, but a formal blessing on the village green.

'Thank you, Mama,' I say. She knows all that that encompasses, and as I feel the tears begin to sting she makes a gesture as if to push me away.

'Go and get yourself a good seat in the cart. You've got a long journey.'

Grateful to her again for releasing me I cross the dusty ground to climb into one of the carts. The women shuffle along the seats to make room for me and as I nod my thanks I notice how festive our white headscarves look. They belie our boots, our coats and warm jackets which are all too much for May. Where will we be in December?

It's not long before the queue at the clerk's desk has gone and those who are leaving are on the carts. Our Nazi escort gives a signal and we're off, flanked by several grinning soldiers watching another delivery of livestock. People call 'Goodbye' and 'God bless' as our drivers click their tongues to their mares and I turn to my own little family. Mama has one hand on her breast, but she's raised the other in what cannot be described as a wave. I see Lyubka and Verochka falter, but Mama's lips move and they pretend to smile as they wave me off. They begin to shrink behind the curtain of dust as we gather speed along the lane and I have to turn away. I look instead at our mares, bravely pulling us along, one accompanied by her faithful foal, which trots close to its mother's flank.

As the beloved fields begin to fall away I make myself focus on the trees which line the lane – linden, walnut, cherry. As we pass the outskirts of the forest, I look straight ahead at the stout back of our driver. All I have left of my beloved partisan is hidden in my bundle.

Chapter 3
England 1990

Lyuba groaned when she heard the bell ringing for the next lesson. She checked the noticeboard as she left the staff room.

'Have you got a cover?' asked her friend Jan.

'Yes,' complained Lyuba. 'I've got so much to do.'

She hurried along the corridor to supervise a History lesson for an absent colleague, trying to control her frustration at not being able to complete a hundred and one tasks of her own in the next fifty minutes. She set up the work which the GCSE group had been left, then, as she patrolled the classroom to ensure that each pupil was settling to the essay, her eye fell upon a shelf of books to the left of the teacher's desk. *The War in the East* seemed to leap out at her. She lifted it off the shelf, wondering whether the title referred to Europe or the Far East. Flicking open its pages she saw a chapter headed *Ostarbeiter*. As she read the opening lines of the chapter her heart began to thump:

'*Germany was facing a manpower crisis at the end of 1941, so Hermann Goering instigated a recruitment campaign in Ukraine from January 1942, drawing young men and women to German factories and farms as Ostarbeiter, workers from the east, but, in actual fact, slave labourers…*'

She stopped reading, flipped forward to the pages of photographs, and saw Eastern European women bundled in ill-fitting coats, their heads covered by headscarves and all carrying some kind of makeshift luggage. The description beneath the photograph read, '*Unknown Ostarbeiter departing for Germany; probably Kiev 1942.*'

Lyuba felt her mouth go dry. Mama would not be in this photo as she had been taken from Western Ukraine a year later, but she had been taken like this. Lyuba turned the page and saw another photograph of two long cattle-trucks stretching away from the viewer. Between them, crowds of men and women were clambering into the trucks, watched by German soldiers in long military coats, belted at the waist, their pistols clearly visible. She scanned the caption: '*Young Belarussians being shipped to Germany as forced labour 1943*'. Had this been Mama's experience, too, she wondered and felt her chest aching with tension.

'Miss, Miss!'

She pulled herself back to the classroom and turned to face the students. 'Yes?' she asked, as she scanned the room for the pupil who had spoken.

A heavily made-up girl in the far corner beckoned her. 'I'm stuck,' she said as Lyuba approached.

'OK. Let's have a look. Where have you got to?'

Lyuba dealt with the enquiry. However, the girl's question had not only shattered the silence, but had opened the floodgates as one student after another sought help or reassurance, or simply work avoidance. She dealt with their problems, but by the time the bell announced the end of the lesson, Lyuba had had no opportunity to return to the book.

She popped her head around the door of the History Department's office. 'Year Ten were fine. They've taken their work with them to finish for homework.'

'Great. Thanks,' replied one of the History staff.

'Can I borrow this?' Lyuba held up the book.

'Yes, sure.'

Lyuba hurried away along the teeming corridor with her

treasure clutched to her chest.

***

Vera heard the phone ringing and sighed. She had just returned from working the night shift and was on her way upstairs to bed but she was alone in the house so she had to answer it. She dropped down the stairs again and lifted the receiver.

'Hello.' She made no attempt to hide the weariness in her voice.

'Hi, Vera, it's me,' she heard Lyuba say. 'I just wanted to catch you before you went to bed.'

'OK. You caught me.'

'Sorry. Are you half-asleep?'

'No. Go on. What's the matter?'

'I was looking at a book I found at school,' began Lyuba.

Vera's heart sank. So it was not an emergency concerning their father or Lyuba's daughter. Only more of what she saw as a growing obsession in her older sister. 'Lyuba…'

'I know. I'll be quick. I found some photos of women going to Germany to work.'

'Was Mama in them?'

'No, of course not but what happened to those women could have happened to Mama.'

'What do you mean?'

'Well, they look so afraid and so beaten. Even though they're only queueing to get on the train to Germany.'

'We still don't know if that's what Mama experienced.'

'It says that the Germans worked them to death.'

'Not all of them. Mama wasn't the only survivor.'

'I know but…'

'Lyuba, I've just come off my shift. Can we talk about this another time?'

32

'Oh Vera, I'm sorry. I was looking at this book last night and I couldn't wait to ring you. I'll show it to you at the weekend. Are you coming to *Tato's*?'

'Yes, on Sunday.'

'OK, I'll show you then. You go to bed now and have a good sleep.'

'Thanks,' said Vera drily, putting down the phone.

But sleep would not come. As she gazed at the daylight brimming around the edges of the curtains, Vera tried to stop her stomach from churning at the thought of Mama, at sixteen, hurrying along with other slave labourers. She could not help thinking of her own daughter, Lydia, with her spiky hair, being completely ill-equipped to deal with enforced exile, despite the ample attitude of an adolescent.

***

The three grandchildren had cleared the table and could be heard squabbling in a friendly fashion in the kitchen.

'I washed last time,' complained Simon.

'Because you're the youngest,' said his sister, Lydia, slapping him playfully with a tea towel.

'Yes, and we're tidier,' said Valeria. 'We know where everything goes.'

'What sort of work did Mama do in Germany?' asked Lyuba, turning to Taras.

Her father ran his hand over his face wondering why his dead wife's first life had suddenly become so important to his eldest daughter. She's like a dog with a bone, he thought. She won't let go of the idea of Natalya independent of her. But then neither he nor his wife had wanted to visit their past lives on their children. They had wanted to protect them from all knowledge of the indescribable horrors they had seen and the terrible heartache they had suffered.

'*Tatu?*'

'Yes, I heard you. She was a servant for a German family.'

'Was she? I've read that's how some of the *Ostarbeiter* were used.'

'We weren't *Ostarbeiter.*'

'What do you mean?' asked Vera.

'We were slave labourers yes, but those of us from Halychyna never had to wear the OST badges that other Ukrainians had to wear.'

'OST badges?'

'Yes. To identify you as a slave labourer from the East.'

'Like the yellow star?' asked Adrian, Lyuba's husband.

'And 'P' for Poles, yes.'

'They liked to categorise people, didn't they?' said Tom, looking at his father-in-law.

'Oh yes. *Alles in Ordnung.*'

'What?' asked Vera.

'They're a very tidy people.'

'So was Mama,' said Lyuba, remembering her mother's efficiency around the house. The routines and order. Everything clean and shining. Always sweet smelling.

'Are there any photos of Mama in Germany?' asked Lyuba.

Her father pointed to the sideboard. 'There might be some old photos in there, but I don't think either of us had any from Germany.'

'Shall we have a look?' asked Lyuba, glancing at her sister.

Taras sighed. He had once asked Natalya, as their daughters were growing up, to tell them about the war years and she had refused. 'Let them have their youth. We didn't, so they should.' Then somehow, as the girls grew into women, the subject had not been re-visited.

Taras watched as his eldest daughter sifted through the old papers. She and Vera made neat piles on the table but they were a disappointment. There were business letters relating to long-forgotten transactions, old postcards and advertisements, but no clue to their mother's past. Lyuba found only one photograph of herself and Vera peering into a cot at a new baby.

'Oh look, Vera. This must have been when Nadiya was born.'

'Weren't we lovely?' laughed Vera, passing the photograph to her husband.

Tom grunted.

'Three little girls,' mused Lyuba. She wondered if Mama had deliberately replicated her lost family, but then thought again of the age difference between Vera and Nadiya. Their youngest sister must have been a later 'mistake'. She smiled to herself. It would be a brave person who suggested that to Nadiya.

'Do you think we made up for them?' she asked Vera.

'I hope so,' said Vera.

Tom handed the photo to Taras. Lyuba watched his face and was relieved to see the ghost of a smile. 'That's a nice one,' he said. 'We took lots of photos of the three of you when you were little.'

There was a shriek from the kitchen.

'I hope you're not making a mess in there,' Vera warned.

'They're alright,' said Taras. 'They're only young.'

'They're Mama's age when she had to leave home,' said Lyuba.

'On her own,' added Vera.

Chapter 4
Western Ukraine 1943

When our cart reaches Ternopil, I see so many others, I can't count them. They're pulled up in some sort of order on a field outside the town. A German soldier with his rifle slung over his shoulder motions to our driver to pull in next to a cart already spilling its passengers out. We have no time to look about us as another soldier appears with his *'Raus! Aussteigen!'* He herds us towards the road which is full from edge to edge with men and women, like us, hot in their coats and winter boots. We line up across the width of the road, behind those already there. The occasional grey uniform is visible along the verge in case we run amok. But we don't. We don't even complain when they keep us waiting. We just put our bundles on the ground and shift our weight from foot to foot hoping to get moving soon. Further away from home.

The last village we saw has silenced us. From a long way off we had been able to see the smoke across the fields.

'What's that? We didn't hear any artillery.'

'Nor any planes either.'

We strained our eyes towards the plumes of smoke which separated as we approached and saw several distinct fires.

'That's Vohivtsy,' said our driver.

We watched without speaking as we drew nearer to what had once been a village like ours. The road went right through the middle of a dozen houses on either side, all of them bright with red and gold flames. The black smoke clogged the sky with its dark stink.

The horses flinched and the driver slowed them down. 'It's

all right, my beauties. Let's keep walking. Just a bit of smoke. It won't hurt you…' Then his mares saw the other horses, as we did.

There were two German soldiers on horseback, checking that the houses burned to ruins. They looked completely incongruous with their metal helmets and grey uniforms, the soldier's paraphernalia, while the horses looked like they always do – large, gentle creatures with flowing manes and tails, the farmer's helper. They were walking towards us, so the driver slowed a bit more.

'*Was hast du da?*' one of the soldiers demanded.

'*Ostarbeiter,*' muttered our driver.

'*Wohin gehst du?*'

'*Nach Ternopil.*'

'*Dann gehe. Heil Hitler!*'

Our driver nodded, but realised that wouldn't be enough so grunted, '*Heil Hitler!*' He flicked the reins and our mares moved forward slowly, keeping their eyes on the other horses. The foal stayed hide to hide with her mother.

As we passed, our driver called out, 'What happened here?'

One of the soldiers flicked his eyes at us. 'Who are they?'

'As I said, workers for Germany.'

'Then their village won't have been burnt, will it? *Heil Hitler!*'

'*Heil Hitler!*' our driver repeated, but as he put some distance between himself and the soldiers he muttered, 'Bastards.'

The rest of us had sat mute, our hands in our laps, as we passed the cottages whose roofs were ablaze, only the triangular timbers visible against the leaping flames. The walls were still holding the fires, although flames poured out of doorways and windows. The only things left intact were the garden fences. There was no sound other than the roaring of the fires. The acrid smoke blinded us and made us cough as the wind shifted. The driver clicked his horses on and we began to pick up speed. We bowed our heads into our bundles. This could have been our village. As we left burning Vohivtsy behind we glanced up and our eyes met. We are at the violent mercy of these monsters.

Stop it! I focus on where we are at this moment on the outskirts of Ternopil. All I can see now, before and behind me, are literally hundreds of us, maybe thousands of young men and women waiting to be transported to our labouring future in Germany. We hear a far-off whistle blown and a faint shout of '*Marschieren!*' Eventually, the wave of movement reaches my row. We pick up our bundles and step forward. I keep my eyes front and my teeth clamped together.

We walk for about five minutes then the houses begin and we're walking along the main street which becomes a wide boulevard. I recognise the direction – we're heading for the station. My stomach churns even though I knew this was what we were going to do. People stand on the pavements watching us go. No one's cheering, or waving, or even speaking. They're silent. Just watching us as if somehow we're wrong or shameful. I bow my head for a moment feeling myself blush with guilt. Then my heart rebels. Why should they make me feel bad? I feel bad enough already. I have to go. Do they want my mother and sisters to be turned out of their house? Or shot? To hell with them! How dare they just watch? As I look up to glare at them I see an old man sitting on the kerb, leaning on his stick, his rheumy eyes saying he's seen it all before. Ukrainians being marched off like beasts, enslaved by others.

The pace slows as we reach the station. We close up on the row in front then wait. We shuffle forward to a barrier of soldiers who are separating us between two stationary goods trains. I have never seen such long trains. I can't see the front of either of them.

'*Nach links,*' they gesture to the women.

'*Nach rechts,*' to the men and, as couples realise they're going to be parted, I hear the wails go up.

'No! No!'

'They said we'd be kept together.'

'This is my wife…'

But there's no pity here. People are pushed aside, the woman in front lurching into me as the soldier prods her away with the butt of his rifle. I put my hand out to steady her, but mostly to protect myself and, as we pass the grey cordon, she rushes across to her husband returning quickly with a bundle tied with string. I clutch mine to me, all I have left of my man. At least hers is there across the platform, alive…I grit my teeth again ignoring the pain under my left breast.

We're funnelled into single file as we walk alongside the train. I can see women hauling themselves up into these trucks, their headscarves slipping against their shiny hair. I look at the trucks again. Surely these are for animals. They certainly stink. The line is severed just ahead of me and we're ordered into an empty wagon. The soldier says nothing, merely waves his rifle at the open door, and we turn at his signal. There are two women in front of me. The first hands her bundle to the woman behind her then raises her foot over half a metre into the air to try to get it on the footplate. She grips the side of the wagon and hauls herself up. She takes both bundles from the next woman and helps to pull her up. I watch, wondering if I'll manage, then I've got my foot up and I've pushed my weight up. For a ridiculous moment, I'm reminded of mounting a horse. One of the women has my hand gripped firmly and I'm up. I turn around and do the same for the girl behind me. I get a quick glance at the teeming platform. The men are boarding their train, the officers patrolling up the middle, observing everything with their hands clasped behind their long leather-coated backs. Their practised efficiency tells us that we are only a few among the many they've packed off to the Fatherland to slave for their victory.

I turn away from the noise, into the sharp smell of urine. The truck consists of four wooden walls with a wooden floor and a wooden roof. No seats, no toilet, nothing, although the floor is covered in dirty straw. I make for the opposite wall to stand near a rectangle of light, hoping this air flap will remain open for the journey. I don't put my bundle down yet. I wait to see how many of us will be packed into this space.

Eventually the flow into the truck halts. We're standing shoulder to shoulder. I don't know how many of us there are. I guess maybe thirty or forty as the door slides closed and slams out the light. A shudder ripples its way among us as we realise there's no going back. We're packed in like cattle, but each of us is completely alone in the gloom. We stand and wait, straining our ears. I recognise the German orders as, further along the platform, other women board our train.

I lean against the truck wall and become aware of the girl on my right. She's put her fingers into mine and is clasping my hand. I squeeze back, but shut my eyes.

At that moment a sharp stamping of feet marches back towards our truck followed by a shout of '*Halt!*' There's the clang of the padlock and the metal bar being flung back and we're torn from our private pools of misery into an alert anxiety for what is to come. I blink against the light as the door is opened again to see the dark outlines of two young women being pushed up into the truck. They stumble against the nearest passengers, but are held up by the crush of people. There's no room for them to fall and I get a brief glimpse of their pale young faces before the door is slammed shut and re-locked.

There's a shocked silence and, when the sound of the marching boots has retreated, a wondering whispering. Who are these girls? But I guess before the word is murmured: 'Runaways.' I feel a flicker of admiration for them. They're not going to be bullied. Perhaps we could control our own destinies if we wanted to. But then I remember the smell of the burning village.

The train lurches and we stumble against each other. We begin to move with a screech of metal. This releases voices and there are calls of 'Goodbye, Ternopil!' 'Goodbye, Ukraine!'

There's a sob to my right, but an older voice calls out, 'Steady, girls. We're going to work. We'll be back.'

The cry goes up: '*Dopobachenya!*' Until we meet again.

***

Everything that happens over the next few days takes us hundreds of kilometres from home. In this wagon we are all village girls, but I doubt any of us has ever had to live like this. We doze standing up because there's no room to lie down. We eat what we've brought until there's nothing left then we simply wait for our captors to feed us. For that is what we are, prisoners of the Germans who don't care how we might deal with our toilet needs. It has to be done in the already filthy straw. Just as we think we can't be humiliated any further, the train comes to a halt.

I hear the doors of the other wagons being opened and the shouted order, '*Aussteigen!*' as the guard approaches. The doors to our wagon are thrown open. We're alert, ready to see what they'll do to us. We're ordered out onto an area of rough concrete and marched over to some huge barn-like buildings…except these are not barns. We're lined up again and I make myself grateful for the sun which is shining on me. I lift my face to it, glad to feel its warmth after the dark days in the wagon. We shuffle forward.

Inside the building we stand in line while women in white

nurses' uniforms keep order. But again there's no need. We're compliant. I peer around the others to see some sort of inspections are taking place. I suppose when a farmer wants to buy a cow or a horse, the animal has to be examined.

I glance around trying to calculate how many hundreds this hall holds, but I give up. Too many. There's only a noise of abrupt questions and quietly given answers as we shuffle forward. I see ahead of me men in white coats checking teeth and glands, nurses checking heads of hair. After which we're divided: some sent into a side room and others straight ahead to another large space.

I open my mouth to say 'Aaagh' then pull my plait loose as the girls ahead of me have done. We stand with our hair rippling down our backs. A girl's glory. The nurse gestures me to sit with my back to her. She examines behind my ears and then parts my hair repeatedly, making my skin crawl. But it's only fear not the lice they're looking for. I'm directed straight ahead. I can't help glancing into the side room as I pass, my heart lurching at what I see. Girls seated, a buzzing shaver being passed over their scalps, their hair falling in swathes to the floor.

I swallow and move forward into the room ahead. We're told to strip. I can already see white bodies entering a grey space beyond. I remove my clothes folding them in a tidy pile. I tell myself that we're all women here and I used to bathe with the girls in the river. There's nothing to fear. But my heart pounds as I step into the blind space of the steam. I try not to pant or scream and make myself breathe evenly. In and out. In and out.

I step forward with arms outstretched. I see more ghostly shapes like mine standing under hot sprays of water. I find myself such a spray and let the heat pound my head and pour down my face, taking my tears with it. I let myself cry – no one can see me or hear me. But as the sobs subside I tell myself, that's enough. They haven't killed me yet and I'm not going to let them. Roman would be disgusted with me if I gave in.

***

We're loaded onto the train again and resume our journey, although this time it's only hours before we reach what turns out to be our destination. When the train halts, we're ushered off and lined up in twos. I turn to look at another train across the tracks. It's also made up of cattle trucks, but the train isn't as long as ours. It seems to be mostly women who are being loaded onto it. In the group I can see there are several swollen bellies, but the rest of the women are skin and bone. Another woman is brought to the train on a stretcher.

'*Divchata*! Girls!' one of our number cries. Some of them turn their heads towards us. They're Ukrainians, then.

'Where are you going?' the same girl asks.

'Home.'

'Home?'

We look at one another.

'They're sending the sick and pregnant home,' says the girl next to me.

'Looks like it,' I say.

'How did they get to be so sick, though?'

That's easy. They're so thin, presumably they haven't been fed. Or not properly. They're coughing, some are bent over like old women, and yet they're not much older than us. So we're to be worked to death.

'Why did they bother with the delousing if that's what's going to happen?' asks a girl with a shudder.

'So that we don't infect the Germans,' I say.

There's not time for more as we're marched away from the station along a road that leads to what might be a military camp, but will be our temporary home. There's not much talk. Our hearts are as heavy as our feet.

Chapter 5
England 1990

As the bell rang to signal the end of the school day, Lyuba dismissed her students then waited until the chaos on the corridors had subsided before pursuing her errand to the History Department. She knocked on the door and entered the staff office where a very pink female member of staff was trying to hold back tears.

'I told Jason he had to finish the paragraph before he could go home but he just got up and left,' she gulped.

The Head of Department glanced up at Lyuba.

'I'll come back later,' Lyuba murmured.

'No, it's alright,' and she gave her a quick smile before returning her attention to her young colleague. 'Jason Roberts? Did you write in his planner?'

The novice shook her head.

'Did you tell him to finish it for the next lesson?'

'I didn't get a chance. He just barged out of the room as soon as the bell went.' She looked at Lyuba as if for confirmation.

Lyuba nodded sympathetically. It took time to learn how to convey the illusion of control in a classroom. Sometimes a newcomer simply had to wait out the first year of mistakes.

'Let me see his folder before the next lesson then I'll have a chat with him. OK?'

The girl nodded and left the room.

The Head of Department turned to Lyuba with a little shrug. 'What can I do for you?' She smiled.

'Sorry, if I interrupted.'

'Don't be. She's really struggling with her Year Ten boys. We have the same conversation most Wednesday afternoons.'

'It's hard for them though.'

'Yes, it is. She'll either learn and stay…or leave teaching.'

'I'm here to ask a favour, Jo.'

'Fire away.'

'I'm after some information.'

'What on?'

'The deportation of Eastern Europeans by the Nazis. You know, the *Ostarbeiter* programme.'

'That's a bit esoteric.'

'Yes.' Lyuba paused. 'I don't know whether you know but my mother died recently.'

'Yes, I was sorry to hear that.'

'Thanks. Well, she was taken by the Germans in 1943 as a slave labourer. I wanted to find out more about them.'

'Of course you do. There's not much written on the subject and it's not something we have much on in school. You could try the University library.' She looked at Lyuba's downcast face. 'But I could lend you a video.'

Lyuba looked at her expectantly.

'I don't know how much coverage there is of this subject but it's worth a look,' she said as she scanned the shelf of videos. She took down a box with a brown cover. 'It's the 'World at War' series. It's pretty good, although I don't know how useful it'll be.'

'I'd like to have a look at it.'

'Sure. Let me have it back when you've finished with it.'

'I will.'

'Didn't your mother talk to you about her experiences?' Jo asked as she handed the box to Lyuba.

'No, that's just it. We knew she'd been taken to Germany as a slave labourer but we never talked about it. Now I wish I had.'

45

'Well, I hope this casts a bit of light for you.'

Lyuba hurried into the house, dumping her heavy schoolbag in the hall as she called, 'Anybody home?'

'I'm here,' replied Valeria clattering down the stairs.

'For a beautiful young woman you make a lot of clumsy noise.'

'Hello to you too, Mum.'

They hugged one another then Lyuba said, 'Where's your father?'

'In the garage.'

'Go and fetch him. We'll eat and then I've got something for us to watch.'

'Oooh, sounds exciting,' said Valeria.

'Well, I don't know about that but I hope it'll be interesting.'

After their meal, Adrian and Valeria settled themselves on the sofa as Lyuba inserted the videotape into the machine.

'So what's the mystery?' asked Adrian.

'No mystery. I borrowed this from our History Department.'

Adrian and Valeria exchanged a glance.

'History?' asked Adrian.

'Yes, look…' said Lyuba as the strains of the theme music from the series 'World at War' rang out from the television.

'Lyuba…' began Adrian.

'It's an episode about Germany between 1940 and '44.'

'Yes, but why do you think we might want to watch it?' asked her husband.

'I'm hoping it'll cover the question of slave labourers. Besides that, it might tell us what Mama went through.'

'That seems unlikely,' said Adrian.

'Well, never mind. Shush now. Let's just watch it.'

The programme began with Hitler's early successes in

Western Europe, showing the streets of Berlin full of goose-stepping soldiers and ecstatic cheering crowds. It passed on to the invasion of Russia.

'Operation Barbarossa,' said Lyuba. 'There might be something after this.'

'Mum…' began Valeria.

'Just watch, Val.'

As the commentator began to talk of the *Reich*'s need for labourers of all kinds, Lyuba sat forward on the edge of the sofa. When he talked of sweeping up swathes of workers in Ukraine, there was a brief shot of half a dozen healthy smiling girls, all in white headscarves, the peasants who became slave labourers. Lyuba held her breath as there were pictures of armaments factories. Then the commentator turned to the subject of Stalingrad.

'Is that all?' asked Lyuba.

Adrian looked at his wife. 'It's not finished yet. There might be more.'

There wasn't. The programme went on to cover the Allied bombing of German cities and Hitler's declaration of 'total war' as his country struggled to cope with shortages and defeats.

When the credits rolled at the end, Lyuba slumped back in her seat. Valeria jumped up to stop the tape. 'They were covering lots of ground,' she said.

'Yes, but people like Mama only warranted a few seconds.'

'The programme has such a broad sweep,' began Adrian.

'He couldn't even say 'Ukraine' properly,' said Lyuba. 'Where is 'Ookrine' anyway?'

Valeria sat down beside her mother and rubbed her back. 'It doesn't make what *Baba* and *Dido* went through any less,' she said.

Lyuba blew her nose. 'And those false photos they used. Propaganda. Those girls weren't happy. Mama lost everything.'

'We know, we know,' said Adrian, moving to sit on the other side of his wife. He stroked her hair.

Between them, he and Valeria held her for a few moments. Valeria kissed her cheek. 'She survived, Mum. She was lovely. She wasn't ruined.'

But the hole in Lyuba's heart refused to be healed as she lowered her head into her hands and wept.

Chapter 6
Bavaria, Germany 1943

I wake completely, in a split second, my heart pounding. Roman is above me on the path, waving and smiling. I smile back at his dear face feeling such love for him. The sun is shining, we're walking in the spring wood, then I realise I'm not at home. I'm not anywhere I recognise. I feel the metal edge of the bed. The lumpy mattress smells of dirty straw. Wrapped tightly in my blanket I remember the ticks trying to bite me in the night. I make myself open my eyes to see the grey light of dawn coming through the window opposite reflecting off the whitewashed walls. I'm in a long, narrow room lined on both sides with the same beds as mine. They're all occupied. The camp. That's where I am.

I drop my head back onto the mattress closing my eyes. I'm not ready to remember all of that yet. I search for my pictures of Roman again, but only find the last one – no, not quite the last one – of him smiling at me, encouraging me. 'Come on, we're nearly there.' I feel as if my heart will break as he stumbles and falls. The hot tears flood the corners of my eyes. They spill over pouring down the sides of my face. I want to howl, but stuff the end of my sleeve into my mouth as I weep for my husband. My husband…for such a little time.

My heart thumps at a sudden thought. He turned! He turned away from the source of danger to tell me we were nearly at the top. What if he hadn't turned? My tears dry suddenly as I replay Roman's actions. He saw we were almost at the summit, so he turned to encourage me… so he didn't see the enemy…so he was shot. He didn't know he should duck because he had turned to me. Oh God! Please don't let that be what happened. That he died because he wanted to lift my spirits. No, please, not that. This time I really might howl except I can't get my breath and I sit up, fighting for air.

The girl in the next bed is beside me so quickly she must have been watching me. She's rubbing my back in a circular motion murmuring, 'It's alright. Just breathe in and out. Nice and slow.'

After a few moments the choking sensation eases and I find I can breathe again.

'That's it,' she croons. 'Take small breaths, in and out.'

I turn to look at her. She smiles nodding encouragement. She's one of the runaways from the train. 'You're doing really well. Keep breathing.'

For a moment I want to laugh at this most basic of advice. I try to smile my thanks. Before either of us can say anything else there's a shrill whistle and the shouted order from outside, '*Alles aussteigen!*' My thanks are lost in the bustle of thirty young women trying to make themselves presentable for the first glimpse of the camp in daylight.

The night before, all we'd seen as we marched up the road were the barbed wire and the floodlights which immediately made the night outside the camp much darker. Within the high gates were rows of barracks. We were led to a space between them where some kind of armed militia ordered us to halt. They were not in Nazi uniforms, wearing instead dark belted jackets, grey trousers tucked into boots, soft caps on their heads. They just counted us into barracks.

We line up in the yard before a huge man who seems to be in charge. He's quite tall and very wide with a big belly which pushes the brass buttons of his military coat forward. The buckle on his belt also glints in the light as it leads the way for the rest of him to follow. He's wearing a peaked cap over a completely round face, the bottom half of which is encircled by a second roll of fat. He has a small black moustache which is only the width of his fleshy nose. I feel a hysterical desire to laugh.

When we're all gathered he shouts instructions at us in German, so that most of us only hear loud guttural noises, but then one of ours translates: 'We're to be registered, issued with our documents and our jobs will be assigned. We're to go back to our barracks to wait until we're called.'

We file back but the muttering doesn't begin until we're safely indoors.

As I sit on my lumpy bed to wait, my neighbour sits opposite me. She has a pretty face with a gentle expression, her blue eyes are sympathetic.

'How are you feeling now?' she says, her earlier help having given her permission to ask.

'I'm fine,' I reply. 'Thank you.'

'I have a little sister who finds it difficult to breathe sometimes,' she says. I can see her worrying about who will rub that sister's back and whisper comfort to her now.

'I have an older sister who has no difficulty breathing,' snorts the younger runaway as she joins us on her friend's bed.

They grin conspiratorially at one another then the older girl says, 'I'm Olena. This is my friend, Olha.'

Olha has shiny dark hair parted in the middle and plaited, her braids crowning her head, making her look like a Ukrainian princess.

They both give me open smiles while I calculate how little I can tell them. 'I'm Natalya,' I say.

'Have you had this breathing trouble before?' asks Olena.

I say I haven't.

'My sister used to get it when she was upset.'

'Well, it's pretty upsetting to wake up here,' I say.

She smiles. 'It might not be so bad. They say we could work in lots of different places, like farms.'

I can see they'd like to be on a farm. It would be like home.

'We're used to hard work,' says Olha, although she doesn't look old enough to be used to work.

'We'll have to go where we're sent,' says Olena.

Olha raises her eyebrows. 'Only while they've got their guns.'

Olena shakes her head at her younger friend. 'We've seen enough of guns for the time being.'

I'm surprised that they both titter at this statement. Maybe it's a way of coping with our circumstances. They make jokes; I couldn't breathe. I think about the rumours I've heard of how the labourers are used. I never paid much attention to them before because it was never going to apply to me. I was staying at home until the fighting was over, until Roman and I could have our own cottage. I swallow carefully. 'Well, we'll see.'

Right on cue, our barrack is called out.

***

We line up outside and are marched in single file, first to face a camera to have a photo taken for our passes, then we're led to a table where a skinny clerk is sitting. He's in Nazi uniform – presumably the Militia can't be trusted to create our identity cards. When my turn comes he asks my surname and I give *Tato's* name in the easy lie. He types my names onto the form. Beside 'Occupation' he simply puts '*Arbeiterin*' – a female worker because to the *Reich*, that's all I am now. He takes my date and place of birth, asks me my faith. Then the key question:

'Marital status?'

'Single,' I reply as I expect to hear a cock crowing loudly somewhere. He writes down '*ledig*' believing my lie. Why

52

shouldn't he? I'm nothing to him, except another worker from Ukraine. Then he stamps and dates the pass with the town name of Ingolstadt. We both sign it and I'm dismissed.

It's not until the following day that our passes are ready. They're distributed by the most senior of the secretaries. She's a well-built woman with wire-framed spectacles and neatly rolled hair. Her gleaming white blouse sets her apart from the dark-clad young women crowding around her. The excitement of seeing ourselves glued to the card with our details is soon overshadowed by our selection for work.

We're ordered out onto the *ploshcha*, the field of assembly, with our few belongings. Thousands of us. Lined up with gaps between each row wide enough for someone to walk up.

'What now?' mutters Olha, the mischief gone from her blue eyes.

Olena stands on the other side of her, but I hear her reply. 'Let's just see what they do.'

For a moment I envy their closeness.

As we wait, we see German men approaching from the staff barracks. They fall into two distinct types: farmers and what must be factory owners. The first group are stockier, ruddy faced and they've not bothered to change out of their overalls. They look as well fed as the second lot, although these men are dressed in suits and ties. They stand in two loose groups in front of us, looking us over.

Then our fat *Kommandant* emerges from his office with a stiff looking woman. She's tall and thin with a rigid posture. Her clothes tell me she must be rich: a suit in good cloth, a fur stole around her neck, soft leather lace-up shoes with a low heel and a felt hat picking out the moss green in her suit.

The *Kommandant* tells us all to remove our headscarves.

Bewildered, we obey.

The woman walks up and down the rows without smiling,

her lips held tightly together, her nostrils pinched as if she's trying not to smell us. From time to time she nods pointing at one of us. The *Kommandant* directs the girl to a nearby bus with a flick of the head. The women she chooses are the smarter, slimmer, fairer ones. As she approaches me, I feel my stomach turn to liquid. What is she choosing for? It surely can't be for prostitution. She looks much too proper for that. Housework perhaps? The fact that she looks at us as if we were animals makes my skin prickle with humiliation. We are truly *Untermensch* and they are the masters. At the flick of a finger our fate is decided.

As she passes me she flips the wrist of her gloved hand and our fat *Kommandant,* whose face is glistening with sweat, jerks his head at me. I glance at my neighbours before joining the group boarding the bus. As before, we all sit silently. I wonder why neither Olena nor Olha has been chosen. They look like perfectly nice village girls. I regret that our brief friendship has ended so quickly, although that might be for the best. The comfort of friendship invites confidences.

When the bus is full, I examine the other girls carefully. Beneath our headscarves we are all fair-haired.

We're driven back towards the town and travel through suburban streets to a church. The severe woman has followed us in a chauffeur-driven car. She orders us into the church hall with a brusque gesture. We clatter through the doorway onto the bare but shining floorboards and see that the hall is already occupied by several groups of German women. The air is not only laden with the scent of coffee and sugar, but also laced with the sweetness of their perfumes. Their expectation that the world has been ordered for them tells us that these *Hausfrauen* are the wives of officers. They know exactly who they are and what they're entitled to. Their husbands are doing important work for the *Führer*, so at the moment, they can call upon anyone or anything in Europe to support the grand campaign. I swallow the bile at the back of my throat and lower my eyes. I'm here to survive if I can and to make the lot of my mother and sisters easier.

We Ukrainian girls form two lines. The smartly dressed women, who have been pretending not to look at us, now approach as our guide addresses them.

'*Heil Hitler, meine Damen.*' She smiles at them. 'Here are the Ukrainian workers selected to help you in your homes. As you can see, they all look strong and healthy so should be able to fulfil any task you set them in your houses. They will also be able to look after your children as they come from large families.'

How does she know that I ask myself? Do they assume that all peasant girls come from large families?

'Please come forward and select your maid.'

I decide I won't look up to be chosen. I won't show any weakness. But then I think I won't let them humiliate me either. So I raise my eyes and meet those of a meek-looking woman. She has dark hair drawn back in a soft bun at the nape of her neck. Her tan felt hat matches her dress and jacket. She has a pretty brooch on one lapel. She nods at me and half-smiles as she sees me taking in her appearance. Her look is direct with her straight dark eyebrows, an aquiline nose, a thin mouth – her face seems all lines, as if a child has drawn it with a ruler. But it's softened by a wistfulness in her dark eyes. She might be a good mistress, I think, as I step forward to follow her.

After introducing ourselves we go through the brief formalities of registering mistress and servant, then we leave the church. We walk out into a tree-lined avenue where we cross the road to wait at a tram stop. I try to look at her from the corners of my eyes while she's trying to peep at me. We take the number seven tram and she pays for both of us. As we pass the commercial part of town, I see one or two stores are boarded up, a yellow star painted on one of them.

When we reach our stop she steps forward and tugs the cord running below the ceiling. There's a ping and the tram pulls to a halt on another tree-lined avenue. We alight and Frau Kuhn walks briskly up to a smart square house. She points at the front door, but then leads me by a path to the rear where we enter an open door into a small space and turn left into a kitchen.

The sound greets me first. Shouts of '*Mutti, Mutti!*' accompanied by the deeper tones of an older woman, clearly exhorting some order from the children.

There's a scramble while Frau Kuhn is clasped at the knees by a little girl. She leans forward to pick up a smaller boy. An older boy approaches with a smile which says he'd like to be clasping his mother, too, if only he weren't so grown up. He satisfies himself by standing at her side.

The admonitions of '*Nein, nein, Kinder,*' have come from a large matron who has risen from her seat at the kitchen table. I look at her more closely. If I'm to have difficulty in this household, it will come from her. She's avoiding looking at me from the fleshy folds around her small eyes, as she continues to focus on the children. I see she's as tall as me, but much wider. The children would not be able to find comfort on the solidity of her lace-covered chest, nor in the firmness of her corseted belly.

She straightens up and looks down her nose at me. She neither steps forward nor extends her hand.

Frau Kuhn says, '*Mutti, unser Dienstmädchen*, Natalya.' And to me, her servant, '*Meine Schwiegermutter*, Frau Kuhn.'

I'm not sure what type of mother that is but guess it's mother-in-law. I wonder if she's expecting me to curtsey, but she'll have to be satisfied with, '*Guten Morgen, meine Dame.*' I mentally thank *Pani* Zenya for her German classes. Frau Kuhn

Senior might be expecting a country girl, but my manners are better than hers as she simply replies, '*Guten Morgen.*'

Frau Kuhn disentangles herself from her youngest standing her children in a line. She says to them: '*Kinder*, this is Natalya, who has come to help us.'

I hear a derisive sniff from the matron, but I don't take my eyes off these three children who it will be my job to look after.

Frau Kuhn points to her eldest child. '*Klaus, neun Jahren,*' she says and holds up nine fingers. I haven't yet revealed to her how much German I know or that the months of lessons in the village school taught us more than courtesy phrases. Besides, I'll learn more about them if they think I don't understand what they're saying.

Klaus steps forward smartly and says, '*Heil Hitler!*' by way of greeting, giving me the Nazi salute at the same time. He's dressed in *Lederhosen*, a moss-green sweater and knee-length grey socks.

I nod. Am I supposed to reply '*Heil Hitler*' even to a nine-year-old?

Frau Kuhn smiles her approval then points to her daughter. '*Jutta, funf Jahren,*' pronouncing the name Yutta.

Jutta still has the bloom of a baby despite her five years: round cheeks and soft limbs clearly visible in her blue woollen dress with its smocking across the chest. She hangs her head and won't look at me, but Frau Kuhn prompts her to say hello, so I get a mumbled '*Morgen*'.

Then the little boy lurches forward with a grin and I drop my bundle to catch him before he falls on his face. '*Hans, zwei Jahren,*' says his mother with a fond smile. Hans is dressed identically to Klaus and is a little version of him, except for the charm of his baby status. If he's heard of *Herr Hitler* it hasn't yet impinged on his consciousness.

'Children, I am going to show Natalya our house. You can

57

stay here with *Oma* and you will see Natalya again later.' She gestures to my bundle and beckons me to follow her.

I pick up all I have in the world and follow her back into the vestibule. We climb up two flights of clean, well-lit stairs to a landing with two doors. She opens the door on the right to reveal a full lumber room, then the door on the left revealing a small bedroom. The room is plain but clean. It's smaller than its floor space as the ceiling slopes under the roof. There's a narrow bed to the left of the door, a table and chair under the window which looks out over the sloping roof tiles to the tops of the trees. As I turn to the right I see Hitler's face gazing at me from the wall above the wash-stand.

Frau Kuhn points to my bundle which I put down. She also points to my jacket so I take it off and hang it on the hook on the back of the door.

'*Komm.*' She proceeds to give me a tour of the house.

We go down one flight of stairs and along a landing. I'm shown the children's bedrooms. The two youngest sleep in the same room, Klaus sleeps alone, then there's the master bedroom. Everywhere Hitler looks out sternly – he will watch all of us eating and sleeping. Although I notice there's no image of him in the bathroom. Some respite then. Possibly also respite from the mother-in-law. She appears to have no bedroom.

We look at the rooms on the ground floor and, besides the kitchen, there's a dining room, untidy with the children's toys, and a day room with comfortable sofas. But by far the grandest room is Herr Kuhn's study. It runs the length of the house, with windows from floor to ceiling so it's filled with light filtered by the crisp net curtains. There are two large sofas and ornate occasional tables, but the room is dominated by a huge desk, backed by a wall full of bookcases.

'My husband works in here,' says Frau Kuhn. 'When he's home.'

I nod, unsure of what she expects me to say to this. In any case, I'm not supposed to have an opinion on anything. Then I wonder if she means he's in Ukraine. Is he in my country?

She offers no explanation. We return to the kitchen and she shows me where the vegetables are kept. I'm to help her prepare lunch.

***

Several days later, Frau Kuhn gives me a postcard. I'm allowed to write to Mama, Lyubka and Verochka to tell them I'm safe. Perhaps I'm safer here than I might have been in a factory. The card is plain with a space for their address on one half of one side which leaves me one and a half sides to write on. But what to say? Where to start? I find it difficult to choose what to tell them. The list of what to leave out is easy…the fear, the grief, the loss.

So…

'Good day, my dearest mother, and my dear little sisters, Lyubka and Verochka. First of all I want to tell you that I am alive and well. I am safely housed here in Germany working with a kind family. They have three lovely children. I think of you every day. Keep well, my dear ones, and hopefully we will soon be re-united.'

When I've finished writing, the longing for our house with its warm kitchen, the bright garden and pink orchard just beyond the little window is so palpable that I feel as if, were I to close my eyes, I would hear Verochka calling to the hens. I can smell the blossom from the orchard and then, before the tears can overwhelm me, I open my eyes to take my postcard downstairs to Frau Kuhn. She'll look at it before it's posted, but I doubt she can read Ukrainian. Besides there's nothing which needs to be hidden. I suppose they have been kind. I haven't been beaten and I've been fed. Alone in the kitchen after they've eaten, but fed. The younger children are lovely with their mother. They're still shy of me, although they're beginning to follow their mother's instructions to follow my instructions. Frau Kuhn will give me a purple stamp with the *Führer*'s head on it to send my message home. Perhaps they'll be able to reply.

Chapter 7
England 1990

Vera glanced down at the watch pinned to her breast. 'I'm calling it. The time of death is 11.16.'

There was a little sigh from her colleagues around the bed then the Staff Nurse drew the sheet up over the face of the old woman. Her features had relaxed in death and already she looked less wizened.

Vera turned to the young Nursing Assistant. 'Please close the doors to the bays and side wards. I'll ring the mortuary.'

She walked to the reception desk, calm in the hospital routine. After all, this particular death had not been unexpected. The old lady had been ailing for some time.

The porters arrived looking for Vera in her royal blue Sister's uniform. She supervised the transfer of the body, gave instructions for the doors to be re-opened and the bed and its surrounding area to be thoroughly cleaned. At the handover to the night-shift, that particular patient's condition merited only a sentence.

'She died this morning.'

As Vera left the hospital she noticed the cherry trees flowering on the avenue. She was reminded of the impatience her mother would have felt for those trees which would bear no edible fruit. Natalya used to pack her garden with food.

'You don't know what real hunger is,' she would say when the girls came rushing in from school, calling, 'We're starving, Mama, starving!'

Mama. She felt the dip in her stomach at the memory that her mother was no longer there to plant her vegetable garden, to decry her neighbours' waste of good growing ground. Mama. Bending over her tender plants in her old trousers. A scarf over her hair.

Vera hurried to her car. She fumed with frustration as she drove in the early evening traffic. 'Come on. Come on, you fool. Get out of the way.'

At last she reached the sanctuary of her own house and hurried in, calling, 'It's me. Where are you?'

Only her husband would answer. She knew both of the children had planned to go to the cinema. But Tom was there. Big, burly and ready to give her a hug. She found him in the kitchen and clung to him longer than was her habit.

'Hard shift?' he asked.

She nodded. 'We lost one.' To her horror, she burst into tears. Even as she cried she was thinking, 'But Mrs Johnson was just another patient.' Why on earth was she crying over the inevitability of an old lady's death? She was behaving more like Lyuba than herself.

Tom continued to hold her. 'It's alright,' he murmured. 'It wasn't your Mama.'

Instead of feeling comforted, Vera wailed more loudly. She wept as she had done as a child. Her face was wet with tears, she was dribbling and her nose was running.

Tom handed her a large cotton handkerchief and she cried herself into it, giving way completely to what she would normally have dismissed as self-indulgence. Some minutes passed before she was able to steady herself. As her sobs became quieter she dried her eyes. She shook her head at the glass of wine Tom offered her, going instead to the sink to wash her face.

He stood behind her and rubbed his hand across her back. 'Why don't you have a shower while I finish dinner? You'll feel better when you've had a wash and something to eat.'

She nodded. 'I will.' She tried to give him an apologetic smile before going upstairs. As she stood under the hot water she thought that she might weep again, but she didn't. Her grief had overflowed and, while she felt exhausted by it, it would not overwhelm her again today.

Tom was right. After they had eaten they sat together on the sofa, glasses of wine in hand.

'Better?' he asked.

'Yes. I'm sorry.'

'No need.'

'I know I was crying for Mama not my patient. But I wasn't expecting it. I was fine at work. It was just when I got home.' She turned a grateful face to him. 'Thank you.'

'There's nothing to thank me for.'

'I know, but I'm glad you're here.' Vera leaned against her husband. 'Would you mind if I invited everyone for lunch on Sunday?'

'Everyone?'

'Well, *Tato*, Lyuba and Nadiya.'

'Of course not. It might help you to be together.'

'I think it might.'

***

Vera's father and sisters had enjoyed the unexpected lunch together. Now Lyuba lifted a soapy saucepan from the sink as Vera said, 'You haven't told Nadiya about the photo have you?'

Lyuba shook her head.

'Are you going to?'

'Yes, but it's not just up to me, is it?'

'No. We should tell her but maybe not today when we're all here.'

'No, let's do it when there are just the three of us.'

'I dreamt of Mama last night,' said Vera.

'Did you?' asked Lyuba. 'What did you dream?'

'It was all a muddle. I was trying to sort a problem out and there were lots of colleagues from work around. I was weeding a raised border.'

'Gardening?'

'Yes. I don't think I was at the hospital but Mama was with me.' She paused. 'She wouldn't speak to me. Not as if we'd fallen out, but just as if it wasn't her place to speak. To say anything.'

'That's odd.'

'Yes. There were feathers falling.'

'Feathers?'

'I can't remember it very well. *Tato* was in the background too. But I have a clear memory of Mama in a navy blue dress following me around, not speaking to me, even though I spoke to her.'

Lyuba dried her hands and put her arms around her sister.

'It's OK. It wasn't sad and it hasn't made me sad…I don't think. But maybe it means she's moved on.'

'Maybe it does.' Lyuba thought it made complete sense. There was much she wanted to know, and maybe Vera did too. But their mother had not told them and now she never would.

Nadiya bounced into the kitchen. 'What's wrong?' she asked in an instant change of mood.

'Nothing,' said Lyuba. 'Vera dreamt of Mama last night.' She watched as Nadiya metamorphosed from a confident woman to the little girl she had been. She pushed herself into their hug, just as she had done as a toddler. 'Oh, Mama.'

The three women held one another tightly as the pain of their loss re-asserted itself.

Chapter 8
Bavaria, Germany 1943

I wake just after dawn to the sounds of the birds in the trees beyond my open window. I hear a blackbird then the skirling of the swallows begins. The weather's getting much warmer. It can be hot here under the roof but I like it. I can't hear much from the Kuhns below so I can pretend I'm independent of them. I turn my head towards the early light and catch sight of our *rushnyk* – mine and Roman's. Right now it's hanging over the picture of the *Führer*. I've tacked the centre of it over his portrait and left the two long sides hanging down, instead of pinning them out like wings. Pity that it hides Hitler's face completely.

A spurt of anger ambushes me – they killed Roman. What for? So that they can go on taking from others to live their wealthy lives. We had lives, too. I tuck the hatred away as I swing my legs out of bed. Frau Kuhn has given me a plain old dress of hers and a large white apron with a bib. To save my own clothes, she said. To keep me neat and tidy I think. I put them on, becoming the Kuhn's servant. I say my prayers and go down to the kitchen to begin preparing breakfast. I don't think Frau Kuhn has got used to my early rising yet. Perhaps she thought she'd have to teach me to get up. She has no idea about life in the village. Up with the sun to milk the cow, feed the hens, work the fields and our own vegetable gardens. Dawn till dusk. But with other people, always with others, Mama, Lyubka, Verochka, the girls in the village. My eyes sting with a loneliness which threatens to gag me as I find myself humming.

'Dear mother of mine, you didn't sleep the whole night through

And led me through the fields beside the village…'

Why this song? It always snags in my throat and here it is making me feel sadder than I already am.

Frau Kuhn saves me.

'*Guten Morgen*, Natalya,' she says as she comes into the kitchen.

'*Guten Morgen*, Frau Kuhn.' I don't have to try to be polite to her. She's always decent to me. She wouldn't have shot Roman…unless he'd been threatening her children. She wouldn't have shot him for an idea. Perhaps. She switches on the light although its low wattage makes little difference to the early morning kitchen.

'I don't know how you can work in such gloom, Natalya.'

I smile and shrug. There was little light in our cottage, yet I wouldn't have described it as gloomy.

'*Die Kinder,*' she murmurs.

I go on to the second task of my day, rousing, bathing and dressing the children. Klaus looks after himself, of course, taking pride in being independent of the women of the house. Jutta needs some help, especially with her hair. I brush out her bedtime plait and side part the hair on top. Then I comb it smooth and roll it around a small comb so that it sits in a pleat front to back. I brush the rest of her fine hair, splitting and braiding it into two little plaits. I'm quick and gentle with her so she doesn't fidget too much. I know she's still finding it an invasion to have me do her hair rather than her mother. Which is why Frau Kuhn remains below while I look after the children as she has taught me to. I keep my mind focussed on Jutta as my fingers mechanically bind the three strands, trying not to think of Lyubka and Verochka as little girls, or even now, combing out their long tresses themselves, sometimes combing each other's hair.

I leave Hansi till last. I lift his baby warmth from the cot, which he's still sleeping in despite his two years. I've tried to harden my heart against him, but it's very difficult when he clings softly around my neck. Sometimes when I've rocked him to sleep, I've had to barricade my mind against the thoughts of Roman's babies…none of whom will now be born. When I told Mama I wasn't pregnant, I didn't really know. I hoped against hope that I was. But the time has been and gone. I'm not pregnant.

I take the children down for their breakfast of porridge made with the milk and butter Frau Kuhn Senior brings from the country. The wife of an officer and with a martinet for a mother-in-law, my mistress suffers no food shortages in this household. Yet. There is rationing. However Frau Kuhn seems to be looked upon sympathetically by the butcher and the baker. Or perhaps they enjoy an officer's patronage. There's been an outcry in the region as the government has rationed beer. In this household of women and children, we haven't missed it. After breakfast, I take the children to the bathroom to brush their teeth. The younger ones squirm at the taste of salt in their mouths, but Klaus sees himself as a brave soldier who wouldn't deign to long for toothpaste.

We settle the children to play in the dining room while Frau Kuhn and I set to work cleaning the downstairs rooms in her orderly routine. Today we start on her husband's study. He's away somewhere, fighting. She hasn't said where. Maybe she doesn't know. Maybe she sees me as a security risk. His study is always kept clean so that if he should come home at any moment it would be ready for him. We even put in fresh flowers from the garden though nobody but myself and Frau Kuhn sees them. I dust and polish carefully. She's impressed on me that nothing must be damaged here so I work with concentration.

I dust the framed photographs. Since I've never met him,

I'm drawn to the family portrait he keeps on his desk. He's in his SS uniform and I can see the four silver pips of a *Sturmbannführer* on his collar. Klaus and Hans lean against him. All three have the same cowlick on the right side of their foreheads. Father and eldest son look straight into the lens while Hansi is having a childish fidget, despite his mother holding his hand. Frau Kuhn isn't looking into the camera but away past her boys, looking serious like the rest of them but somehow sad. Jutta is on the end of the group, her arm linked through her mother's for protection and looking sideways into the camera as if she doesn't quite trust either the photographer or his apparatus. They look exactly like what they are, a well-set up German family, doing the *Führer* proud, although Frau Kuhn has no fourth child to merit the Mother's Cross.

'No, it's mine!' I hear shrieked from the playroom. Frau Kuhn and I arrive simultaneously to find Klaus standing above his little brother, his face red with anger.

'*Mutti!*' They both appeal to Frau Kuhn, Klaus furiously and Hansi with a wail, a lead soldier held firmly in his chubby fist.

Klaus has his German soldiers set out on the table, the officers inspecting a parade of men. He's fiercely proud of these figures which his father bought for him and he keeps them tidy at all times. Needless to say, I'm not allowed to dust them. Hansi has probably even dribbled on one.

'Come, Klaus,' says Frau Kuhn. 'He's only little. Let him have one to play with.'

'He's ruining the parade,' shouts Klaus, close to tears despite himself.

'Come Hansi,' Frau Kuhn tries again. 'Let's see what else we can find for you.' But he's not to be drawn back from the impasse either and now cries real tears.

'Is it time for a glass of milk and a bit of cake?' I ask.

Frau Kuhn nods. We usher the children into the kitchen and I offer Hansi a finger of cake which he exchanges for the lead soldier. I pop it into my apron pocket and, with a conspiratorial smile from my employer, we establish peace among the boys.

After their snack, Frau Kuhn picks up Hansi and taking Jutta by the hand, leads them to the big armchair in the corner of the dining room for a page or two of their storybooks. I take a soft, damp cloth and show Klaus how to tidy up his infantryman. He tries not to scowl at me as he takes both from my hands, then he rubs vigorously at the soldier, as if he'd like to erase all trace of his brother. I leave him to it.

I serve lunch to the family. When the little children go down for their naps and Klaus rests in his room, I stand in the kitchen and eat mine before clearing everything away. Later I take the children to the park with Frau Kuhn. She informs me that she will show me the routine so that in future I can take them alone. We tidy them up, their clothes, their hair, and then I help them with their footwear. Both boys have sturdy brown leather lace-up boots. Klaus doesn't need my help but as I pass his boots to him I see the swastika on their soles. My heart bumps for a moment. Even here. On a child's shoe! There's no swastika on Jutta's. She has a little girl's dainty shoe with a strap and a button. No evidence that she belongs to the Third Reich. I swallow my revulsion, giving the children and their mother my bland face.

The park...There were such places in Ternopil, but not in our village. Who had need of a park when we had meadows, forests, and rivers? But here! The expanse of smooth, green grass. The trees – some of which I've never seen before. Frau Kuhn introduces me to one glory which she calls a tulip tree. It's a towering beauty with green leaves shaped like cats' faces and pale lemon, cup-like flowers. I see linden trees. In a flash, Mama

69

is opposite me, an old bed sheet in our hands as we stretch it between us with its load of blossoms. We'd leave them in the sunshine to dry. I wonder if Frau Kuhn and I will gather blossoms for tea. I gaze at the flowerbeds which are deep and full of colour. I try not to stare, but can't help myself. If Mama could see this. I think of her carefully nurturing the dahlias in our garden adoring their late summer colour. She'd love this. Beyond the beautiful manicured space, my heart lifts to be in the fresh air and I realise how much I've missed being outdoors. The green spreading away from me, the width of sky above me could almost be home. Oh, to be home…

I turn away from the sky and the pain in my chest to encourage the children to run about on this grass which no beast has ever cropped. Surely no one will ever go hungry here. So much pasture. No wonder they just marched through our villages treating us like animals.

Klaus is running in circles with a toy plane in his hand making engine noises which Hansi vainly tries to copy. Jutta is tugging off her cardigan in the sunshine. Frau Kuhn sits on a neat rug she has brought while I stand pretending to care for the safety of these three lucky children, whose father may be away fighting but who haven't had to watch him being dragged from the house by men in green or grey uniform - it really doesn't matter which - then beaten and shot in the yard.

So it goes on. The daily routine. I have no complaints. I work hard, but I'm safe in this house. No one comes looking for me. Although I don't feel so safe when Frau Kuhn shows me a new task. One afternoon, while the children are having their nap and Klaus is reading, she gets out the best china. She takes me into the sitting room and shows me how to set it out. Filling the coffee pot with cold water, she demonstrates how to pour it for an imaginary drinker. I nod at each stage of her training, assuming that I am to serve important guests.

This dry-run also explains why we spent the morning baking. The kitchen is still delicious with the smells of *Apfelstrudel* and *Sachertorte*. I have added these names to my growing list of vocabulary, although I doubt I'll ever find a use for them. These words weren't in the *Wörterbuch* I was given when I arrived. It was full of useful objects like 'knife', 'fork' and instructions which my mistress might give me: 'Clear the table!' 'Scrub the floor!' However, Frau Kuhn's gentler manner presents me with a frilled white apron which I'm to wear over the plain black skirt and blouse she has given me from her own wardrobe. I am to look and act the part of a housemaid, so it's made clear that I do not need to wear my habitual white headscarf. Alright then.

The children are farmed out with their grandmother for the morning. When the guests arrive I see they're the same sort of women who looked us Ukrainian girls over when we were brought from the camp. They are comfortable and confident, expecting only what they think is their due. Their husbands' status not only protects them from the nation's push to include everyone in the work force, but also allows them to hold on to luxuries increasingly missed by their proletarian sisters. '*Kinde, Küche, Kirche*…' Hmmm.

There's a lot of chatter as they take their seats in the crowded sitting room, full of their flowery scents, overlaid with the smell of lipstick and powder. Their shining heads bob like so many sleek, well-fed crows. Frau Kuhn gives me the signal to bring in the coffee and cake. I show my training hasn't been wasted by attending carefully to each woman.

'She looks a tidy body,' says one of them, as I pass the full cups.

'Clean, too,' sniffs another. 'Although you can always recognise them.'

'Yes, you can. That fair hair fools nobody. They're all

degenerates.'

'Huh,' says another, 'they're certainly *Untermensch* as our dear *Führer* has said. Do you know what mine did the other day?'

I close my ears to move around the rest of the group, politely offering plates of cake to go with their coffee. For a brief, hysterical moment, I wish I still had the pistol Roman taught me to shoot with, but blood on the carpet wouldn't save Mama and my sisters.

Frau Kuhn asks me in a low voice to make another batch of coffee so I leave the room for the sanctuary of the kitchen. I gaze out of the window, waiting for the water to boil and watch a group of starlings on the lawn, pecking and poking in their sleek iridescence. I make the coffee carefully. I will be meticulous and polite. They can't touch me. I return to the sitting room.

'Well, I won't be travelling to have my hair done!' exclaims one of the young matrons as I re-enter.

'You may have to, my dear,' purrs another. '*Meine Friseuse* has told me she's running dangerously short of products for permanent waves.'

'It's outrageous! How are we to keep standards up if we can't get our hair done?'

I don't know whether to laugh or cry at these spoilt women. I think of Mama with her hair tucked under her headscarf, the girls with their plaits. I close my mind as I re-fill their coffee cups.

After they've left, Frau Kuhn and I gather up the debris and when my hands are deep in soapy water washing the precious china she says, 'Thank you, Natalya, for this morning. I could not have done it without you.'

Grateful tears prickle my eyelids, but they disappear as she adds, 'We raised a good sum to help in our *Führer*'s campaign. So it was worth it. *Danke schön.*'

It's kind of her to thank me. Certainly not many of her friends can thank their *Ostarbeiter* for work they're expected to do, but…to help raise money for Nazis to maraud across Ukraine?

'*Bitte schön*,' I murmur, as I accept the small cup of coffee she offers me.

As I prepare for bed that evening, I find myself wondering about the other girls I met so briefly in the camp and wonder where they are now. Some might be like me working to keep one house spotless and one family fed. Not like the hard work we used to do in the fields. I know I've been lucky, but I feel like the canary the *Pan* in our village, the lord of the manor, had when I was a little girl. Fed, watered, its cage firmly closed. I'm not allowed to go anywhere except where my employer takes or sends me. I wonder about the other girls…the ones who weren't chosen for domestic work. I try to recall the name of the girl who helped me to breathe and can only remember her kind simple face, her friend with the dark crown of plaits. They had big square hands like mine, but theirs are probably not in soap suds or stirring a pot. Perhaps they're working in a factory or on a farm. They'll be in a group. I imagine them gossiping, the comfort of others sustaining them as they speak Ukrainian together. Will I forget my own language as I acquire more German?

I say my prayers and look out at the night sky, wondering if Mama and the girls can see the stars, too. Is it a clear night there? I can send another card to them soon, but I long for just one word from them. I lie down on my clean, comfortable bed making myself thankful for it. I will hold on here. I just need to wait.

I'm changing the bed linen with Frau Kuhn, the double bed which only she sleeps in now unless one of the younger children has a nightmare, when I see her glance out of the window to the front of the house. She stiffens. I edge around to see what's frightened her. It's only the postman, wheeling his bicycle away from their letter box at the front gate. She drops the pillow she's encasing in a fresh cover and without a word rushes downstairs. I watch from behind the curtain as she almost runs down the garden path and unlocks the letter box to remove one letter. She barely looks at it before clasping it to her breast as she hurries back to the house.

News from her husband?

I finish changing the bed on my own and scoop up the linen to take to the basement for washing. I check on the children as I pass the dining room and continue downstairs to the washing machine. There's no sign of Frau Kuhn so I start the sheets in the machine, return to the kitchen to check the time and fetch the children for their elevenses. There's still no sign of their mother even after we've returned to the dining room and are tidying the toys from their first scattering of the day. Then she goes past the room with barely a glance at the children so I continue with my work. I think I hear her go into her husband's study from which she doesn't emerge until the children have had their lunch and have settled for their afternoon nap. She comes to find me in the kitchen, closing the door behind her.

She's been crying. That much is clear. I wonder if he's died. Is he wounded? She tries to speak, becomes choked, waits then tries again.

'Natalya, what can you tell me about the eastern part of your country?'

I look at her blankly. 'The east? I've never been there.'

'But what is it like?'

I falter and then give her the snippets I know. 'It's more Russified. The people speak Russian more than Ukrainian.'

She's waiting for more.

'There's industry. Coal. Steel.'

74

'Is it far?'

I wonder if she's lost her wits. 'From here?'

She looks bewildered. I realise she isn't asking about kilometres. I can't tell her that it might as well be the other side of the moon. 'Ukraine's a big country,' I say, when she doesn't speak.

'Tell me what the weather is like now.'

I look out of the window, knowing she's seeking some kind of reassurance that I can't give. So I focus on the weather. The end of July. I begin, 'It's hot and sunny. So dusty in the fields and lanes that we go swimming in the river…' I stop. I can't go on either. Standing at the water's edge, watching over Lyubka and Verochka. Wanting them to be good swimmers, but aware of the Dniester's strong currents. Before I can stop it, an image of Roman flashes up on the screen of my mind. His grinning face and naked torso rising up out of the water between my sisters, where he has swum up behind them, the spray arcing up in rainbow crystals as they shriek with surprise at his sudden appearance and the mayhem of their laughing, splashing battle. My tears overflow. It's my turn not to be able to speak, but it seems to pull my employer out of her own hell.

'Oh, Natalya, I'm sorry. How thoughtless of me.'

I shake my head, but won't put my sorrow into words.

She gives me her own handkerchief with its R for Renate embroidered in the corner. I mop up my tears, trying to swallow my sobs. I hold my breath then let it out little by little.

'I'm sorry,' she says again. 'You must miss them.'

I nod. I won't tell her more. I clutch my dead husband and my living sisters to my own heart.

'I had a letter you see,' she begins to explain across the gulf. 'My husband seems to be in eastern Ukraine.' She pauses. 'There's been a lot of fighting.' She adds as if to comfort me, 'He's not hurt.' Then more quietly, 'Not physically.'

I wonder if he's gone crazy. But what do I care? She sighs. So I take pity on her meeting her eyes.

'It's hard for all of us,' she says.

'Perhaps he'll get some leave.'

She shakes her head. 'I don't think there's any chance of that at the moment.'

She gets up putting water on to boil. The letter peeps out of her apron pocket. I see Hitler's face on the red stamp marked *Feldpost. Sturmbannführer* Kuhn has had time to write, however hard the fighting. Frau Kuhn makes us some tea and we sip it, thinking of our loved ones in Ukraine.

Our quiet moment is brief though as we hear Klaus's impatient cries to his baby brother. As we both rise she says, 'The park, I think. We all need some fresh air.'

Much later as I tidy the kitchen one last time before bed, I notice Frau Kuhn's apron hanging on its peg behind the door. The letter is still in the pocket. She's gone to bed with a headache. I pause. Then I lift the letter out with finger and thumb. I shouldn't, but I do. I shouldn't open it, but I do. He is senior enough not to have had his letter censored.

'*Dearest Renate*,' it begins and although I struggle with his handwriting and with the German, I understand enough. They're fighting at Kursk. Or were. Back and forth, back and forth. Finding the Russian soldier more bloody-minded than they'd imagined. What did they expect? He refers to them as being everywhere, like rats. That's all we Slavs are to these Nazis. Sub-human. And the numbers… Stalin can call on his Mongol hordes. He won't care how many of them die for the Motherland. I think I read that the Germans haven't enough equipment, although I'm not sure. He seems envious of the Russian T34's – the German tanks aren't nearly so manoeuvrable. Perhaps the loss of so many of his comrades has made him bitter. There's a list of names – Otto, Manu, Uli, who have died, one of dysentery. A brief, bitter description of Gunter's double amputation. '*We couldn't save either of his legs, both cut off at the knee. But at least the Sanitäts-Ju lifted him out of this hell.*' No wonder the letter doesn't end with '*Heil Hitler*' but simply with his concerns for his family.

'*Kiss the children for me. Tell the boys I fight so that they won't have to. As for Jutta, I fight so that she will be able to live in the luxury of peace. I kiss you, my dearest. All my love, Dieter.*'

So what was it that upset her so much? The fact that he's in danger? Or the fact that he seems so angry? At whom? The leader who isn't mentioned? Loss of faith is a great danger for a soldier. I think of Roman and the partisans I knew who carried their faith like armour. The *Ukrainska Povstanska Armia* motto: Believe in your own strength and ignore obstacles. Without that, an army might as well give up. Maybe Frau Kuhn has peeped into the future and found it terrifying.

I fold the letter carefully and put it back as it was, wondering where that leaves us Ukrainians. Kursk is a long way from Mama and the girls, but it's nearer than Stalingrad. The Red Army is pushing the Nazis west. I wish again that I'd had a letter from home. Just one word.

The following day, I'm ironing in the basement when Frau Kuhn Senior arrives with our black market supplies from the countryside. I can hear her talking to my mistress in the kitchen. It's obvious *Oma* has sent the children away to play while she grills Renate on her peaky looks.

'So what's happened?'

'Nothing, *Mutti.*'

'It must be something. You look terrible. It's Dieter, isn't it?'

'He's fine, *Mutti.* Nothing for you to worry about.'

'When did you get a letter?'

There's a pause then a sigh. 'Yesterday.'

'And?'

'As I say, he's fine.'

'Show me the letter.'

'*Mutti*, it's addressed to me.'

'Show me the letter. He's my son.'

There's a longer pause during which I imagine Frau Kuhn has crumpled and passed her precious letter to her mother-in-law. The old woman must read it quickly because then she exclaims, '*Gott im Himmel! Kein 'Heil Hitler'.*'

'Shhh, *Mutti*,' urges her daughter-in-law. 'The children.'

Their voices lowered, they hiss back and forth at one another.

'What's happening to my son?'

'*Mutti*, you've read what Dieter says. They're badly equipped. They're dying in great numbers. You know how Dieter feels about protecting his men.'

'Renate, this is treason. Anyway, it's the Russians' fault. Those *Untermensch*!' she spits out.

'Yes, it's the enemy, too. And their winter. It was so hard. It was the second time our men had endured it so it's no wonder…'

'No wonder what?' pipes nine-year-old Klaus.

'Oh, Klauschen,' says his mother. 'I thought you were playing. Where are Jutta and Hansi?'

'What were you saying about *Vati*?' I imagine him sticking out his bottom lip in that stubborn way he has.

'He's fighting for our victory, Klaus,' says the old woman, her voice like treacle now. 'He'll come home a hero, you'll see.'

'Yes, and he'll kill all those Russian swine!'

'Klaus, you must not use such words. Now fetch your brother and sister. *Oma* has brought us some treats.'

I carry the full laundry basket up the stairs. As I pass the kitchen, I say, 'Were you calling me, Frau Kuhn?'

'Oh, Natalya. The children are going to have their elevenses. You can finish your work since their *Oma* is here.'

'Very well,' I say. I mount the stairs to put the laundry away hearing the old woman again.

'Natalya! Why do you bother to use her name? She's one of those degenerates, too.'

'No, *Mutti*. Natalya is Ukrainian. Dieter is fighting the Russians...' but I hear no more as I distribute their clean laundry in their cupboards, my heart both lightened and darkened. I'm glad the Germans aren't having it all their own way, but if the Russians are pushing them west, will they reach us again? I catch myself thinking 'us' but remember I'm not there. It will be Mama, Lyubka and Verochka they might reach. Unless the partisans intervene. They were growing stronger when I was still at home. If the Russians do come, will I be able to return? They might treat me as a traitor for serving the Nazis. I try not to let the trembling of my heart show as I go back downstairs to finish this German family's ironing.

***

It's a warm sunny day. In the dappled light of the Kuhn garden, I'm hanging out the children's laundry as they play beneath the trees when Frau Kuhn comes hurrying around the side of the house, a letter in her hand. Another missive from the east, I think, as I bend to lift a little shirt out of the basket at my feet.

'Natalya, Natalya!' she calls, coming towards me waving the letter.

Then I realise. My stomach ripples with fear and I drop the shirt I'm holding. I run the few steps towards her, asking, '*Für mich?*' It is for me. A whole letter from home. In an envelope. I

79

ease open the edges carefully, unfold the sheet of paper, and there it is. My mother's handwriting. At first I can't see for tears, but then I begin to make out: '*Nasha dorohenka Natalya…*' My head swims.

In the distance I hear Frau Kuhn say, '*Kommt Kinder,*' and I'm alone in the warm sunlight with my mother and sisters.

They hope I am well. They are well. The harvest is in so they were all working in the fields, including little Verochka. Mama says I wouldn't recognise them, they've grown so much since I left. But I would. I would.

Mama says they have been good girls helping to gather and store the vegetables from the garden. I feel the absence of our garden in a hollow space as big as the Kuhn's garden and for a moment am confused by the sunlight. I look around me. This is not my home. This is several days' travel away. This is weeks and months away. How did I get here?

The cow is well and the hens. Why is Mama telling me that? Then I understand. To tell me their food sources are safe. She adds that a grey mist lingers in the village. So the Germans are still there. I'm surprised by Mama's little subterfuge, but am glad she's trying to tell me what's happening.

She finishes as I would expect. '*Buvay zdorovenka…*' and I will. I will stay healthy and I will return to them just as soon as I can. At the bottom of the page, Lyubka and Verochka have signed their names. Verochka has drawn me a sunflower beside hers. I kiss the paper their hands have touched and read it again. And again. Whatever is really happening at home, they are well enough to write cheerfully. Even if they aren't, they want to comfort me with their love so I must accept that they're well. That all is well. In a village where the Nazis are in charge while their compatriots in the east are being driven back towards the west. But for now, or whenever the letter was written, my three are safe. I wish I could accept my mother's kiss in person, bending my head as if she were beside me. But she isn't. I fold the letter and put it in my apron pocket.

As I bend to lift Jutta's dress out of the laundry basket to hang it on the line, I grieve for my little sisters. They won't be girls for much longer. The impossibility of hugging them to me is like a knife in my breast.

Chapter 9
England 1990

Nadiya entered the crowded carriage of the Underground train glancing around for an empty seat. There were none so she fixed her eyes on a teenager who stood up, his blush rising with him. She took the proffered seat as if it were her due. She sat perfectly still, looking straight ahead for the rest of her journey. She rose at her station and made her way out of the carriage onto the bustling platform. She did not hesitate in her path nor step out of the way for anyone else. When she reached the escalator Nadiya held onto the moving banister, her glove protecting her from any contact with others. She gazed upwards, not seeing the people crowding the escalator, neither those travelling away from her, nor those descending. She held her head erect until she reached the top of the moving stairs then glanced down to step onto the immobile floor of the Tube station. She presented her Travelcard to the blank face of the guard and tapped her stilettoed way across the shiny floor out into the dark street. The pavements were glossy with rain. She put up her umbrella for the five minute walk to her flat. Again she made a point of not registering faces around her. She avoided the puddles and the people as delicately as a cat.

She reached her home, a ground floor flat in an Edwardian terrace, letting herself in through the communal outer door to her rooms. As she entered, she pursed her lips to kiss the air to her cat.

'Kotyk!' she called.

A grey cat rose from the armchair stretching his back. He yawned then stepping onto the arm of the chair, jumped onto the table in the centre of the room. He approached Nadiya purring and brushed himself against his mistress's arm.

Nadiya stroked his silken head. 'There you are. Have you had a busy day, my kitty?'

She slipped off her black woollen coat, stepped out of her stilettoes and walked across to the kitchenette to put on the kettle. The cat followed and wound itself around her legs.

'I know, I know. I'm a terrible person.'

Nadiya reached for a sachet of food from the cupboard and emptied it into the cat's bowl. She poured him some water then opened the fridge door. She sighed. She hated shopping for food. She would have to have a supper of hummus and crackers.

'Never mind, Kotyku,' she said. 'It's almost bedtime.'

Nadiya had gone for drinks with her colleagues from the magazine where she worked. She thought of Nigel, the editor, as she munched on her crackers, leaning against the worktop.

'Come and eat with us,' he'd said.

'I can't,' she'd told him glancing at her watch to suggest she had another appointment.

'Who is it this time?' he'd asked with a smile. 'A rich banker? Someone from the City?'

'Never you mind,' she had smiled back.

'Never you mind…' But she did mind.

As the kettle boiled, she reached for a mug then put it back. She took a glass instead and poured herself the last of a bottle of white wine from the fridge. She crossed to the armchair, sat down and gazed across the room at the blank television screen. The cat leapt onto her lap and kneaded her legs before curling around to sit down in a coil, his tail flicked over his nose. Nadiya relaxed into the chair back, still hearing the echo of her own 'Never you mind'.

There was no date with a handsome rich man. There hadn't been since Mama's funeral. She knew she had become critical of almost every man she encountered. She didn't know how it had come about, but it felt like a long time since she had met someone who interested let alone excited her.

Her gaze travelled to the mantelpiece with its large family photograph: her nephew and nieces, her sisters and their husbands, Mama and *Tato* centre stage on their last anniversary. How had they done it, she wondered. Mama and *Tato* married for over forty years; her sisters with their good, steady men…who were sometimes dull, she admitted to herself. But there was no disputing how settled Lyuba and Vera were. And not just because of their children.

She stroked the cat's fur. 'We don't need anyone, do we?' she murmured as the cat snuggled itself more indulgently into Nadiya's dress. She sipped her wine. She liked being alone. Her flat was small, but it was hers. No one could enter without her permission. There might be little food in the fridge, but there were fresh flowers in a vase on the table.

What had Mama said? 'Don't worry. You have plenty of time. There'll be someone for you. If there's not, then you're strong enough to live for yourself.'

She would have to be.

She finished her wine and lifted the cat one-handed to her chest. She got up carrying the suspended cat through to her bedroom where she put him down in his favourite spot in the centre of the bed.

She brushed the loose hairs from her dress, hanging it in the wardrobe and chose another black dress for the following day. She laid out clean underwear and new tights, then went back to check her shoes for scuffs. She wiped the patent leather clean and brushed the shoulders of her coat before hanging it up ready for the morning.

She cleaned off her make-up and applied night cream, checking the corners of her eyes for wrinkles. As she leaned towards the mirror, she wondered if she would become a lonely old woman, obsessed with her cat. Then she dismissed the thought.

She climbed into bed and lay on her side. The cat shifted its position curling up behind Nadiya's knees with a loud purr.

Chapter 10
Bavaria, Germany 1943

I push the pram while Frau Kuhn has a firm grip on her handbag containing the food coupons. We walk slowly through the aisle of fruit and vegetable stalls. Frau Kuhn points to the expanse of the town square beyond, explaining how it used to be full of traders on market day, but now there are only two rows of them. We check the prices on all of the stalls then make our way back, buying expensive potatoes and onions.

'Why don't we grow our own?' I ask her.

'Where?'

'In the garden.'

'But there's no place for them.'

'We could make a place. I could dig a bed.'

She looks at me as if examining me.

'Perhaps,' she says.

It seems obvious to me. Any fool can grow potatoes. We should dig up the useless lawn and plant food. Later when we're back in her kitchen, I say, 'What happens to the things the stallholders throw away?'

She looks at me blankly.

'At the end of the market.'

'I've no idea. Do you think they have things to throw away?'

'Maybe.'

There's a pause. I'm not really supposed to go out alone, but presumably I can with her permission.

'I could pop along and check.'

She looks at me for a long moment. 'Alright. But be careful and come straight back.'

'I will.'

In the darkening afternoon I jump on a tram, Frau Kuhn's empty basket tucked against my side. When I get off at the square my heart sinks to see others rooting through the debris. But I'm here so I might as well look. I start at the far end of the line of ghostly stalls rifling through the rubbish to find the hard stalks of cabbages. I could use these for soup, so I take the best of them. At the next stall there are a couple of crumpled paper sacks. I open them out. One contains dust, but in the bottom of the other I strike gold. A couple of handfuls of tiny potatoes no bigger than the top of my thumb. I tip them all into the basket.

'Hey, you!' I hear but ignore it. I'm not the only one foraging and if I look up, it will signal guilt.

'Hey, you, *Ost*!'

I ignore him again. I'm from Halychyna so I don't have to wear the hated blue and white OST badge. So how does he know? I begin to walk towards my tram stop, hoping he will just go away. He doesn't.

I hear his footsteps clattering over the cobbles towards me. My back feels so wide and flat, such a perfect target that it seems impossible that a bullet should not shatter my flesh. I swallow my nausea. I'm doing nothing wrong. I have my mistress's permission to be here.

He grabs me by the arm spinning me round.

'*Was willst du?*' I shout, hoping my accent is good enough in this short question.

He looks at my chest obviously wondering where my badge is, while I take in his soft cap with its wreathed eagle in a green border telling me he's *Ordnungspolizei*. He's armed with a pistol, but it's still in its leather holster.

'What are you doing?' he asks.

I show him my basket.

'*Papiere?*'

I reach into my coat pocket and hand him my workers' identity card. He flicks it open, checks my face against the photo and, just as he says, 'Name?' there's a shout from across the square. He looks up. Three of his colleagues have surrounded an old man.

'*Du, Jude!*' shouts one of the officers.

My *Orpo* flicks the pass back at me. 'Get home!' he snaps before trotting across the square.

I don't look back. I try to breathe normally while I head for the nearest side street. I want to work my way around the square to the tram stop without exposing myself in that huge open space. I hurry along the street making for a deep doorway where I stand well back to wait. Then I hear two shots. They're so loud they seem almost beside me but they're over the roofs of buildings opposite in the open square. Shouting follows and I cringe back, seeing the old man in my mind's eye. I imagine him lying on the uncomfortable cobbles and wonder what sort of a threat he posed to three well-built men. My breath shortens while I wait for more shots. I close my eyes to be surrounded by trees in full leaf on a green hillside in the *Karpati* with a stream rushing by. I daren't open my eyes to see Roman's bloody body lying at my feet. I want to scream, but am interrupted by the clanking of the approaching tram. I peer out of the doorway. Coming towards me, bell ringing, is the beautiful sight of the number seven tram.

I step forward, put out my arm and, miraculously, the tram stops. I board it and am whisked away from death and danger. I stand, swaying, holding onto the ceiling strap, trying to breathe evenly. I don't make eye contact with any of the other passengers, but as I pretend to watch the buildings passing by, I check there are no uniforms on board. Only civilians. I breathe more slowly but I don't relax. Even when I've alighted, I hurry along the pavement to the Kuhn's gate and around the back of the house to what, for the moment, seems like a blessed door.

'Is that you, Natalya?' calls Frau Kuhn as I enter.

'Yes, it's me.'

She comes into the vestibule as I hang up my coat.

'Everything alright?'

'Yes,' I say.

She glances in the basket. 'Not very good pickings?' I can see her wondering why I bothered. I don't know why I bothered either. I don't have enough words to explain to her that her people are too keen on death. That they smash and destroy others in their arrogance. That their violence is profligate.

'Don't be disappointed,' she says.

'Some vegetable stock and seed potatoes,' I mumble. My words won't come out properly.

'Well, then,' she says and, with another glance at me, she returns to the children.

I give myself a moment to gather enough energy to help her put the children to bed. All I want to do is to lie down in the privacy of my room to try to absorb what has just happened but it will have to wait.

I do my chores and when they're finished I drag my weary body up the two flights of stairs to my attic room. I close the door on the Kuhns and the rest of Germany and lie down on my bed. The luxury! To have a place where I can let my face do what it wants. Where I don't have to pretend to care or to be innocent. I ache from the day's events so I turn on my side closing my eyes to seek out a place to be happy.

I see them…half a dozen young men in a motley mixture of uniforms, coming towards me along the river bank. The cows were at my back, grazing on the rich green pasture beside the Dniester while I was watching the sunlight on the water. A girl daydreaming.

'Hey, girlie,' one of them called.

I remember turning towards them knowing them instantly for partisans, but wondering where they had come from. The river plain behind them was flat and wide, apart from a row of willows which followed the stream flowing downhill to join its bigger brother. As they came nearer the one who had called to me spoke again.

'So which village are you from?'

'The one up there,' I said pointing up the hill to the trees.

'Where?'

'Beyond the trees.'

'You're scaring her,' said another voice and, as I looked at the owner of it, my heart turned over in my chest. He was smiling at me and I had an impression of curls and light. I felt as if I'd been struck dumb.

'We've been following the river,' he said. 'We seem to have lost track of how far we've come.'

'It's Krasivka,' I said, determined not to simper.

'There,' he said. 'You see, Vasyl, you just need to ask nicely.'

Vasyl glowered. 'Why don't you tell her our life story while you're about it?'

'That would be foolish,' said the handsome one. I noticed that both he and Vasyl carried ancient rifles, while the others had stout sticks.

'It gets very muddy further up,' I said. Even now, remembering, I blush at my stupidity.

'Muddy?'

'Yes. You'll have to come a bit inland to get around it…If you're going upriver.'

'What about crossing the river?' asked Vasyl.

'Nicely, Vasyl.'

'Please,' added Vasyl, trying to stretch his lips into a smile.

The handsome one laughed, his blue eyes meeting mine, inviting me to laugh at his colleague too.

I couldn't help smiling back. I wanted the moment to go on and on, but again caught myself feeling silly, so I turned to the river to give them a sensible answer. 'It's fairly deep,' I began pointing the way they'd come. 'The current is stronger near the bend. But here,' I took a few paces away from them, 'this is the shallowest part.' I pointed toward the water. 'You can see that there are flat stones under the water. They carry on almost to the other bank.'

I looked back at them. They were all watching me intently.

'Is it deep here?' asked the handsome one, coming to stand beside me.

'Not really. Not at the moment. Up to here.' I patted my thigh.

'We could cross here, Vasyl,' he said. 'It might be easier than further upstream.'

'It is,' I said. 'You have to go beyond the next village before you can make an easy crossing. There are boats, though.'

There was a silence. I could see them thinking about what I'd said then Vasyl seemed to come to a decision. 'We'll cross here.'

The handsome one looked around. 'A line of willows, the woods mounting the hill, the broken stones over there on the ridge. What is that?' he asked, turning to me.

'The quarry.'

'And the NKVD?' asked Vasyl.

'In the village,' I said. 'But there are more of them further up.'

'Many?' he asked.

'Enough,' I said.

He looked at me again and for a moment the sunlight dimmed.

'They shot my father.'

'*Divchyno*,' said the handsome one touching my arm.

91

'Show us the crossing again,' said Vasyl, 'please.'

I turned back to the river bank showing them the stones beneath the water. 'Here.'

They began to approach the riverbank.

'I'd take off your trousers before you cross,' I said as I made to turn and walk away.

The handsome one leaned in towards me. 'I'm Roman and I'll be back.' Then with a grin, 'No peeping now.'

I found myself smiling like an idiot again, so I made myself turn my back on them to walk away.

'And you?' Roman called.

'Natalya,' I called back, without turning.

Chapter 11
England 1990

Vera stared at her reflection in the hall mirror as she waited for Nadiya to pick up the phone. Finally, a voice said in breathy tones, 'Hello?'

'Nadiya, it's Vera.'

'Oh, hello. What's wrong?'

'Nothing's wrong. I'm just ringing you because Lyuba's birthday's coming up.'

'Oh yes.'

'I thought I'd take her out for a meal. Do you want to come with us?'

'It depends when. Work's mad at the moment.'

'So an evening would be better than lunch?'

'Yes. What day does her birthday fall on?'

'Thursday. She'll probably go out with Adrian and Val that day. Are you free on the Friday?'

'I'll have to check. I might have a date.'

'Well, let me know as soon as you can. I really want to take her out. I don't think she's coping at all well with Mama's death.'

'None of us are.'

'I know, but she's getting obsessed with researching DP's in Germany and who knows what else.'

'It's just her way of coping. You know she likes to have all the facts.'

'Yes, but she's trying to find out things which no one can really tell us.'

'*Tato* can.'

'But does he want to? They had a hard time in the camps.'

'I know. OK, Vera, I'll check my diary and I'll let you know.'

'Alright,' sighed Vera, wondering why Nadiya could not admit to needing her older sisters as much as they needed her.

***

The three sisters entered *La Vie Française*, Lyuba's favourite restaurant, where they were offered a table in the window.

'No, can we have one further back, please?' asked Vera, dreading the thought of passers-by peering in at a tearful Lyuba. But it might all go well, she thought. They might have a lovely evening.

The sisters settled themselves at their table, Nadiya glancing around but then dismissing the couples and groups of friends as unworthy of any attention. She smoothed the back of her skirt as she sat down then reached into her handbag for a parcel wrapped in silver coloured paper with an elaborate silver bow.

'Happy birthday, *sestrichko*,' she said, passing her gift to Lyuba.

'Thank you, Nadiya,' said Lyuba, leaning forward to kiss her youngest sister on the cheek.

'Open it, then,' said Nadiya smiling in anticipation.

Lyuba undid the bow removing the paper tidily.

'You're not going to re-use the paper, are you?' asked Nadiya and all three women grinned conspiratorially, remembering their mother's hatred of waste.

'No, but don't tell,' said Lyuba as she lifted the lid off the box inside the wrapping paper. More silver tissue rustled as she pulled it apart to reveal several strands of heavy silver links interspersed with garnets. Lyuba lifted the necklace out, stretching it between both hands. 'Oh, Nadiya, it's beautiful. Thank you. But you shouldn't have spent so much.'

'That's my business,' said Nadiya. 'Yours is to enjoy wearing it.'

'I will. It's lovely.' She leaned forward to kiss her youngest sister again.

Nadiya didn't mention that she had been gripped by a superstitious need to buy Lyuba something expensive to shield her from death.

The waiter brought the menus and placed them before each of the women. 'Today's specials are on the board. The soup of the day is wild mushroom.'

'Thank you,' said Vera. 'Shall we do my present before we order?'

Lyuba smiled. 'If you'd like to.'

Vera passed Lyuba a package wrapped in purple paper. 'Happy birthday.'

'Thank you.' Lyuba unwrapped the paper and drew out a fine silk scarf like a magician, holding it up in both hands to see it properly. 'Oh, I've wanted one of these for ages. Did you get it at the craft shop at the Abbey?'

'Yes. I don't know how many times I've seen you looking at them.'

'Because they're beautiful…but very expensive. You shouldn't have,' she added, leaning forward to kiss her sister. 'Thank you.'

A young waitress approached them. 'Are you ready to order yet?'

'We will be in a few minutes,' said Nadiya. 'In the meantime, will you bring us a bottle of champagne, please?'

'That's a bit extravagant,' said Lyuba.

'My treat. Besides we all deserve it,' said Nadiya.

When the champagne was served the women chinked their glasses.

'*Nazdorovya*!'

They sipped their wine and then examined the menu, although they were all drawn to what they knew the restaurant did best – the home-made pate and the venison stew.

Later, the waitress approached again. 'Would you like to see the dessert menu?'

'Not for a moment,' said Lyuba, as Nadiya topped up their glasses with red wine.

'That was delicious,' said Vera, 'but I'm not sure I'll be able to manage a pudding.'

'Nor me,' said Nadiya. 'I'll have a coffee, though.'

'They do a good strawberry shortcake,' said Lyuba.

'Mama's strawberry pudding,' said Nadiya.

Both of her sisters responded with sighs, remembering the confection of warm custard and fluffy egg whites bejewelled with juicy strawberries.

'Her *Sachertorte* was my favourite,' said Vera.

'She must have learned to make that in Germany,' said Lyuba. 'I doubt they would have eaten it in the village.'

Vera and Lyuba exchanged a glance. 'And certainly not in the mountains with the partisans.'

'What?' asked Nadiya.

'What do you mean?'

'You two. You know something I don't. As usual.'

'No, we don't,' said Vera. 'Not really.'

'We found a photo,' said Lyuba, 'of Mama before she left home.'

'And?'

Lyuba reached down for her handbag and, withdrawing the photograph, passed it to Nadiya.

Nadiya looked at the image briefly then flicked the photograph over. '*My dearest wife,*' she breathed. '*Roman*'. She turned it over again to examine the faces of the two figures. 'He's very handsome.'

'Nadiya!' exclaimed Lyuba.

'What? He is. You can see why Mama was in love with him.'

'But it's not *Tato*.'

'No. It was 1943. She hadn't met *Tato* yet. So what happened to this one?'

'Killed by the Nazis,' said Vera.

'Poor Mama.'

'He was a partisan so they married secretly. Then when he was killed *Tato* said she thought they'd been betrayed. Mama had to go to Germany as a slave labourer to avoid suspicion,' explained Vera.

'So *Tato* knows?'

'Mama told him before they were married.'

Nadiya looked at the faces again. 'Mama's first love. How romantic.'

'What about *Tato*?' asked Lyuba.

'Her second love obviously.' Nadiya looked closely at her oldest sister. 'She loved *Tato*.'

'I know.'

'So what's wrong, Lyuba?'

'I don't know. I think I was shocked, that's all.'

'Because Mama didn't confide in you?'

'No, but we didn't know.'

'We didn't need to,' said Nadiya. 'If she'd had a child by him it would have been different.'

'Besides she was very young,' said Vera.

Lyuba sighed. 'I feel for *Tato*.'

'There's no need,' said Vera. 'He knew about Roman yet he still wanted to marry her.'

'Don't you feel sad for him?' Lyuba persisted.

'No,' said Vera. 'Think about it. He got to marry Mama himself and they lived the rest of their lives together.'

'But now…'

'Now he has us three, our husbands, our children. He might not have had any of that without Mama. Look at how many old Ukrainian men have never married. All those sad *samitni.*'

'Not only does he have all of us, but we're all part of her, too. *Tato* was lucky,' said Nadiya.

Lyuba turned to her. 'You'll find somebody.'

'Oh, this isn't about me...or about you,' said Nadiya. 'Both of them lost all they had but they found each other and started a family of their own. They were happy with that.'

'Yes, I suppose so,' said Lyuba.

'What is it, Lyuba, that really upsets you about this?' asked Nadiya. 'Why can't you let it go?'

'I feel as if I lost Mama twice. She died and then I discovered this about her. I feel as if I've never known her.'

'That's silly,' said Nadiya. 'We know enough. She loved us.'

'Yes, she did,' said Vera.

Chapter 12
Bavaria, Germany September 1943

There's no point in trying to take the children to the park today. It's windy and threatening to rain. There's a storm of red and yellow leaves flying past the window as I encourage them with their painting. It will keep them busy for a few minutes at least. Hansi particularly loves the mess, slapping slabs of colour onto squares of unused wallpaper. Klaus is producing a meticulous battle scene in which the grey forces overwhelm the green in waves of victorious stick men. Jutta paints a face and I don't ask whose. She has clung to her mother more over recent weeks as Frau Kuhn becomes quieter and greyer. There have been no more letters from the Front. While she tries to hide her anxiety from the children, she doesn't succeed with her daughter. Jutta climbs onto her mother's lap as often as she can, which isn't as often as she'd like because Renate is trying to make the children more independent. But Jutta's having none of it. She senses danger.

September was a month of shocks. The British bombed Munich. Twice. That's less than a hundred kilometres away. Then the Italians surrendered. Now we even see bombers going over in the daytime. Frau Kuhn Senior comes with smaller and smaller quantities of black market food. Somehow she reconciles her use of a thriving black market with her continuing admiration of the *Führer*. My mistress has made it very clear there's to be no waste. The coffee and cake party of early summer would be unthinkable now. Even for an officer's wife. I introduce her and the children to *varenyki* – our flour and potato dumplings, so tasty with a little onion and butter, although I know how lucky we are to have these modest items.

The *varenyki* provide a distraction for the children. They learn to roll and cut the dough, to make the little parcels. As we work, Hansi plays with a handful of dough, but the other two take the task seriously. Frau Kuhn works with us.

'Did your mother teach you how to make these, Natalya?'

'Of course. All of us girls could make *varenyki* from a young age.'

Jutta pipes up. 'Girls? What girls?'

'My sisters.'

She stops trying to pinch the dough together to look at me properly. 'Where are they?'

Klaus snorts with derision. 'In the east, you little fool.'

'Klaus, please don't be rude to your sister.'

I tune out the family row to continue slapping and pinching the dough, making rows of floured dumplings. For a moment it could be Mama's kitchen with Lyubka and Verochka making supper.

'Natalya, Natalya!' cries Jutta, calling me back to Germany.

'Yes, what is it?'

'Look.' She holds up a sticky grey mess which not even she will want to eat.

'That's wonderful. Want to do another?'

***

Frau Kuhn hands me a postcard, the second one of the month which I'm allowed to send home. I shake my head and go up to my room, returning with some precious notes. *Reichsmarks*, fives, with the face of a stern youth on one side.

'I'd like to send these to my mother,' I say.

She nods leading me into the *Sturmbannführer's* study. She takes an envelope from the desk tidy, opens a drawer and removing a clean sheet of crisp white paper places them both on the desk. I try not to weep at her generosity. Paper is in such short supply and envelopes almost impossible to buy. I feel as if she's raiding Dieter's store for me.

'*Setz dich.*'

'*Nein, danke.*' I shake my head. I could no more sit and write to Mama at this desk than fly. '*In meine Kamera,*' I say softening it with a smile. She nods as I take the precious paper up to my room.

Two whole sides. I wonder how I should use it. I have hundreds of questions for Mama, but that's almost a waste of paper. She'll know I'm hungry for news. I turn the thought around to think of Mama wondering about me…

28 November 1943

Dorohenka moya Mama, dorohenki moyi sestrychki…

How dear they are to me, especially now that I can't take them for granted. So I tell Mama since I rarely go out of the house alone and I have nothing I need to buy I am sending her some money.

Yesterday we had our first snow. I'm sure you must have had yours already. The children were thrilled although Frau Kuhn and I kept the shutters closed until they were dressed and had had breakfast. We knew we'd have a mutiny on our hands if we let them see the snow as soon as they got up. They loved playing in it although Hansi found it difficult to walk in. He kept tipping over into the snow and laughing. Jutta tried to build a snowman but she had to struggle on her own. Klaus wouldn't help her. He cleared a path around the house to the gate. So there you have the three children I look after, Mama. When we brought them indoors, we had to change their clothes completely. Despite their red cheeks, they would soon have taken cold…

I don't tell Mama that we leave the children in bed as late as we can in the morning to conserve precious supplies of fuel. There has been no new delivery of coal since I arrived and even officers' wives are now struggling to get hold of the basics. The redoubtable Frau Kuhn Senior struggles to get wood for us from her contacts. I think of the woodpile along the whole side of Mama's house and am so glad there will be enough wood for them this winter. I don't tell Mama that the bitter cold has surprised Frau Kuhn. Apparently it's much colder than usual this winter, just to add to everyone's woes.

I warmed them up with a good bowl of borshch, Mama, just like you used to make for us girls...

I pause, steady my breathing and continue.

Frau Kuhn showed me how to make her cabbage soup but I think the children now prefer the taste of our borshch. The children's grandmother brought us some beetroot from her village. There's room in Frau Kuhn's garden to grow some vegetables but she doesn't seem to have thought of doing this. She could easily grow potatoes, beetroot and cabbage. There's not one fruit tree in the whole garden. Lovely flowers, but you can't eat those. However, we have enough to eat and she has said I can plant some vegetables in the spring...

I don't tell them how careful we are now to eat everything... slowly.

Last night, after the children had gone to bed I helped Frau Kuhn to make a board game for Klaus. I think she intends to hide it for him for Christmas. There are few toys for sale this year so we are making a game with hand drawn maps of a village, some woods and a river, with squares and counters so that Klaus will be able to play a game of war. As we sit colouring in the blues and greens, I can't help but remember our lovely hills. Are the woods full of snow at the moment?

I stare out of my window and see the long meadows falling away to the trees which line the river in the valley bottom. I paint it white with snow and people it with the shrieks of youngsters, sliding down the hill on whatever they could find. The three of us could just fit on *Tato*'s wooden sledge. We would go hurtling down with the others, the wind whipping tears from our eyes as we yelled with laughter. I sigh.

Well, that's all for now, my dear ones. Stay well and hopefully we'll all be together again soon. With all my love…

***

Frau Kuhn receives a reply before I do. One frosty morning I watch her sprint down the path to retrieve the letter which has just been placed in our mailbox. The way she hurries back to the house tells me it's from Dieter, not from Mama. I let out my breath and continue with the dusting. Then I relent and go to check on the children. Klaus has his men on manoeuvres on the dining room table, as he creates the battle terrain with the green chenille table cloth. Jutta sits at her little desk with an old drawing book of Klaus's colouring with the stubs of some crayons. Seeing me, Hansi picks up his train and waves it.

'Good boy,' I say. 'Where's your train going?' I ask as I squat beside him.

'To *Vati*,' he grins.

Klaus tuts moving around the table so he has his back to us.

'I'm drawing a picture for *Vati*,' says Jutta, not to be left out.

'I'm sure he'll love it,' I say.

I leave them to their toys. I take my dusters and polish into the *Sturmbannführer*'s study, but I stop short when I see Frau Kuhn at his desk poring over a large atlas. She looks up at me, her face ashen, her eyes huge.

'Natalya…'

'*Entschuldigung*,' I begin to apologise.

'No, no. Come and help me,' she says. Again I wonder if her husband has died. She points to the map. 'The Dnipro. The river. Where is it?'

I move my finger west of hers. 'Here.'

She looks up at me in horror and then peers into the tiny text of the map. She traces the river north to Kyiv, south to Kherson… then she spreads her palm across the Ukrainian land to the east. 'All those young men,' she breathes. 'All dead for nothing.'

After a moment, she says, 'Where are your family?'

I point to the land west of the Dniester. 'Here.'

She nods. 'Good.'

'For now,' I murmur.

She looks up quickly. 'Yes, for now.' She draws her finger to the right, to Stalingrad, then drags it to the left. Past the dead at Kursk. To the Dnipro.

'Red with blood,' she says in a low voice.

'Pardon?'

'That's what my husband says,' she whispers.

'The Dnipro was red with blood?'

'It's not the Dnipro, it's the Don.' Klaus storms over to his mother. 'Here, *Mutti*.' He points at the river to the east. 'It's here.'

We both stare at him appalled. How long has he been in the room?

He leans towards his mother from the opposite side of the

desk. 'Look, *Mutti*, here. You've got it wrong.'

'Yes, you're right, Klauschen,' she says. 'Silly me.'

He looks up at her and I see he's fighting the trembling of his lips. '*Vati* is here. They're beating the Russians. Our *Führer* said so.'

'Yes, he did, *mein Kind*,' she says gently and I will her to hold back her tears. '*Vati*'s beating the Russians.'

They stare at one another, then Klaus breaks away.

'I'm going to get my soldiers to kill them all,' he shouts as he stomps back to the dining table. 'They're not going to push us back across any stupid Ukrainian rivers.'

***

Klaus's games with his soldiers become more serious after his tenth birthday. He must join the *Deutsches Jungvolk* by law, but no law is needed to force him into the ranks of regimented children. His eagerness is palpable.

Frau Kuhn has managed to obtain his uniform despite the clothing shortages and he struts about the kitchen in his khaki shirt and black shorts. He keeps adjusting the woggle on his black neckerchief in his anxiety to be gone to his admission ceremony.

Frau Kuhn enters the kitchen with a tidy Jutta, who has been allowed to join her mother to see Klaus admitted into the ranks of boys who want to be men.

'Come, Klaus,' says Frau Kuhn. 'Let's practice your oath once more.'

'I know it, *Mutti*. There's no need to practice it.'

'Just once, Klaus. *Vati* will be so proud of you. I'm sure Hansi and Natalya would like to hear it as they're not going to be at the ceremony.'

'Oh, very well,' and he deigns to recite, in as deep a voice as he can manage: 'In the presence of this blood banner which represents our *Führer*, I swear to devote all my energies and my strength to the saviour of our country, Adolf Hitler. I am willing and ready to give up my life for him, so help me God.'

Frau Kuhn represses a shudder at the thought of her own child dying while I repress one at the thought of any child dying in such an unworthy cause.

'Come, *Mutti*,' says the little *Führer*. 'We don't want to be late.'

Hansi and I are left to our own devices. We prepare *Lebkuchen* together, measuring and mixing flour with Frau Kuhn's carefully hoarded ginger and cinnamon. We pour in the melted butter and honey from their grandmother and Hansi takes a turn at stirring the dough. He enjoys moulding the cookies most and I give him a handful to roll into a sticky ball, while I roll as many other balls as I can. When they're all on the tray, I let Hansi squash them flat with his plump little hand. We put the biscuits in the oven to bake then I stand him on a stool at the sink, where we pretend he's helping with the washing up. He splashes the water, enjoying the mess.

We remove the scented biscuits from the oven and after they have cooled, Hansi and I test one for flavour. We keep the rest for Klaus's triumphant return. He marches into the kitchen slapping his *Deutsches Jungvolk* badge with its white Sieg rune on a black background onto the table in front of me.

'*Du*,' he says, 'sew this onto my uniform.'

Frau Kuhn has hurried in after him. 'Klaus, please don't be rude to Natalya.'

'It's alright, Frau Kuhn,' I say, 'but I thought soldiers sewed their own badges on.'

Klaus looks nonplussed.

Frau Kuhn gives me a little smile. 'Of course they do,' she says. 'Perhaps you could show Klaus how to do it.'

'With pleasure,' I say.

***

Some days later, I'm washing the worst of the mud off the boys' knee length socks when Frau Kuhn calls down the basement stairs to me.

'Natalya, could you leave that for a moment and come up here, please?'

I climb the stairs, wiping my hands on my apron. As I enter the kitchen, I see Frau Kuhn Senior standing, one hand clenched in a fist at her side, her other arm protecting Klaus who stands beside her. They're both looking at me accusingly, so I turn to my mistress, wondering what I can have done wrong.

Frau Kuhn says, 'I'm sorry, Natalya, but I must ask you to show me your room.'

'Sorry!' snorts Frau Kuhn Senior.

Her daughter-in-law gives her a quick glance.

'Of course, Frau Kuhn,' I say. 'Now?'

'Yes, please,' she replies.

I lead the way and at the turn in the stairs, I see Klaus and his grandmother following. I can't imagine what they hope to see. I've made my bed, as usual. My few clothes are hanging on the back of the door. Then my heart lurches…The photograph of Roman and me is displayed on the table.

As we climb up to the second floor, my heart pounds more swiftly. At least he wasn't in uniform in the photo. He's wearing a suit over his embroidered *sorochka*. I will not give the photograph up and decide that I will do whatever I must do to keep it. They will not rob me of this precious memento.

I open the door to my room taking a couple of steps towards the table. I turn to the others, my body screening the photo and, as I am placing my hands behind my back Klaus screams,

'There, I told you so. She's betraying our *Führer*!'

I look at him open-mouthed to see him pointing at the

portrait of Hitler, which is obscured by the two halves of my *rushnyk* hanging down from the picture hook.

'This is what we were warned of at *Heimabende*,' says Klaus.

There's no point in feeling angry at the indoctrination Klaus is subject to every Wednesday evening at his *Deutsches Jungvolk* meeting.

'It's a disgrace!' exclaims the old woman, as Frau Kuhn steps forward to touch one side of my *rushnyk*.

I want to laugh with relief at the banality of my crime, but know I'm not out of the woods yet. My fingers find the photograph and while they're all staring at the sliver of the face of a monster which is still visible, I slip the photo into my apron pocket.

Frau Kuhn raises the fabric of the *rushnyk* to reveal the hateful face. 'Natalya?'

'Frau Kuhn?'

'See! I told you she'd covered him up. She's a traitor!'

'Quiet, please, Klaus. Let Natalya speak.'

'*Mutti*, we should call the *Ordnungspolizei*.'

'No, Klaus,' says Frau Kuhn more firmly. 'I want to hear Natalya speak first.'

'Huh,' grunts the old woman. 'Let's hear what the *Untermensch* has to say.'

Frau Kuhn looks at me. 'Natalya, could you tell me why the portrait of our leader is covered over?'

'By accident, Frau Kuhn,' I say.

'By accident?'

'Yes, Frau Kuhn. This is called a *rushnyk*,' I say as I lift one side of the fabric and drape it over the corner of the picture frame. 'It's traditional in Ukrainian houses to place such an embroidered cloth over our holiest images. Like this,' I add, as I lift the second side of the *rushnyk* over the second corner of the frame. 'We have shrines like this in all our homes.'

'Oh, I see,' says Frau Kuhn and I think I hear relief in her voice. 'There you are, Klaus. Natalya isn't showing disrespect to our *Führer*. It's a Ukrainian way of honouring important people.'

'Not just people,' I say. 'But God too.'

As expected, I see a spark in Klaus's eye, although the old woman doesn't look convinced yet.

'We usually hold the ends of the rushnyk with a nail or a tack driven into the wall,' I explain, holding up one end to demonstrate, 'but I didn't want to damage your wall, Frau Kuhn.'

'That was very thoughtful of you, Natalya,' says Frau Kuhn. I have no way of knowing if she's taken what I've said at face value. But that's of little consequence as long as the *Orpo* aren't called. I'd rather live with the *Führer*'s face than be incarcerated in some German prison.

'She should fix those ends up, shouldn't she, *Mutti*?'

'Yes, Klaus. Natalya, I'm sure we can find a hammer and a couple of nails in the basement.'

I nod, wait a moment, then realise they aren't going to let me off. They're going to witness my attempts to honour their beloved *Führer*. So I say, 'I'll go and have a look now, shall I?'

'Yes, please,' says Frau Kuhn.

'I'll go with her,' says Klaus, as if he thinks I might not want to find a hammer and nails.

We trot down the stairs to the basement. My footfalls are light. Klaus stomps behind me. I feel his childish hands itch to be holding a rifle at my back. What was he doing in my room anyway I think, then tuck that thought away to be examined later.

I kneel to open a cupboard. The hammer's easily found among the *Sturmbannführer*'s neatly stacked tools. Klaus pushes me aside reaching in for a cardboard box full of assorted nails.

He pokes through them and lifts out two long ones.

'Those are too big,' I say.

He ignores me and sets off upstairs. I'm not going to let a child hammer huge holes into my *rushnyk* so I take the box upstairs hoping Frau Kuhn won't want her wall damaged by nails long enough for Christ's palms.

I don't hurry after my little Nazi. I have the hammer after all.

His mother is as sensible as I had expected. She chooses two small tacks from the box, while I have another thought which I set aside for later. What were those women looking at while I was downstairs?

We tap the tacks into the top corners of my *rushnyk* . When it's done, we all step back to admire the manic face, now framed by a white cloth with its bright bands of embroidery.

'There, that's much better,' says Frau Kuhn. 'Now Natalya is like the rest of us.'

'Hardly,' says the old woman, as she turns to go down the stairs. 'Come, Klaus.'

'Make sure you keep it like that,' he says, as he follows his grandmother.

'Yes, it would be better so,' says Frau Kuhn quietly.

'Of course, Frau Kuhn,' I say as I pick up the hammer and the box of nails to return to my washing in the basement.

I make myself keep my own thoughts at bay until hours later when I finally go to bed after the last of my chores is complete. I close the door of my room and leaning back on it take the photograph out of my pocket. I look at it for a moment wondering what sort of dreamland we were inhabiting, that we thought we'd be allowed to be happy.

But where to put it now so that it's safe from little fingers?

I could put it under my pillow. But that's too girlish. Or under the mattress. But again, it's an obvious place. I look around the room. There's only the small table and my empty sack on the floor. My eyes travel the walls coming to rest on the now-garlanded portrait. I smile to myself. The perfect place. I lift the bottom of the frame away from the wall tucking the photograph of us behind the image of the man responsible for Roman's death and my enforced exile. He can now be responsible for guarding the picture of our love.

As I lie on my bed, eyes wide open, I let myself explore my unmasking as a traitor. Klaus must have come to examine my room alone, perhaps to look for something to incriminate me. Then he must have brought his more-than-willing grandmother to witness my evil action. I should have expected it. This is not my home. Not even temporarily. I'm not free to leave, or even to come and go to the town. I'm not allowed in their churches, nor in the theatre, nor even in some shops. Although I am allowed to do my mistress's shopping for her. Klaus reminded us all that *Ostarbeiter* are subject to even harsher laws than the general German population. We can be imprisoned and executed for any perceived crime against the State. Where there are so many of us, we're expendable.

I realise that Klaus has done me a favour. I had relaxed and become complacent. Vasyl told us we must always keep our guard up. Never trust the enemy. Klaus showed me today that a German child can point the finger at a Ukrainian adult with mortal consequences. I turn on my side resolving to keep sharp eyes in a bland face.

***

I cut the stiff wallpaper into strips half a centimetre wide and several centimetres long. Then I start to fold them together one by one.

'What's that?' asks Jutta, climbing onto the chair beside me.

'Wait and see.' I go on folding, adding another strip to my

structure.

'What's it going to be?' she asks with the edge of a whine in her voice.

'Nearly done,' I say. With a last fold, I turn the paper angel to face her.

'Oh, *ein Engel*,' she breathes. 'Let me.'

I begin again, taking a couple of strips in my hands. 'Here you take one too. Hold these bits of paper like this. Now fold it here…' So we go on, slowly folding, Jutta's tongue helping her to concentrate.

When we've finished, it's not a bad job for a five-year-old.

'Another one,' she says and we continue to fold, Jutta in wonder.

Frau Kuhn enters the room.

'Look, *Mutti*. I've made angels.'

'How lovely,' says Frau Kuhn. 'Did Natalya show you how?'

'Yes. We've made lots.'

'You could hang them on our Christmas tree,' says Frau Kuhn. She smiles at me. 'Is this another Ukrainian tradition, Natalya?'

'Yes, it is.' I don't add the explanation that we'd have made them from straw, sitting around the table together, creating a large one to hang above the stove, and small ones to hang from boughs of fir decorating the room. Nor that my mother's kitchen would have been scented with baking and that we'd have sung carols as we'd worked. Home…

I'm jerked back to the Kuhn's by Klaus striding into the room in his black and khaki uniform.

'Look Klaus, an angel,' says Jutta, holding up one of her creations.

He stops to glare at her, then rips the angel from her hand, throwing it to the floor and stamping on it. Over Jutta's screaming, he's yelling: 'Religious rubbish! It's all rubbish!'

112

Frau Kuhn looks as shocked as Jutta. 'Klaus, stop it! You're upsetting Jutta.' She tries to grasp his arm, but he throws her off. 'Klaus, stop this right now.' Again she tries to pull him away from the trampled scraps of paper, but he pulls back with a much greater strength than she expects and she stumbles against him. He moves aside letting her fall to her knees. 'Klaus, go to your room at once!' she cries.

'Gladly. I won't spend another moment in this hell hole!'

'What has come over you?' asks Frau Kuhn in horror.

'Our *Führer* says we must love only Germany. We must think only of victory. We should not be wasting our time with this nonsense.' With that he marches out of the room.

There's a moment's shocked silence and even Jutta sits open-mouthed as she watches her kneeling mother gather up the broken angels from the carpet.

'I'm sorry, Frau Kuhn,' I begin but she interrupts me.

'No, Natalya. There's no need for you to be sorry. The person who should be sorry…' She stops herself, biting her lower lip, but can't help her eyes flickering to the portrait on the wall. He glares back. There's no room for two gods in Germany.

Frau Kuhn gets up swallowing her tears. How can she defend her children from the madness in this country? Her home is not inviolate. The children mix with others. Especially Klaus with his *Deutsches Jungvolk* meetings and his habit of listening to the radio, in what we thought was a sad attempt to follow his father's progress. But his young mind has simply absorbed all of the hatred and bile which pours out of the *Volksempfänger* with its eagle and swastika.

Christmas can only be a sad affair. The children receive a gift of apples from their grandmother, who also manages to provide a small tree. Frau Kuhn searches out some candles from last December and when they've been arranged in the tree and lit, their gentle light illumines the faces of Hansi and Jutta as they hum along with their mother's singing of '*Stille Nacht*'. But she can't finish the first verse. Klaus won't come downstairs and Dieter is somewhere in the tight grip of winter. She bows her head trying to smile at her two youngest children. Even Frau Kuhn Senior wipes a tear away. I stand in the doorway hoping with all my heart that mine are warm and well.

I slip out of the house to stand in the snow-filled yard and look up at the cold sky. There's a sickle moon shining so sweetly it can only be oblivious to the misery down here. The same goes for the twinkling stars. But I draw comfort from the fact that Lyubka and Verochka might, at this very moment, be going from house to house through the village with the other youngsters singing carols.

I hum to myself, '*Nova radist stala…*' A new joy came to the world. Who will save us though, I wonder. But before I can reach a hopeless conclusion, I'm called back inside by Frau Kuhn.

Chapter 13
England January 1991

Lyuba slipped into the sitting room as soon as she saw her father begin to test the CD player in the dining room. The strains of her mother's favourite Christmas carol followed her. '*Nova radist stala…*' She hummed the next phrase as she bent to her task but was soon interrupted.

'Oh, you startled me!' she said as Taras entered the room. She was on her knees looking into the back of the sideboard for a book she thought she remembered seeing among Mama's magazines. She had always ignored the closely typed pages of '*Nashe Zhitya*', '*Our Life*', the magazine for the women in the diaspora…just as she now realised she'd taken little notice of the fine detail of her mother's cooking. To her embarrassment, she was not entirely certain how to make the first course for the Christmas Eve meal. One of the most important meals of the year and she would have to tell her father she had not paid enough attention.

'What are you looking for, child?'

Lyuba blushed. 'Mama's little recipe book.' She rummaged a bit more. 'You know, the yellow and brown one.'

'It might be in a drawer in the kitchen.'

'I'll just finish looking here,' mumbled Lyuba, reaching for another pile of soft-backed books. As she drew them forward, she felt more hopeful. One of the books had a brown plastic spiral spine. She pulled it out of the pile breathing a sigh of relief. 'The Art of Cooking Ukrainian Style' she read.

Her father watched her as she turned the pages to the section on Christmas Eve and its first course, *kutia*.

Taras looked over her shoulder. 'You know how to make *kutia*.'

'Well, I do and I don't. I always helped Mama, but if I have to do it on my own, I'm not sure that I can.'

'Of course, you can. Look at the recipe. Is there anything there that you don't know?'

'No, although this tells you to use pecans. Mama always used walnuts.'

'Because we had walnuts in Halychyna.' He took the book from her hand. 'This was produced in Canada. They'd have had plenty of pecans there.'

Lyuba read the recipe again. It mentioned wheat, poppy seed, sugar, honey and nuts, which was everything she could remember of the sweet chewy first course of *Svyat Vechir*. She had helped Mama make it year after year, but to make it alone…

Taras left the room while Lyuba read through the other recipes for the holy meal. She and Vera had agreed to split the work between them. Nadiya had said she'd bring the poppy seed cake for dessert.

'From the deli, no doubt,' Vera had said.

'Never mind, at least she's contributing.'

'Here,' said Taras, coming back into the room. He held out a photograph to Lyuba. It was another small black and white print showing a girl of three or four kneeling on a chair beside a table. She was stirring something in a large bowl which was being held steady by a smiling woman.

'Mama.'

'And you,' said Taras. 'You were always helping her.'

'Yes, helping her. But she was the one who knew everything.'

'Never mind. You can carry those things on now.' He leaned over to give her a rare kiss on the top of her head.

'There's nothing to be afraid of. It's only cooking.'

'Only cooking…' To some extent it was. All three daughters had sat around the kitchen table with their mother, pinching together the dough parcels of cheese and potatoes or shredded cabbage and, at Christmas, the smaller mushroom dumplings to be added to *borshch*. They could do it again, even without their mother's supervision.

As they gathered in their father's house for the first Ukrainian Christmas Eve, everyone was on their best behaviour, making an effort to be cheerful, as if they always ate this most important meal of the year without their mother. Her place was set but empty. The traditional empty seat for the unexpected guest.

They stood for the prayer, their father leading them in '*Otche Nash*', the daughters and grandchildren joining their voices to Taras's, the English sons-in-law bowing their heads, all in their embroidered shirts and blouses, every one of which bore Natalya's hand. As the prayer finished, Taras spoke the usual blessing, remembering 'those who cannot be with us'. There had always been a large group of characters off-stage, throughout the girls' lives, the relatives 'back home' who would also be celebrating Christ's birth that night, beginning their feast with the appearance of the first star of the evening. But tonight, the enormity of their mother's absence was almost unbearable and, as Taras passed around the *prosfora*, the blessed bread, a sob escaped Lyuba. She tried to swallow it as all eyes flicked to her in panic. She gave an apologetic smile.

Nadiya picked up the cut-glass bowl of *kutia*. 'I can't wait to taste this. It looks delicious.'

Vera's daughter, Lydia, giggled. 'It's just the usual grey mess, Aunty Nadiya.'

'Still delicious,' said Nadiya, as she dolloped a couple of spoons into her father's dish. 'Enough, *Tatu*?'

Then she served herself a portion before passing the bowl to Lydia. 'Here you are, Miss Picky.'

'Oh, I know it's delicious. It just doesn't look it.'

The bustle of passing the bowl around the table gave everyone a task while Vera left the room to check on the *borshch* simmering in its pan.

'Mmm, this is good *kutia*, Aunty Lyuba. Just as good as *Baba's*,' said Vera's sixteen-year-old son Simon. The mention of the beloved name made the three grandchildren smile.

'Thank you,' said Lyuba.

'Yes, it's good, Lyuba. Mama would have been proud,' said Nadiya. 'Although what she'd think of me buying *makivnyk* I don't know.'

There was some laughter at this as the dangerous moment passed. Lyuba heard Taras breathe a sigh of relief and saw him pat Nadiya's hand.

After the *borshch*, while they waited for the *varenyki*, Taras and the grandchildren joined in the singing of the carols coming from the CD player. His face was serious as he sang, but Vera and Lyuba, peeping in from the kitchen, saw that he was happy that they would still join in, that they didn't deny what was theirs.

'How do you think he's coping?' Vera asked Lyuba as they lifted the dumplings into Mama's best serving dishes with their red and black pattern.

Lyuba looked up, surprised out of her own loss. 'Coping? I don't know. He seems calm.'

'But too quiet.'

'What are you two muttering about?' asked Nadiya, appearing between them and encircling their waists. 'Tell me.'

Vera and Lyuba smiled at this refrain from their childhood.

'No…' began Nadiya.

'*Tato*,' said Vera. 'Is he coping?'

'He's sad,' said Nadiya. 'But he would be. He adored her. She was so lucky,' sighed Nadiya, picking up the sauce boat of onions and butter.

After the *varenyki*, eaten only in superstitiously odd numbers, everyone managed a *holubech* or two, before sitting back groaning in their chairs. As usual, the cabbage parcels were eaten in smaller quantities but would make tasty leftovers.

'Can we have a break, Mum?' asked Val.

Lyuba nodded, smiling. 'I think we all need one.'

'In that case,' said Taras, 'I'll get the letter.'

Taras leafed through the stack of letters behind the framed photograph of himself and Natalya with the three grandchildren which stood on the mantelpiece. He withdrew a pale blue envelope bordered with the red and blue flashes of an airmail letter.

'Oh, is it from the aunties?' asked Nadiya.

'Yes, from Verochka and Lyubochka,' said Taras.

'Isn't it funny how those old ladies are stuck with the names they had when they were little girls?' said Lydia.

'That's because that was how *Baba* remembered them,' said Taras. 'To your grandmother, they were always the little sisters she'd had to leave behind.'

He unfolded the fragile paper, reached for his spectacles and began to read.

'*Dorohenka nasha rodyna,*' he began…'Dearest family,' translated Nadiya for the sons-in-law, Tom and Adrian.

'*On the occasion of the birth of Christ, we would like to wish you all happiness, health and a long life. We know that for you this Christmas will be a difficult one…*' Taras swallowed but continued, '*without your beloved wife, mother and Baba. But she is with God, you can be sure. She was the best of sisters to us and we know she looked after all of you with the same love. We were not*

119

lucky enough to have her with us most of our lives yet we felt her presence and her warmth. Be sure she is watching over you now with the same love she always showed you in her life.

We are getting old, dear ones. Our only wish now would be to see some of your lovely faces before we die. If only God would make this possible. In the meantime, we kiss you and bless you. May God keep you safe and well,

Lyubka and Verochka.'

'Well,' said Taras, 'I'll write to tell them how we are.'

'It's an idea, though, isn't it?' said Lyuba.

'What is?' asked Taras.

'To go to Ukraine.'

'Not yet.'

'Why not?'

'Because we don't know how things are going to work out.'

'Isn't that Gorbachev making things more open?' asked Adrian.

'Yes, *glasnost*.'

'And it's two years since the Berlin Wall came down,' added Tom.

'Yes,' said Taras. 'but that's not the same as Ukraine being independent and having control of her own borders. The Russians are still in charge. I know it's difficult for you to understand because the English have been free for so long, but we Ukrainians know the Russians well. Even when, especially when, they show a smiling face to the West, they can't be trusted. They could still hang people like me in the village. We need to wait and see before we think about travelling there.'

Chapter 14
Bavaria, Germany Spring 1944

The last of the snow has melted, so while the children rest after lunch, I have marked out a rectangle in the far corner of the garden for our vegetable patch. Frau Kuhn watches as I peg out the string to mark the border. I drive the old spade I found in the shed into the ground. I lift the soil as I work along the line of the string, turning brown earth. It looks quite good, but it's not as good as our black soil at home. I lift and turn, lift and turn, working up a bit of a sweat. Frau Kuhn continues to watch.

'I feel I should help you, Natalya.'

'There's only one spade. Besides, I've missed this.'

'The simple pleasures, eh?'

'Oh yes,' I say, then save my breath for my digging.

When the children waken, it's Frau Kuhn who does the afternoon's work with them, tidying them up, giving them a drink, entertaining them. Eventually, I have to give in. I've been working hard as a housemaid, but I've lost some of my ability to keep on digging as I used to. When I go into the house, I leave my muddy boots at the door to dry, wash my hands and nails of the garden dirt and join the family in the dining room among the toys.

'Finished?' asks Frau Kuhn.

'Not quite but I will tomorrow. Then perhaps the children will help to plant the potatoes.'

'Oh yes,' says Frau Kuhn. 'Remember, *Kinder*, we have the potatoes ready with their pale roots, don't we?'

The potatoes I foraged and some which the old woman

brought from her village contacts have been germinating on the kitchen window. The children have been fascinated as the little nubs have become tentacles.

'Huh, I'm not helping,' says Klaus.

'No, Klaus, we can all do a little work,' says Frau Kuhn.

'I'm no peasant,' he says turning his back on us.

'Well, perhaps only Hansi and Jutta will want to eat the potatoes when they're ready,' she says mildly.

'I'll help, *Mutti*,' says Jutta.

'Of course you will, my darling.'

'First the potatoes,' I say, 'and then the beans.' I have hoarded those seeds too from last summer's bounty, every time Frau Kuhn Senior brought us bartered vegetables.

***

Some days later we take a holiday from our chores.

'Come on, *Mutti*,' growls Klaus through gritted teeth. He runs down the garden path and is almost out on the pavement.

'Wait, Klaus,' she says. 'We're coming,' as she hurries Jutta and Hans towards him.

Klaus flies through the gate and runs to the tram stop only to have to wait again. He's looking feverishly for the tram to take us into the town centre. For we are all going. Even me. Although why I should want to celebrate the *Führer*'s birthday…

Klaus is wearing his dark shorts and khaki shirt with the black bandana around his neck. His *Deutsches Jungvolk* badge is neatly sewn onto his left sleeve. Klaus made a poor attempt to do it himself so Frau Kuhn took pity on him re-sewing it more tidily. He has his soft side cap on, too. He's immensely proud of his resemblance to his heroes and keeps checking that his socks are pulled up to his knees. Little Hansi has no such grand uniform, of course, but his mother has found him some dark shorts and a tiny khaki shirt so he can resemble his almost grown-up brother. Jutta is wearing a flowered skirt and a white blouse with short frilly sleeves to honour the April sunshine. She carries a small bunch of narcissi from the garden, although there will be no *Führer* at our parade to receive them. But she is proud of her role – the giver of flowers. Frau Kuhn is wearing her best pre-war suit, a fitted jacket over a long straight skirt. She has also glanced at me to check that I look smart. I don't know whether she's noticed that I've chosen to wear black.

The tram clanks towards us. We manage to find a seat for Frau Kuhn. She takes Hans on her lap while Jutta stands by her knees. Klaus pretends not to be with us, although he's forced closer to us as the tram fills up on its way into the centre of the town. When we shuffle off the tram, the square is already thronged with people.

'I told you we'd be late!' storms Klaus.

'We're not late, Klaus. Look, there's your *Jugendschaft* over there…' Before she has even finished speaking, Klaus has run over to join his group of identically clad boys. I see an older boy ordering him into line with the other *Pimpfen.*

Frau Kuhn leads the way into the crowd, carrying Hans, while I keep a firm grip on Jutta's hand. She returns my grip, perhaps feeling as intimidated as I do by all these people.

'*Entschuldigung, Entschuldigung,*' says Frau Kuhn as we try to make our way to the front of the crowd. I don't take my eyes off her forest green hat, especially as it's a preferable sight to the red flags hanging from every building and every window, their black and white centres revealed intermittently by the light breeze. It's more difficult to avoid seeing the small flags clutched in hot hands, ready to be waved in adulation. I wonder at the irony of such beautiful weather on this day.

We come to a halt, becalmed in a sea of women and children. I bend at the knees to lift Jutta, despite her weight. She and I are both getting a little panicky and she might feel less alarmed if she can see over the heads of the crowd. I wonder if the people around me are as aware as I am that I'm a foreigner. They must be. Their sense of themselves is so acute, they know exactly who belongs and who doesn't. Even holding a German child won't save me. I'm a slave here, barely tolerated, not acknowledged. Although Frau Kuhn is.

'Renate, Renate!' we hear to our right. I see a couple of the faces from the coffee morning. Frau Kuhn falls upon her friends, feeling braver in a group of officers' wives and their children. I stand behind them, Jutta released into the safe care of little German girls.

I turn to see the men at the front of this gathering on the *Rathaus* steps. They have plenty of space and a good view. The officers and mayor will take the salute on behalf of their revered leader, while opposite them sit several rows of soldiers who are relaxed, legs stretched out, hands lying loosely in their laps. But one or two have their arms folded. I study their faces. Not for them the shining excitement on the cheeks of the children. Some of them look drawn, even downcast, but, as the trumpets sound for the start of the ceremony, they sit up a little straighter.

I give myself a shake. I'm surprised by the sympathy I feel for these men. I remind myself that it was soldiers like these who shot Roman. Kill or be killed. I am in the lion's den. My heart thumps as I look around for other maids, other *Ostarbeiter*. But I can only see families like the Kuhns among the vibrant young women in their brightly coloured dirndls and bodices. All now wave their little *Hakenkreuze* enthusiastically while an officer takes the salute on behalf of his *Führer*, one of the soldiers giving it left-handed, his right being held in a black sling. He's the only wounded soldier on show. Later I realise why when he's awarded a medal for his outstanding bravery. An example to his comrades and to all of the younger males in the crowd.

The parade passes in a cacophony of sound. The *Deutsche Mädel* smile broadly while the Hitler Youth look serious. The band doesn't need to provide the rhythm for the soldiers and sailors who follow. They're all marching towards a future which surely can no longer be as bright as it once was, despite the home-made banners claiming that their buildings are broken but their hearts are not. We all know the Russians and the Americans and the British are coming, but the crowd cheers hysterically as if they can hold back defeat by the volume of their roars. Behind the Hitler Youth march the boys of the *Deutsches Jungvolk*.

Frau Kuhn sees him first. 'Look, Jutta, Hansi. It's our Klauschen. Wave children. Wave to your brother.'

Klaus keeps his eyes front pretending not to see or hear his mother.

***

Only weeks later, Klaus is kneeling on the armchair, his ear pressed against the mesh speaker of the radio, despite the fact that the broadcast can be heard across the whole room. I have to remind myself that he's still a child at ten, but the stricken look on his face belies that. The Red Army has retaken Crimea and hundreds of German soldiers have been killed or taken prisoner.

Frau Kuhn knows it's pointless trying to drag him away from the radio. When the broadcast ends he climbs down from the chair and goes over to the table where he has laid out the map of Europe. I watch him looking for Crimea. He traces his finger south from Kursk and Kharkiv but he can't avoid seeing Crimea to the west. He looks and looks, his finger travelling east again, but if his father and the millions of troops stationed in the east can't change the direction of their journey, this one boy won't either.

Frau Kuhn puts her arm around his shoulders. '*Vati* isn't

near Sevastopol.'

He throws her off. 'Of course he isn't!' he shouts as he strides from the room.

She dips her head.

Later, hunger drives Klaus down for supper. Frau Kuhn makes sure he gets the biggest piece of bread and jam. He eats as if re-fuelling.

'This jam is delicious, isn't it, children?' Both she and I know it's the last of the hedgerow fruit I gathered last year. Who knows where we'll get sugar to make more?

I clear away the supper things and as I boil the water to wash the dishes Klaus brings in a basket of wood. His one chore. He dumps the logs noisily by the stove.

'*Danke*, Klaus,' I say.

'Don't speak to me,' he hisses. 'I would kill you all.' He stomps out of the kitchen.

I know. I swallow the stone in my throat as I sink my hands into the water. You've already done it. You and yours killed my husband a year ago and would kill the rest of us. I've been trying to distract myself for days now from the exuberant green of May, every flicker of which takes me back to a smile, gunshots and the weight of a dead man in my arms. The pain in my chest becomes unbearable as I choke on the sobs which rebel and rise noisily, forcing themselves out of my mouth. My tears drip into the sink to mingle with the washing up water as I hold onto the tiled edge of the worktop. Grief tears through my body like some fierce genii. There's nothing I can do but wait until the storm has passed. Eventually it subsides so that I can let go of the sink and bury my face in my apron for comfort. I'm letting my sobs die away when I feel an arm around my shoulders and I turn to Roman, not caring how he came to be here.

'There, there, Natalya, don't cry,' says Frau Kuhn, stroking my back. 'There, there.' She rocks me as one would a child.

126

It almost undoes me again, so I pull back from the luxury of love and wiping my face on my apron say, 'I'm sorry.'

'There's no need.'

I can't look into her dark eyes observing me with such sympathy.

'We all long for what we cannot have,' she says.

I nod. I long for what I have lost.

'We can only try to live.'

I nod again.

In my next letter home, I write that I am well. That the garden is growing. We will have our own food. I don't say that I thought I had my grief under control, but one year later it has refused to be boxed in and is rampaging through my heart. I want my husband. I want my mother and my sisters. I want my home.

Chapter 15
Bavaria, Germany September 1944

I get up at six as usual, but the mornings are getting gloomier as September progresses. I dress, go down to the kitchen, wash my face and hands at the sink. Before I start my chores, I'm drawn to the garden. I open the back door stepping out into the misty space. Even in the town it smells like autumn. The grey damp air swathes the trees as I walk into its blinding mist. I close my eyes and breathe deeply. It smells a little like home. As I take deep breaths I think I could fetch a basket to go looking for mushrooms, the little *pidpenki* I used to search out with Verochka and Lyubka. Perhaps if I open my eyes I will find I have only been dreaming. I will be in our garden about to let the hens out…

The hens! I hurry to their pen to let them out of the coop. They're bumping about and burbling at one another. As I open the little door they burst out, their voices raised in protest as they realise I'm empty-handed.

I give myself a shake. It's no good dreaming. I'm here in Germany until somebody in authority says I can go home. But it's too big a thought. For a moment I want to wail at the impossibility of what I would like.

'Natalya?' I hear Frau Kuhn call from the back door.

'I'm here, Frau Kuhn. Just letting the hens out.'

As I go into the house she says, 'You gave me a fright. I came down and found the door open.'

'I'm sorry.' I start to prepare the children's breakfasts. 'Frau Kuhn, does anyone gather mushrooms in the park?'

She looks at me as if this is another of my crazy notions.

'Mushrooms?'

'Yes. At this time of year we would always gather mushrooms to dry them for the winter.'

'I don't know,' she says.

'I'd like to look.'

'Very well. We can go this afternoon.'

'It's best to gather them in the morning,' I say. 'But we could check for possible places.'

In the afternoon we take the children to the park. They all complain that they don't want their sweaters. Jutta has torn hers off, sleeves inside out, and thrown it down.

I pick it up off the grass saying to Frau Kuhn, 'Little girls who throw their cardigans away don't want to know where the secrets are.'

'No, they don't like secrets.'

'Secrets?' says our little fish.

'Can't tell,' I say.

'Give me my cardigan.' She almost stamps her foot.

I pass her the offending garment and hugging it to her chest she says, 'So where is this secret?'

'Under the trees,' I say.

We wander towards the rougher border of trees at the far end of the park.

'It's a long way,' complains Jutta.

'Oh yes, it is. For little girls,' sneers Klaus.

'I'm not little. I'm five.'

He doesn't even deign to look at her.

As we reach the trees I say, 'We need to look for fallen branches, or tree stumps, to find the *pidpenki*.'

'*Pidpenki*?' asks Jutta.

'*Deutsch!*' exclaims Klaus. 'Speak only German.'

'I would, Klaus, but I don't know the word for it.'

'*Mutti!*' he shouts.

'Alright, Klaus. Calm down. Natalya means a kind of mushroom. *Pilze*, eh, Natalya?'

'Thank you…' I begin, but am cut off by Jutta wailing, 'Mushrooms? Is that the secret?'

'Now, Jutta,' begins her mother.

I have to swallow my irritation as I long for the silent mornings, we three girls each with our own basket, wandering apart but in sight of one another, bending to pick the little honey-coloured mushrooms growing in clumps. Searching out the familiar places and always on the look-out for new ones among the misty trees. Bending and searching as if suspended in some magical world. Then seated around the table in Mama's kitchen, threading the mushrooms onto cotton to dry. Perfect for adding a burst of flavour to winter meals.

'*Muttiiii!*' Jutta's mouth seems to have done the impossible and become a square.

Frau Kuhn and I exchange a glance.

'What about hide and seek instead?' I say.

'Oh yes,' says Frau Kuhn. 'Hansi and I will hide together.'

But even Hansi has caught the mood. He pulls his hand away from his mother's. '*Nein!*' He sets off alone on his sturdy little legs to hide behind the nearest tree trunk.

Jutta immediately calls out, 'I can see you.'

We hear a wail from behind the tree.

'It was a stupid idea anyway,' says Klaus. 'We're not yokels or refugees looking for mushrooms.' He strides away from us in the direction of home.

Frau Kuhn watches his receding back helplessly. I want to tell her to let him go, but he's her son. We gather the other two obstinate children and then we tramp them around the park, trying to wear them out.

Later, Frau Kuhn says, 'Do you think it's worth a look in the morning, Natalya?'

'Yes, Frau Kuhn. It's definitely worth a look.'

'Then go on your own when you get up. I'll see to the children. Take my basket.'

'I will, thank you.' I wonder if she knows I'm not thanking her for the basket, but for the moment of freedom.

I go to bed full of anticipation at being able to get up alone and go out alone and come back only when I've finished my search for German mushrooms. During the night I wake up suddenly. Fully awake with the decision fully formed. I won't go to the park to look for mushrooms. I doubt there are any there anyway. I'll head out of town to look in the woods and hedgerows. I doze until the sky begins to lighten then I get up quietly leaving the house armed with Frau Kuhn's basket.

It feels ghostly, moving forward in the mist, what's visible of the hedgerow still monochrome except for the red splashes of berries on the hawthorns. But I'm not afraid. The mist protects me from prying eyes and prodding bayonets. I keep my footsteps light. I remember the forest craft Roman taught me. I head for a stand of trees across a field of stubble. I enter the wood scanning the ground for edible mushrooms. I'm soon rewarded by the sight of a vigorous clump by the stump of a tree. I bend to pick their delicate domes, my nose full of the lovely scent of autumn – the fallen rotting leaves, the peaty soil under the trees, the mushrooms themselves and am transported…

I had reached out to pluck a group of *pidpenki* and as I rose up again, someone had grasped me around the waist clamping a hand over my mouth. I had gasped and tried to scream, to warn Lyubka and Verochka, who weren't far away among the trees. But I had been held tight against another body when the same person whispered in my ear.

'Natalka…'

I tried to turn my head, but heard the whisper again.

'Don't scream.'

The hand around my face had loosened its grip and I had turned to face my partisan.

Roman.

He had grinned putting a finger to his lips.

I pointed to my upturned basket and he had shrugged. He had taken my hand leading me behind the great trunk of a sweet chestnut and kissed me...

My head swims, even now, when I think of that first kiss. I had only seen him once before beside the river with the other partisans and yet we had kissed as if we were honouring a bargain already made. I had turned my face up to his as he enfolded me in his arms. Roman!

I close my eyes, but the image has gone. He had helped me to pick up my spilled mushrooms and had slipped away before my sisters saw him. I remember hugging the secret of his kiss to me as I walked home with Lyubka and Verochka, who were crowing at the poor harvest in my basket. All that day I had caught myself smiling at the memory of those kisses. Then I had hoped they might be the first of many.

Now, I know there will be no more kisses. My arms feel empty and my lips cold. I stand watching the mist beginning to lift a little among the trees. Their trunks gradually appear, adding depth to the wood, but I still can't see the way out. I bend to look for more mushrooms.

Chapter 16
England February 1991

Lyuba shivered inside her fleece as she went out into her father's garden.

'Let's leave this till another day, *donechko*. It's too cold,' said Taras.

'No, *Tatu,* it's fine. I'll soon warm up when we start work.'

'I can do this on my own. I have plenty of time.'

'I know you do, but I'd like to help you. You and Mama always worked together in the garden, so I'd like to help you now.'

'Come on then,' he said going down the path to fetch the tools from the shed. He brought out a spade and a pair of secateurs. 'Can you start on the roses? I'll dig the ground over for the potatoes.'

'OK.'

Her father followed her to the circular bed which was overgrown with weeds. The rose bushes would be glorious with scent and colour in the summer.

'Cut them here…' he began.

'I know how to prune roses, *Tatu.*'

'Alright then,' he said and crossed the path to the other side of the garden to work on the vegetable plot.

Lyuba began to snip the roses. She focussed only on the branches in front of her. Choosing the point where to cut, she fell into the simple rhythm of the work. She threw the cuttings onto the path to be collected later and progressed from one dark spiky bush to another.

A sudden gust of wind chilled her and a full-blown memory

of visiting her mother's grave assailed her. It had happened a few weeks before. They had all gone, *Tato*, Vera, Nadiya, the men, the children, to visit Mama on the first anniversary of her death. They had taken a large bunch of their mother's favourite yellow roses. They had talked of her around the grave while they tidied away the winter debris. *Tato* had led them in a prayer for their mother and then he had spoken to her.

'Natalya, we're all here. The girls, the *svati*, the children.' He had paused.

Lyuba remembered the feeling of horror that her mother was somewhere beneath the soil, in a tight box, then her mind had fled from the rest of that image. Her father's next words had been ripped away by the blustery wind which always seemed to blow on that hill. Lyuba had hoped her mother's spirit was somewhere safe.

'Mama…'

She shook herself and bent to the earth, clearing methodically between the denuded roses and felt some satisfaction in seeing the clean brown soil between them. She threw the weeds onto the path moving forward to a fresh patch of ground. As she bent to her work again she felt a hand brush across her back. She turned, thinking her father might be ready for a cup of coffee. However he was still across the garden, preparing the soil for this year's planting. She turned in a full circle, but she was alone among the roses.

'Mama?' she whispered.

Chapter 17
Bavaria, Germany Autumn 1944

On another chilly autumn day I cross the road by the station. I hurry towards the queue outside the bakers trying not to see the frightened figures climbing up into the lorries, their yellow stars bright against their dark coats. There are far fewer of these transports now. They've become much rarer in the last year. I assume the Nazis must have found all the Jews who've been hiding. Or most of them. The soldiers prod them forward to the odd cry of '*Jude*!' from passers-by. But the German people have had enough of being bullied by the SS themselves so although they show no sympathy, there isn't the baying I used to hear.

I pass the closed shops displaying their faded stars of David and take my place in the baker's queue only to be followed immediately by Frau Bachmann, one of the Kuhn's neighbours.

'*Guten Morgen*, Natalya,' says Frau Bachmann. 'How is poor Frau Kuhn?'

I'm not deceived by her show of sympathy.

'She's well, thank you, Frau Bachmann.'

'But you're out doing the shopping again.'

'Yes, I am.'

'Isn't she well enough to come out herself?'

'Of course.' I throw her a scrap. 'But she has a lot to arrange for Christmas.'

'Has the *Sturmbannführer* got leave?'

I look at her for a moment. She knows perfectly well that no officer, nor soldier for that matter, is getting leave anymore. It was rare enough last year, but now…we all know the desperation with which Hitler is trying to hold off the Red Army, even in the eastern provinces of his own country.

'No,' I say turning away to shuffle forward in the queue, knowing I could have another hour of this as I wait to buy bread which might have sold out by the time I get to the counter.

I've become used to doing most of Frau Kuhn's shopping for some months now, with her *Muki* card – her ration card for *Mutter und Kinder*. Meanwhile she's been trying to hold herself back from falling into a slippery decline of despair. She has changed too much since last Christmas. The infrequent letters from her husband have done nothing to lessen her fears and she's terrified for her children. I can see that she dreads not only death, but the damage to their hearts and minds.

I could tell Frau Bachmann that the news on Christmas Day that the British had bombed Berlin hit her hard. I don't think she's had a moment's peace since then. It doesn't matter that the cities which have been bombed are far to the north and east of us. She's terrified that we might be next. Neither is she comforted by the posters and handbills telling us to go to our nearest air-raid shelter. She almost fainted when one of the leaflets advised us what to do if we were buried in an air-raid. I've seen her plotting how she might save her children from the disaster of defeat.

I could also tell Frau Bachmann that my mistress sleeps badly, that she's become obsessive about gathering whatever food she can get, that one of her greatest difficulties this year has been keeping Klaus and Jutta in shoes. They've grown so quickly, but there are no shoes to be had in the shops. She and I have cut down some of his father's clothes to re-make them for Klaus, as we have cut down Frau Kuhn's old dresses for Jutta, but shoes are a different matter. Some of the *Frauen*, those smug officers' wives who came for coffee and cake so long ago, now have an informal swapping system. Frau Kuhn has managed to put aside her pride to barter for second-hand shoes for Klaus and Jutta from those with older children. Her fur stole came in handy for that. Hansi, of course, lives in Klaus's hand-me-downs.

My own boots are wearing thin. I stamp my feet in the snow, trying to keep warm. I peer around the woman in front of me to check on the progress of the queue and count another ten women waiting. It's always the women.

Then I see her. Olha, the girl from the camp. I only recognise her because she's still wearing her hair like a regal peasant. She sees me too and comes hurrying up the street to me. We fall into each other's arms as if we're long-lost friends.

'It's you,' she says.

'Yes, it's me.'

'How's your breathing?'

'In and out,' I laugh.

We hug again. This echo of home. Of all that we both miss.

'Natalya,' I remind her.

'Of course, Natalya. I'm Olha.'

The soft Ukrainian vowels bind us. We kiss each other more formally on the cheek then grin at each other insanely. I feel as if I've found my family.

'What are you doing here?' I ask. 'I assumed you'd been sent to a farm.'

She shakes her head. 'No, to a factory. We make parts for tanks.'

No wonder she looks paler than when I met her. Her skin has a yellowish tinge.

'Is it dangerous?'

'Not really. The men do the more dangerous jobs. I just cut lengths of metal all day.' She pauses. 'Or all night. We're on shifts.'

'Shifts?'

'Yes. The factory's working full-time. It's been a bit safer at night lately, with all the day-time raids.'

We both glance around us, but while our neighbours resent our foreignness, they can't understand what we're saying.

'Where are you living?' I ask Olha.

'In the same camp. We walk to the factory every day. It's not far.'

'And they let you out?'

'They do now. Partly because they know we won't run home to the Russians, but also because they need us. Our working hours are better than they were this time last year. We get one day off a week now. But the food is worse.' She takes a long breath in of the delicious smell of baking bread.

'Do they feed you badly?' I ask.

'Oh, we get a slice of bread morning and night with our soup.' She pulls a face on the word 'soup'. 'What about you?'

'I work with a family. I've been with them ever since I left the camp.'

'Is it hard?'

I'm embarrassed after what she's just told me. 'No. Cooking, cleaning. My mistress is more genuine than most.'

'Are there children?'

'Three.'

'Oh, I would have loved that kind of work.'

Even with Klaus's anger and Jutta's tantrums, it must be easier that working in a factory. I smile a little guiltily.

The queue shuffles forward but there's grumbling behind me at Olha's presence. I turn to face the complaints.

'*Sie kauft kein Brot. Sie ist meine Freundin.*'

She isn't here to buy bread. I have only just found this voice from home and I'm not giving it up yet.

'Do you hear from your family?' she asks after I've bought the Kuhn's bread.

'Yes. Do you?'

'Yes.' She pauses. 'I don't think they're telling me everything.'

'Probably not. Are you telling them everything?'

'Of course not.'

'I think things must be getting worse,' I say. 'If the Red Army has come west as far as the radio reports suggest, they must have come through Halychyna by now.'

She looks around to make sure no one is close enough to hear. 'Those Red devils!'

Oh yes, those Red devils. I shiver at the thought of the NKVD marching into our village. Wrecking lives again. They might have looked scruffy and ill-disciplined, but they were implacable in their ruthlessness.

'But we're still getting letters.' I try to smile.

'Yes. My mother writes, but my younger brother, Levko, doesn't.' She sighs. 'I wouldn't really expect him to. He'll be twelve now.'

I can see her longing for her own as vividly as I long for mine. 'We'll see them all again.'

'Perhaps.'

After a pause she says, 'Do you remember Olena?'

'Of course, she was the girl who rubbed my back for me. Is she working with you?'

'She was but she didn't last long.'

That gives me a start, but then Olha explains that Olena's not dead. She was moved with her baby to a children's nursing station.

'Her baby?'

'Yes. It turns out she was pregnant when we left home, although she didn't know it then. The Nazis put all the pregnant women together to have their babies.'

'I had no idea,' I say, staring at her. I feel a bit foolish that I thought I was the only one with secrets. Then I remember the train about to leave as we came into Germany. 'But I thought they sent them home again? We saw those pregnant women when we arrived in München. Do you remember?'

'Yes, but the Nazis seem to have changed their policy.'

'So what happened to Olena?'

'She was sent to work in another factory when her baby was weaned.'

'And the baby?'

'Taken away.'

Now I really stare at her. 'Where to?'

'Who knows? Our best hope is that it's been taken for adoption.'

As terrible as this sounds, we both know it's a far better outcome than the other possibilities.

'What about the baby's father?'

'Oh, he'll be too busy.'

'What do you mean?'

'Well,' she says as she draws a mock-scandalised breath. 'Olena's boyfriend at home was also my sister's boyfriend.'

'Oh.'

'Yes. I have a sister, too. Sofia. She's older than me, but she had no plans to leave home… or Ivan. So she stayed and I left.'

I gaze at Olha not knowing what to say.

'It's alright. I've got used to it now. Olena and I stuck together while we could.'

'But the father…'

'Olena could write to Ivan to tell him, but can you imagine how private that postcard would be?'

'Not at all,' I agree.

'I think Olena wants to deal with all that's happened herself. Anyway, what could Ivan do even if he knew?'

I think of Roman and how excited he might have been to

be a father, but recall the impossibility of looking after a child while fighting with the partisans. I remember my own relief and despair the first time I'd bled after I'd left home.

I'm shaken out of my memories when Olha says, 'So you can see why I worry. Levko's just a boy and Sofia cares only for herself.'

'And your mother?'

'Mama's very strong.'

'Mine is too,' I say. Then I see my tram trundling towards us. 'I'm sorry. I have to go. When's your next day off? We could meet again.'

'Yes,' she says eagerly. Despite being with other Ukrainians in the camp, I see that she's lonely too.

Lonely. I hadn't realised how alone I've been until this drink of water in the desert.

'Wednesday.'

'Alright. I'll try to meet you here. Say ten o'clock?'

'Yes,' she says. 'I'll try to be here too.'

We embrace quickly and I board the tram. She waves her hand, red with cold, as the tram pulls away. *Meine Freundin. Moya tovaryshka.* My friend. I hug the glow to warm my hollow heart which aches with my own losses and Olena's too. How could she bear to part with her baby? How does she cope with the uncertainty of its fate?

The empty feeling keeps returning over the following days. Our babies. All those lovely, sturdy Ukrainian babies. The Nazis really won't leave us anything and I won't ever have my own dimpled baby to gurgle its love while I hold its warm round limbs…

***

Olha and I meet once more before the violent chaos of spring. I see her waiting near the stop as my tram draws up.

141

We're waving to each other like children before I even alight. I jump down and we hug each other, then we set off across the crunching snow to walk in the relative warmth of the almost empty department store. At one time, these shops would have been '*Nur für Deutsche*' to indicate to any Jews and Slavs that, as *Untermensch*, we were not allowed to shop here beside Aryans. But the attitude to foreign slave labourers has changed. They need our paltry earnings in their almost bare shops.

We pretend to examine the few items on show, but we're more interested in each other's stories. Olha tells me about her work in the factory which produces military vehicles. I notice that this time she has kept her gloves on, perhaps to hide her workers' hands.

'The factory was re-organised last year,' she says, 'after the plants at Zwickau and Siegmar-Schönau were bombed. They all transferred here to be able to continue production.'

'Where they'd be safe?'

We raise our eyebrows at one another. Where is safe now?

'You could come to work there,' she says. 'There's always too much for us to do and they treat us better than they used to.'

'Maybe.' Frau Kuhn and her children aren't my responsibility, but despite myself, I have learned to like Frau Kuhn over the twenty months I've worked for her. 'The woman I work for has treated me decently. I can't leave her in the lurch at the moment. I know I've been lucky to work in someone's home.'

'But if things change?'

'If things get worse, I'll have to think again. Is it dangerous work?'

'It can be, but we've all been trained. They'd train you too.'

'I'm not sure I'd like it.'

She looks around to check no one is within earshot. 'There

was one girl who hated it here. She was really homesick so she asked to be sent home.'

'Did they let her go?'

'Of course not. They just laughed at her.'

'Poor girl,' I say, thinking of my own ache for home.

'There's worse. She deliberately injured herself at work, so badly she had to have her arm amputated.'

'No!'

'Then they let her go home.'

I stare at Olha, shocked out of my self-pity.

'But…'

'She was desperate,' she shrugs.

'Would you?'

'Never. I want to go home in one piece. What use would I be to my family with only one arm?'

'Not much,' I agree. We walk in silence for a few moments, thinking how far our loneliness might drive us. Finally I say, 'We have to wait it out. But however long it takes, we will go home.'

She smiles, takes my arm and we quicken our pace as if we were truly walking home.

I return to the Kuhns to find the children shut in the dining room while Frau Kuhn argues with her mother-in-law in the kitchen.

'Where can you go, Renate?' asks Frau Kuhn Senior.

'South. East. Wherever it's safe.'

I stand in the doorway. Frau Kuhn has unlocked the pantry and is bringing out her shrinking store of tinned food.

'Nowhere is safe,' says the old woman.

I look away to hide the shock I feel. She has never shown the tiniest lack of faith in the *Führer* to lead the German people out of the mess he has led them into.

'There must be somewhere,' says Frau Kuhn without

slowing her pace.

'Where?'

'Ukraine. Austria.'

'For goodness sake!' She sees me standing in the doorway. '*Du*! Tell her what's happening in your Ukraine.'

I look at her coldly. She has never spoken to me directly and she can address me as '*Du*'. I am a servant after all. But I am also a person, *ein Mensch*.

Frau Kuhn pauses to look at me. 'What does your mother say, Natalya?'

'She has to be careful what she writes. I know the Russians are back in my village and that they drove out the Germans last year but I haven't heard from her since the autumn.'

'Oh, Natalya, I'm sorry.' I see that she is genuinely sorry for treating me as her mother-in-law has done, seeing me simply as someone who makes her life easier. But I won't show her my fear for my family. That's what their precious *Führer* has brought us to – the inhumanity of only being concerned to save our own. *Überleben*. To survive at any cost. I know that when the time comes, it will be easier to leave them.

Frau Kuhn draws herself up and looks at her mother-in-law. 'Well then, south to Austria.'

The old woman shakes her head again. 'Renate, you have been sleep-walking for the last year. The Americans and the British are south and west of us, the Russians are to the east. So then, go north to the Baltic Sea.' She harrumphs. She must know about the tens of thousands of Germans who are trying to flee from the tidal wave of the Red Army. 'What will happen to your house if you leave it empty? Someone else will take it from you then you'll have no home at all. You know the town has been full of evacuees. You've been lucky so far not to have anyone forcibly moved in here with you.'

Renate sinks down on a kitchen chair, putting her elbows on

the table to rest her head in her hands.

I leave the kitchen, hang up my coat and go to join the children in the playroom.

Chapter 18
England 1991

Lyuba knocked on the old woman's door then entered calling, 'Hello, Aunty. It's me, Lyuba.'

She went along the narrow corridor to what had once been used as a dining room, but was now even more crowded with the addition of an armchair beside the conservatory door. She peered into the room where she saw her aunt nodding in her chair.

'*Dobroho dnya, Teta.*'

The old woman looked about her. When her eye fell on Lyuba, her face broke into a broad smile. 'Lyubka, *donechko.*'

Lyuba advanced, glad of the honorary title of daughter and kissed her aunt's wrinkled cheek. 'How are you?'

'Sit, sit. Or are you in a hurry?'

'Not at all. I've come to see you. Would you like a light on?'

'Yes, put the light on. It's a bit dark.'

Lyuba rose to turn on the light. 'Shall I put the kettle on while I'm up?'

'Of course,' said Olha. 'Especially if you're staying.'

Lyuba made the tea with lemon and honey and brought it through to the old woman. 'There you are. Just as you like it.'

Olha took a sip smacking her lips. 'Just right.'

'When did you first have lemons?' asked Lyuba.

'What do you mean? When did I first have lemons?'

'Well, did you have them in Ukraine?'

'Of course not. They didn't grow in Halychyna.'

'I assume you didn't have them in Germany.'

'Nooo! We were lucky to have tea in the camps.'

146

'Which camp was that?'

'You know, in Bavaria after the war.'

'When you were with Mama?'

'Yes, with your mother.' Olha looked at Lyuba dreamily. 'You sometimes have a look of her. The way you turn your head.' Olha demonstrated, turning her head from Lyuba with a little tilt of the chin.

They smiled at one another.

'She could destroy anyone with that look,' said Lyuba.

'Oh yes. I remember…' Olha paused.

'Remember what?'

'Oh, nothing. You're too young to know.'

'I am not. Besides, if you don't tell me, how will I ever know?'

'What is there to know?'

'What Mama did. What happened to her.'

Olha took a long look at her friend's eldest daughter. 'What is it, Lyuba? What are you looking for?'

'I'm not sure, but I feel as if I didn't know Mama. Her life before us.'

'Of course you didn't. How could you? It was the war.'

'That's what *Tato* said.'

'Well, he's right.'

'But there's so much we girls don't know.'

'Lyuba, your mother wanted to protect you from knowing about all the hardships we went through.'

'Yes, but I'm not a child. I want to know what happened to her.'

'She survived, like all of us here,' said Olha, straightening her skirt. 'It was hard, Lyubochka. But your mother was strong. She looked after all of us.'

'All of you?'

'Alright. Pass me the box.'

Lyuba rose to fetch the large wooden box from the sideboard. She remembered stroking its worn inlaid pattern as a child, but never being allowed to open it alone. She brought it over to Olha and placed it on the small table beside the armchair.

Olha lifted the lid taking out a handful of photographs. She shuffled through them. 'Here we are…'

She passed Lyuba a small black and white photograph. It showed three young women, leaning their heads together and smiling out at the camera. 'Your uncle Dmitro took that one.'

'Oh, it's you and Mama. She still had her *kosi* then.'

'Yes, she wouldn't cut them off.'

'And you had yours. You look like a princess with them up over your head like that.'

'I know but I wanted a modern hairstyle. Your mother was so cross with me when I cut them off.'

'She always said you used to have lovely hair.'

'Not anymore though,' said Olha, touching her thinning grey perm.

'You still look pretty, aunty.' Lyuba looked at the three faces again. 'But who's this beauty? I can't remember seeing her before.'

'That's Marichka,' said Olha.

'She looks lively.'

'Oh, she was.'

'Lots of boyfriends?'

'Lots,' said Olha, nodding her head.

'And Mama,' said Lyuba, seizing her opportunity, 'did she have lots of boyfriends?'

'Oh no. Only your father.'

Lyuba looked back at the photograph. So Olha hadn't known Mama's secret either. 'Why have I never seen this Marichka?'

'She went to America. England would never have been big enough for Marichka.'

'Was she a wild one?'

'Definitely.'

'Did she go from Germany to America?'

'No. We all came here first, but she moved on as soon as she could. She hated it here. The reminders of the war. She said she never wanted to see another bombed out building or ration card as long as she lived. She knew what she wanted alright.'

Lyuba looked closely at Olha. 'That sounds as if she wasn't always nice.'

'She could be better than the rest of us at getting what she wanted.'

'Were she and Mama good friends?'

'Yes…'

'Like you and Mama?'

'Not quite. Our friends often became our family because we had no one else. Your mother and I stuck together because we were on the same train going into Germany. We didn't know each other then but we met again later in the war.' Olha looked down at her hands. 'We stuck together at the end of the war. It was chaos, Lyubochka.' The old woman raised her hand to stroke Lyuba's hair. 'We looked after each other.'

'Like sisters,' said Lyuba, repeating the family mantra.

'Even better than sisters,' said Olha. She turned to look at the photograph on the coffee table beside her. 'She was such a help with Levko.'

Lyuba picked up the photograph. It showed a tall, dark-haired man with an attractive wife and two smiling children. They were in a garden beside a swimming pool.

'They look so well. How are they getting on?'

'Good, good. That was taken a while ago. The children are in high school now.' Olha sighed.

'Are they coming to visit?'

'Levko says he'd like to but they work so hard over there. In America.' She sighed again but then made a visible effort to pull herself out of her sadness. 'And how's your Valeria?'

'She's fine. She'll be going to university soon.'

'That's exciting.'

'For her, yes.'

'But not for you?'

'No. I'm dreading her going.'

'She's growing up. You'll have to give yourself something to look forward to.'

'Well, we're thinking of visiting the aunties in Ukraine.'

'Who are?'

'Me, Vera and Nadiya.'

'Is it safe?'

'That's what *Tato* said but we're British subjects. I think we'll be alright. It would be good to see what Mama's life was like.'

'Perhaps,' said Olha slowly. 'But things will have changed you know. The Russians…'

'I know but it's all we have left.'

'All you have left?'

'To find out about Mama.'

'Don't be upset about your mother, Lyuba. She was a good woman. She helped a lot of people.'

'Yes, but how?'

'A friendly word here, a helping hand there.'

'I want to know what happened to her.'

'You have to understand, Lyuba. As the war came to an end we were all fighting for our lives. Everyone was looking out for themselves. But you had a better chance of surviving if you helped those who were close to you.'

'And you were close.'

'To the end,' said Olha.

Lyuba leaned over to kiss her aunt's wrinkled cheek. 'You miss her too don't you?'

'Every day, *donechko*.'

Chapter 19
Bavaria, Germany 1945

The war engulfs us in January. When we hear the siren we follow the instructions given in the air-raid training. We gather the children, helping them into their warm coats and hats. I pick up the emergency bag by the kitchen door and the gas masks Frau Kuhn purchased for all of us. We hurry along the street to the shelter. We've already done this a couple of times when the bombers coming over were headed for other cities, but it turns out that this time the bombs are for us. We don't know that yet, of course, although we've been expecting it since the Americans and British entered Alsace before Christmas. Frau Kuhn tries to keep Klaus with us. He'd like to march off to help the *Volkssturm* which has the old and the young in its ranks, but as Frau Kuhn often thanks God, her eldest son is only ten and his boyish fantasies will remain just that for now. She carries Hans, who at four would like to walk, but whose little legs can't hurry quite enough yet. Jutta is gripping my left hand, while I heft the roll of blankets strung over my shoulder and carry our supplies in a shopping bag. Jutta would prefer to hold her mother's hand, but she's getting old enough to be reasonable about using me as a substitute. Though a poor one, I know.

We hurry down the steps of the shelter, Frau Kuhn peering round Hansi so that she doesn't lose her footing. We descend into the cold heading for a corner where we can bed the children down between us. I lay out a blanket for them to lie on but they're not ready to settle down yet. They're watching the other people making temporary homes for themselves just as we are. Even Klaus's eyes are wide.

There's been no pushing and shoving as we've made our way here and no one tries to encroach on our space with the children, but I don't doubt that, if need be, these other mothers would fight for their own. I would. If I had any of my own here. I send up a prayer that they're safe as the noise begins.

I imagine I hear the bombs falling, but the noise of the anti-aircraft guns is immense. This town is truly well-protected, our guardian angels being the factories like Olha's which must continue to produce weapons. We huddle under their borrowed wings.

There's no let-up for us though. The noise goes on and on. We can only hold onto ourselves and wait out the exploding inferno above us. I find my teeth are clamped together. I try to smile encouragement at the little ones, but it must look more like a rictus than a smile for Jutta buries her head in Frau Kuhn's shoulder and Hansi gives in to baby tears, fat droplets bouncing down his cheeks. We know heavy bombs have been dropped when the air pressure blows out the candles. We wait in darkness.

When the all-clear sounds, we creep out peering at what remains of the town. Every building is damaged. Windows are blown out, doors are blown off. Some buildings have lost their roofs. And the fires…They seem to be all around us. The air is black and scarcely breathable. I pull my scarf up over my nose and mouth then turn to do the same for the children. Frau Kuhn's eyes meet mine. I read her unspoken question – does she still have a house?

We set off back to the Kuhn's home, Klaus staying close to us this time. We climb between the piles of rubble and hear the fire engines trying to get through to put out some of the fires. I don't imagine they'll be able to put them all out…there are simply too many. What did the Americans drop on us? For it was them. These bombs didn't just destroy buildings, but set them ablaze. Later I hear on the news bulletin that hundreds of planes attacked the town, not just one or two, and that the Americans are using incendiary bombs whose sticky contents can't be easily extinguished.

'They'll kill us all,' whispers Frau Kuhn to me.

It's clear the Western Allies aren't playing games. They will destroy every man, woman and child to defeat Hitler's Germany. I long to shout my identity to the sky – don't kill me, I'm Ukrainian!

Later I carry my mattress down to the basement and lean it against the wall beside the mangle. There isn't room to lie it down permanently, but I will not sleep any longer with my face just a few metres away from passing bombers. I also take my few belongings. I prop the precious photo of Roman and me on the shelf, but there's no room to display my *rushnyk*, so I keep it neatly folded in my bundle with my spare but threadbare clothes. At least I won't have to ignore the image of the *Führer* down here. I've left him to his fate in the attic. When I climb the stairs to the kitchen Frau Kuhn is at the sink gazing out at the garden.

'You've done the right thing, Natalya.'

'I was beginning to be disturbed by the noise.'

She nods. She understands that noise can be life-threatening. 'I don't think you'll plant my garden this year,' she says.

I look out of the window at the vegetable patch I dug and planted last year. We had potatoes, onions and beetroot and I showed the children how to grow salad. But Frau Kuhn's right. The end of this war is coming. Now it will be her turn to be terrified by an unfamiliar uniform and a brandished weapon.

'Have you heard from your family recently?' she asks, although she knows I haven't.

I shake my head. They might be safe. But if those devils of

the NKVD are back, they won't be allowing anyone to send a letter to the enemy. I swallow my fear though and ask, '*Und Sie?*' knowing that she hasn't heard from her beloved Dieter for far too long.

She shakes her head.

We look out of the window at the frozen garden, our shoulders almost touching, our hearts thousands of kilometres away in the east.

That night I dream of home. I'm standing in the lane beyond the little fence but I can't find the gate into our garden. Lyubka and Verochka are inside the house, looking out of the window at me. They both look serious as they beckon me to enter. I still can't find the gate. I try to tell them this, but they can't hear me. I see them turn away from me then Verochka steps back from the window. Mama appears in her place and I can see her lips moving. She's calling me, but I can't hear her. I make another attempt to find the gate as I walk the length of the fence, trailing my hand along it, trying to find the break where the gate should be, but it's not there. When I look up again the house has gone and all is darkness.

I wake with my face wet with tears and feel as if I'm falling into a pit of dread. I try to tell myself that just because I've had no letter doesn't mean they're dead. I dry my face on the sheet. I roll off the mattress to climb the stairs to the back door. I unlock it and lean out, smelling the air, which is still acrid with its scent of fires. I look up at the stars as I send my love to Mama and Lyubka and Verochka in waves, hoping they will dream of me and know that I'm alive too.

I'm fully awake now so I go back into the house and creep along the corridor to the *Sturmbannführer*'s study. I turn the door handle carefully, slip through and shut it as gently as I can. I can't close the curtains as Frau Kuhn would hear me in the room above, so I can't put on the light either. I light a candle instead then take the rolled map of Europe out of the cupboard. Klaus and his mother have studied it during the news broadcasts but now it's my turn. I spread it out on the carpet behind the desk holding down its corners with a paperweight and photo frames. Then I look at where I am now.

To go home I would need to cross northern Austria via Linz and Vienna, then through Slovakia to Ukraine. I let my finger travel east to Ivano-Frankivsk trying not to think of the thousands of kilometres. I ignore the mountains and rivers, but think only that there are no oceans between me and home. I could walk back to Mama and my sisters.

I roll the map up and return it to its place in the cupboard. I put back the paperweight and photographs, plotting all the while. I'm going to search this room in daylight for a map I can take, one I can conceal in my bundle. I'm not going home yet, but I will one day and when the time comes, I will have to make my own way. I blow out the candle and creep back to my bed.

***

Frau Kuhn and I are shepherding the children back from the air-raid shelter late one afternoon when we see what she has dreaded since the bombing began in January. Her house is broken open, part of the building gaping like a smashed skull, its teeth exposed. When we look more closely, we see my bedroom has completely disappeared, as has Frau Kuhn's. All she has left to witness her marital history is some shredded wallpaper flapping in the breeze.

I take Hansi out of her arms as she hurries forward, her mouth open, her breath coming in gasps. I hold tightly onto Jutta's hand, her screamed '*Mutti*!' spiralling up into the air. Klaus runs after his mother, spitting out the forbidden word, '*Schweinehunde!*' but nobody admonishes the boy. We stand in the rubble-strewn front garden while Frau Kuhn runs around the back, her coat flapping behind her. I wait for what seems like an age, my arms encircling the two sobbing children until Frau Kuhn, white with shock, comes back to us.

'Come, *Kinder,* Natalya. It's not all gone.' She takes Hansi out of my arms. Jutta uses the opportunity to get away from me to cling to her mother's skirts with fingers which would have to be broken before they'd let go. Her mother almost stumbles, but she leads us around to the back door and into the little lobby which is intact, as is the kitchen. Although everything is smothered in dust.

I close and lock the door. Then I think, why not? We can pretend we're safe. I join Frau Kuhn in the kitchen. She's still shocked but her eyes show she's planning.

'Natalya, may we join you in your bedroom tonight?'

'Of course,' I say, as if the basement is a sumptuous place of rest.

'Tomorrow, we will go to visit *Oma,*' she says to the children.

'Shall I prepare the beds?' I ask.

'Yes, please, Natalya. That would be very kind.'

I creep up the stairs, looking out into the sky from the first floor landing. The children's rooms at the back of the house are intact. I strip one of the beds and bump the mattress down the stairs, sending up clouds of dust at every step. As I pass the kitchen, I hear Frau Kuhn telling the children, 'We'll be like Klaus and the *Jungvolk* going on camp.'

'What about me?' whines Jutta.

'You'll be a *Deutscher Mädel,*' says her mother calmly. 'We'll go to *Oma*'s and see the hens and the goats.'

'I must join the *Jungvolk, Mutti,*' says Klaus. 'They'll need me.'

'You can't go, Klaus. The *Deutsches Jungvolk* have nowhere for you to eat and sleep.'

'But I have to go.'

'No, Klaus. You will help me take your brother and sister to safety at *Oma's*.'

'But how will *Vati* find us?'

'We will leave him a note, but anyway he would know to look for us where there are no bombs.'

I go down to the basement to give it a quick sweep before putting down the mattress. Frau Kuhn comes down, the children crowding behind her.

'Natalya, if we put your mattress next to this one, we could all squeeze on these.' I see the appeal in her eyes. It's easier this way and more comforting. I cross another line with my mistress. We will share our sleeping arrangements. The *Führer* would have a fit. First she lets me eat with them and now this!

'I'll fetch the duvets,' I say and go upstairs to fetch the warm bedding from the children's rooms.

After Frau Kuhn has arranged the beds, she says to the children, 'I'm just going to pack your clothes for our trip to see *Oma*,' but her words are drowned out by their wailing.

'It's alright,' I say. 'I can do it.'

'Thank you, Natalya.' She gives me a look which tells me to pack everything I possibly can. They will not be returning. She leans back so that the children don't see her mouthing one word, '*Alles*.'

I smile and nod as if we're all on the most delightful adventure. But I ransack the cupboards packing onto the outspread sheets any item of clothing which will fit any of the children. Then I tie the sheets up tight, wondering what Frau Kuhn is going to use as transport. Before I go downstairs, I open the door on the abyss of her room, knowing there's nothing to be saved from the thin air.

I haul the tightly tied bundles down to the kitchen and hear Frau Kuhn trying to reason with Klaus who is insisting that he wants to take all of his soldiers. If he can't be one, then at least he can take the lead figures his father bought him.

'No, Klaus, it's too dangerous,' she's saying. 'The dining room has been damaged.'

But I can see he's adamant so I offer to take him. 'What if I put some favourites into a pillow case?'

'That's very good of Natalya, isn't it, children?' says Frau Kuhn, but they simply stare at me.

So Klaus and I climb up from the basement. I offer him my hand, but he slaps it away contemptuously in a parody of the arrogant men he has so admired and as ever I don't know whether to laugh or cry for this child. What will become of him in this defeated country?

When we push open the dining room door he lets me go first. The window has been blown in, but one wall gapes wide. I glance up at the groaning floor above and withdraw.

Klaus tries to push past me.

'No, Klaus,' I say putting myself bodily between him and the room. 'It's too dangerous. The ceiling could fall in.'

He stamps his foot, furious at me. He tries to push against me, but I hold both of his wrists. 'No, Klaus, I mean it.'

He can't help the tears of frustration which gather in his eyes so I take pity on this little Nazi. 'I'll try to find your soldiers but you must guard this door. If the ceiling comes down, fetch *Mutti*. Remember, a good soldier never deserts his post.' I creep into the dust-laden room.

The children's toys are in the cupboards on the remaining outer wall. I try to step lightly around the table with its load of broken glass and rubble. I reach the waist-high cupboards holding my breath as I ease open one of the doors. I reach for the wooden box containing Klaus's soldiers and then I move along to Jutta's part of the cupboard. I silently curse the fact that the children squabbled so much they each had to have separate compartments. I open a second door, hoping no part of the ceiling can hear me and reach in to feel for her felted dolls. I draw them out, a little bedraggled and dusty, but recognisably her Bavarian boy and girl. The little boy's hat is still attached to his woollen head and the little girl's blonde plaits still have their white silk bows. I tuck them into my coat pocket then stop to listen to the house creaking.

'Natalya,' hisses Klaus.

So he does know my name after all. 'I'm coming,' I whisper back, but I force myself to open a third cupboard door to rescue Hansi's horse. I could not leave *Pferdi* to his fate and face the baby of the family.

I raise myself up slowly glancing at the ceiling. I try not to rush out of the room with my booty. When I look down to assure myself of my footing, my eye falls on an upturned photo frame. I put Klaus's box under my arm to pick up the frame. It's a photograph of the five Kuhns which must have been taken near the beginning of the war when Hans was a babe in arms. The glass is shattered, but the photograph is intact. I clutch it and make for the door. I hold my breath until I've gone through it then hiss to Klaus, 'Close it, quietly.'

We tiptoe away.

When we reach the basement, Frau Kuhn, Jutta and Hansi are all waiting with wide eyes and open mouths. I try to still my heart's sudden pounding as I hand over the treasures.

Jutta immediately bursts into tears when she sees the dirty state of her dolls.

'Never mind,' says Frau Kuhn. 'We'll all have a bath when we get to *Oma*'s house. Say thank you to Natalya for fetching your toys.'

I'm rewarded with sulky mumbles from the children, although their mother gives me her heartfelt thanks for the photo.

After the children have fallen into fitful dozing, Frau Kuhn whispers to me, 'Natalya, I need you to help me take the children to my mother-in-law's house and then we'll come back to salvage what we can.' She looks at me apologetically. 'I know this isn't really your job, but I don't think I'll be able to manage alone.'

'Of course,' I say. 'And afterwards?'

She looks at me sadly. 'Perhaps back to the camp?'

'Yes. How will you carry everything?'

'The children's pram.'

'Alright.'

'Let's try to sleep now.' She shuffles about a little trying to get comfortable without disturbing the children.

I blow out the candle but lie on my back with my eyes wide open, weighing up what I should do next. I'll help her with her children and I'll pack up what remains of her home then I should return to the camp. To work with Olha? Or to work on a farm? But the Americans and the British are coming...

Chapter 20
Bavaria, Germany 1945

We're about a kilometre from Frau Kuhn's when it happens. Two men dressed in civilian clothes are walking towards us. As we draw closer, huddled behind the now empty pram, I see that one of the men is in his twenties and the other is older, perhaps forty. They are unshaven and hatless so I can see their cropped heads. The brighter patch on the chests of their jackets tells me that they've removed the badge identifying them as slave labourers, which would also have told me what nationality they are. They're leering and commenting loudly to one another. They might even be a bit drunk. One of them appears to be swaying rather than swaggering. I thank God that the children are safely stowed with their grandmother.

'Natalya,' says Frau Kuhn in a low warning.

'I know,' I reply. 'But there are only two of them and there are two of us.'

'We have no weapons,' she says.

I can see no one else on the road ahead. I daren't turn around to see what's behind me. I've been watching the hedgerow since I first noticed the men, but have seen no useful sticks. However, we're nearer the town now so there are chunks of masonry and rubble. 'There are bricks,' I mutter.

'No, we can't. We won't be able…'

'Yes, we must. They're not going to get me. Here, take over with the pram,' I say and she does without a murmur of protest.

The men are now twenty metres away calling to us in a language I don't recognise, although there's the odd German word thrown in. We carry on walking forward at the same pace,

162

Frau Kuhn pushing the pram.

'*Fräulein*,' calls the eldest and waggles his tongue at me while pushing two stiff fingers into the fist he's made with his other hand.

'*Was willst du*?' I ask sweetly.

'Oho,' he grunts and then speaks to his friend. He's clearly telling him that he's having me first.

In his hurry he stumbles the last few metres towards me on broken shoes as I bend to reach into the ditch for a hefty chunk of mortar I've been eyeing. I make some space between myself and Frau Kuhn and as he closes in on me, his rancid breath hissing into my face, I slip past him swinging my arm with as much force as I can muster to smash it against his head. There's a satisfying thud and he crumples. As he goes down I kick him hard in the groin for good measure and turn to Frau Kuhn who's screaming.

The younger one has hurled the pram aside and thrown her down on the ground. He's kneeling between her legs leaning forward to press one arm against her throat. With his other hand he's fumbling with his trousers. As I approach him, I see he's fully erect. I rush at him to deliver a downward blow with the brick against his skull. He falls sideways ejaculating at the same time onto Frau Kuhn's legs. She screams again, but manages to struggle out from under him.

He groans trying to get up. As I face him, arm raised, he flops his head onto his forearm. I reach for my mistress's hand and yank her upright. She is trembling uncontrollably so I reach down to help her pull up her knickers. She makes a disgusted sound in her throat, but there's no time for horror. I grab her hand and we run down the road as if the devil is after us. I don't know whether the men are giving chase. We run without stopping to the first of the houses then race into a garden to hide behind a wall which hasn't completely collapsed.

I peer out, but they're not following us. We sink down onto our haunches to catch our breath, Frau Kuhn whimpering quietly while staring at the slime on her legs. I peer over the wall again as my breathing slows and seeing no one, I say, '*Komm!*' We run the last few metres to Frau Kuhn's house holding hands tightly.

We reach the house and let ourselves in. I secure the door behind us. We both make for the kitchen. Frau Kuhn stands trembling at the sink so I help her onto a chair. I pour water into a bowl and find a rag to clean her legs. When I wipe her thighs, her legs shake uncontrollably, but I murmur soothing noises until it's all gone.

'There,' I say. 'Better on your legs than inside you.'

She nods then points at her supplies cupboard. She fumbles at the ribbon around her neck producing a key which she gives to me. 'In the back,' she says.

I reach round and my fingers feel the smooth glass of a bottle. I bring out the *Schnapps* then get a couple of pebble-like glasses to pour us a measure each. When I hand her a glass she manages an ironic grimace. '*Prost!*'

I grin at her. '*Prost!*' I open the cutlery drawer and pull out the two best kitchen knives.

As I sharpen them she gets up out of the chair to pour us a second drink. 'One for shock,' she says, 'and one for survival.'

I hear her trying to control her voice while I keep sharpening the blades. I'm not leaving the house again with only my wits to defend me.

'You're right, Natalya,' she says, watching me. 'We need to protect ourselves. They could have been anybody.'

'Foreign labourers,' I say.

'Yes, but there'll be all sorts coming through. Soldiers, refugees…'

'I know. I'm not giving in to anyone. Not easily.'

'We may have to.'

I raise the knife to examine its blade. Roman and Vasyl had insisted I take part in the UPA training. They wouldn't let me be just a girl who carried messages. I know how to put a knife between a man's ribs, although I've given no thought to the lessons I was taught. I only hope it all comes back to me now when I need it.

'No, we don't have to,' I say as I approach my mistress with the knife held loosely in my hand. 'It's best to push the blade upwards rather than inwards.'

She looks at me aghast.

'Like this.' I hold her shoulder with one hand and with the other I point the blade at the bottom of her ribs. 'Thrust upwards,' I say again. 'If you have the strength it's good to twist the knife too. It makes a better wound.'

She can't take her eyes off mine. Eventually she says, 'You didn't learn that from your mother.'

I put the knife down and start sharpening the second one. It's smaller but better – easier to conceal, easier to handle. 'May I have this one?' I ask ignoring her last statement.

'Of course,' she says. I can see she's wondering what she's been harbouring in her house for the last two years.

'We have to help ourselves,' I say to her. 'Only you can protect your children. And I want to go home.' She doesn't reply and I wonder how much grit she's got in her. 'We have no men to defend us, so we must do it ourselves.'

'Yes, you're right,' she says at last. She shudders. 'We'd better get on with this packing.'

'Yes, but first I'm going back for the pram.'

'No, Natalya, it's not safe.'

'How will you carry your things otherwise?'

She looks about her.

'Those men will have gone by now.' I wave the blade at her.

'I'll be careful.'

So I set off back the way we've just come. No one would know my heart is in my mouth from the way I'm striding along. But I will do this. I need to get Frau Kuhn off to her mother-in-law's so I can go myself, back to the camp…or home…or wherever I end up.

As I leave the town behind I march close to the road listening all of the time. No vehicle passes me although there are other people on foot. An old man sits on a handcart clutching a two-year-old child. It's difficult to see whether it's a boy or a girl. A woman in a ragged black coat is pushing them, trying to steer between the rubble.

I approach the place where we were attacked to see the pram flung on its side. There appears to be nobody near it and I have to admit to being relieved that there are no prone male bodies. I didn't kill anyone then. However, I take the knife out of my pocket just in case. I hold it lightly in my hand as I take the last few steps and peer around the bulk of the pram to see no one's hiding there. I heave it upright and checking around me I put the knife in the well of the pram just below the handle. I pass the family and their cart without comment as I trot along the road behind the pram back to the town. I meet no one else.

When I get back to the house, Frau Kuhn is busy packing. She looks relieved to see me. '*Alles gut?*' she asks.

'*Alles gut,*' I say.

I reach down for my bundle which is beside the mangle I won't need to turn anymore. It's slightly bigger than when I left home as Frau Kuhn has given me a small saucepan and has let me take the towel I've been using. I've hidden the pages I tore from the atlas in the folds of the towel as I won't need them yet. What is left of my earnings I've sewn into the hem of my coat. There are a few *Reichsmarks,* but I have tried whenever possible to convert my cash to goods which won't lose their value when

Germany collapses. I have a couple of small pieces of jewellery which I bought in the *Marktplatz* from people desperate to buy food at inflated prices.

Besides the kitchen knife which is in the turning of my coat behind the buttons, I also have Herr Kuhn's cut-throat razor which I stole from the bathroom. I test the hidden pocket I made for it. It's easy to reach my hand in to draw it out quickly. The mechanism for opening and closing the razor is a lovely piece of smooth engineering and the blade is beautifully sharp. It's a much better weapon than the kitchen knife.

I climb the stairs out of the cellar for the last time to join Frau Kuhn in her filthy kitchen. We refuse to look at it.

'Here, Natalya,' she says handing me my *Arbeitsbuch für Ausländer* with its eagle and swastika on the cover. She has signed me off out of her employment and the authorities at the camp will re-assign me. She also hands me the last of my pay. When she passes me her favourite basket with some of her jars of preserves I almost weep.

I notice that she has placed a note on the table and weighed it down with a heavy stone. It is addressed to Dieter. She sees me noticing. 'I don't want him to think the worst when he comes home.'

'No, of course not.'

We both have in our mind's eye the wounded soldier we saw sobbing on a garden wall, which was all that remained of what must have been his family home. Dieter will surely think to go to his mother's in search of his wife and children.

But Roman won't struggle to find me, although I am lost. Nor will he be waiting in my village when I manage to get home. He will be nowhere I will ever go.

Frau Kuhn must read some of this in my face. 'Good luck, Natalya. Thank you for all you've done for my family. I hope it's not too long until you are with your own family once more.'

'Thank you,' I reply. 'Good luck to you and the children.'

'*Überleben*,' she says. 'That's what matters.'

'Yes,' I say. That's what everyone wants. To survive.

She surprises me by leaning forward to embrace me and I surprise myself by returning the embrace. After all, I've been with her for almost two years. But it's time. I pick up the basket and strap my bundle across my body. Then I step out into the wrecked yard and turn to take the road away from what remains of the devastated town.

I set myself a brisk pace, humming one of Roman's marching songs. I pass the slower traffic of women and children of all ages. There is a noticeable absence of any teenage boys. No one speaks much. There's no exchange of greetings as each person grits their teeth. I notice the old women with their bundles tied onto long sticks. If they can do it we all can.

I feel free and, despite the coldness of the morning, I lift my face to the sky. I consider my options. My papers only entitle me to return to the camp but I could simply turn east and head for home. My stomach flutters as I consider this possibility. How long would it take me to walk back? Even as I begin to explore the idea I see an image of the bloodthirsty hordes in their green uniforms with their red stars. How could I evade the Red Army, which I know from the radio bulletins is hurrying towards Berlin? How could I fend them off if even the efficient *Wehrmacht* couldn't? But to go home…It's too much. The longing to be in my own house with my own family almost overwhelms me and I stumble over the loose ground. I manage to stop myself from falling and come to a halt. I step out of the traffic to take stock.

The landscape around me should be beginning to take on the green veil of spring. There are buds on some of the trees. But those same trees show the scars of the bombing. Some have disappeared altogether in the craters created by the explosions.

Some show their brown root-balls to passers-by. Some have lost great branches which lie scattered and some lean precariously against their neighbours. This is not the hopeful landscape of spring, but it would still be a good time of year to begin the long trek home. There are so many people on the move, one more refugee would surely not be noticed. I can't avoid seeing again the map I've pored over in *Sturmbannführer's* study…across Austria and Slovakia to reach Ukraine, avoiding the dangers of Poland to the north and Hungary and Romania to the south…approximately one thousand five hundred kilometres. If I cross the bridge ahead of me I must go north to the camp, but I could just turn around now and head south-east.

'*Papiere*,' I hear and turn to look into the face of a boy in SS uniform. He's walked forward from his post at the head of the bridge to hurry us on and has his hand out.

I take out my pass with its photo of me, presenting it to him.

'*Wohin gehst du?*'

I tell him the name of the camp. He opens the pages of my pass to see Frau Kuhn's note and dated signature.

He hands the pass back and with a contemptuous flick of the barrel of his rifle he sets me off again in the direction I was going.

Not yet then. The camp first. I plod on. My feet heavier now. But I try to comfort myself with the thought that I'm strong. I've survived two years working at the Kuhns, although it's true the work wasn't as hard as in the fields at home. I've been able to eat. I resolve to keep up my strength in the camp. Then, maybe soon…

My thoughts are shattered by the deep humming of airplane engines so I throw myself into the ditch along with everyone else. There's a row of abandoned carts and prams left on the road above us, but everyone is more concerned about the huge

169

planes overhead. They're flying east to west so they must have already bombed cities beyond this road and they're returning to their bases. It takes me a moment or two to work this out because the blue sky above me is being torn apart by the noise of an aeroplane coming in low. Then I hear the flutter of stick bombs being dropped. I know that these break apart on impact to spread their wicked fire for up to eighty metres, so I raise myself to crawl out of the ditch into the field and crouching low I run in a zigzag pattern towards a line of trees, just in case the pilots decide to strafe us as well. But they don't bother to fly back over the road to see the fruits of their labours, they just continue westward.

I keep running, ignoring the screams behind me. I reach the treeline and am tempted to throw myself down but, just in case the bomber hasn't emptied his load and swings back for another run, I keep jogging between the trees until the ground begins to rise. I slow to a walk trying to get my breath back. I can hear people shouting to one another in the wood behind me but when I hold my breath to listen for any more sounds of engines there are none. I drop my hands realising my bundle is still strapped to me, but Frau Kuhn's basket lies in the ditch. Oh well. If the preserves have survived, they might do someone else some good.

I get my bearings and begin to walk north again in the general direction of the camp but I don't go down to the road yet. I stay under the protective canopy of the trees. Those bombers fly in huge groups so there may be more to come. Even at this distance though, I can hear the disasters beside the road as some voices scream in an agony of physical pain while others wail their loss to the terrifying sky.

The track widens ahead of me then winds around a bend, but amongst the trees I see the grey uniforms of German troops. I step back slowly. From one tree to another I put as much distance as I can between myself and the approaching soldiers, treading softly. I crouch under the shielding darkness of a yew tree keeping perfectly still. It's movement which gives people away. The soldiers keep coming on, but they're not in any kind of orderly formation. There are men on foot, others on motorcycles, their tyres caked with mud. Men and horses are pulling carts loaded with a muddle of equipment. Even from this distance I can see they're all tired. Some are wearing their coats, but many are dressed only in their uniform jackets. All are dishevelled, filthy. The skinny horses have their heads down. I wonder where they've been, or where they're going, but like everyone else they know the Americans and the British are coming.

They rumble and clatter past my hiding place while I crouch low watching the comrades of the soldiers who strode into our village scattering our young men to the forests, the soldiers who would have shot me without a moment's hesitation if my links with the partisans had become known. I'm glad. I'm glad they look pale and hungry, that they're dirty and are armed only with what they've salvaged. The Americans and the British can't come soon enough.

Chapter 21
Germany Spring 1945

I look along the rows of workers. There seem to be thousands of us, most wearing an embroidered blouse or shirt with vibrant bands of colour, the white fabric reflecting the Spring sunshine. The priest in his gilded robes intones while we sing the responses. Easter Sunday Mass was a joyous affair at home but I missed it last year. I sway to the lovely rhythms with so many of my compatriots…all exiles, all displaced and all speaking the same language.

We haven't brought our baskets of food to be blessed as we would have done at home. The front of the church would be awash with the bright colours of embroidered cloths drawn aside to reveal the painted eggs. The yellow and white of the butter and cheese decorated with crosses of pungent cloves would be nestling among the other good things adding to the scent of the sweetly baked *paska* with its crown of decoration. The smell of cured hams underlying it all and for those lucky enough to have horseradish in the garden, a scrubbed white root with its green fringe. I swallow hard. That deep digging of the horseradish had become my job when *Tato* died. I used to try to get the whole root out including the very thin end just as *Tato* did, laughing at how far the clever vegetable had pushed itself into the black earth.

Every one of us must have a similar image of our families preparing for the holy feast. I send up my prayers for Mama, Lyubka and Verochka, that they might be celebrating Christ having risen. I feel a tremor too that, if the NKVD is there, there will be no Mass, only a secret celebration behind closed

172

doors.

I'm torn from home by the hundreds of voices around me singing, '*Khrystos voskres*,' Christ is risen. I join in but am pulled up by the words: '*…i tym shcho v hrobach zhytya daruvav…*' He gave eternal life to those in their graves. It's the word '*hrobach*' - graves - which has snagged me. I see Roman falling on the stony path on a day as sunny as this one almost two years ago and I wonder what happened to his body. I left it there. So did Vasyl. Dragging me down the mountain away from the Germans. Roman has no grave.

My throat is so full of tears I can't sing. I lower my head to let them fall. It's safe. Those around me will diagnose homesickness. But my heart is broken. I feel as if I've been asleep at the Kuhn's and have only now been given my wounded self back. A sob escapes me as I fumble in my sleeve for a handkerchief. Olha passes me hers.

'And for those in their graves, He gave them life.'

Then do it! Give him life again. Give him back to me. Just for a moment. To stroke his cheek. To kiss his lips. To say goodbye.

But there's no help for it. God didn't save Roman. I wipe my eyes and swallow my grief. That's mine to carry until I die, I think. Roman, a smiling visitor in my mind. I send up a prayer for him despite my disappointment in God. Please keep his soul safe at least.

***

We march along the cold road its grassy edges white with a late frost, our feet clanging on the hard ground through the early morning mist. Olha is beside me. We haven't managed to live in the same barrack yet but we have stuck close to one another in the work detail. The *Werkschutz* don't care as long as they get their quota of labourers to the factory gates on time.

173

The sentries on the gates merely glance at us as we stride into the cobbled yard and disperse to our stations. Olha is among the experienced elite, whilst I am given a brush and a barrow to clean up after the craftsmen.

The smell of grinding metal and hot oil is in my nostrils all day as I sweep the aisles in the cavernous workshops. I gather up the curls of discarded metal putting them in a separate bin on my barrow to be re-used. Nothing must be wasted. I've bound my plait away in a tight scarf, tied to cover every scrap of my hair so that the dust doesn't get into it. Some of the women are vain about their hair and show off a front of curls, but I've learned that machine dust won't be washed away by water alone. I'm also grateful for the overalls I've been given. They're too big for me and they're stained, but at least I don't have to wear out my precious clothes.

I try to tune out the din as I work – the banging and grinding, the shouting and drilling. But I'm grateful to be in the machine shop. When I came here on the first day they took me into the smelting shop. I was terrified as I watched the dark silhouettes of bare-chested men manoeuvring the buckets of molten ore from the furnace. It reminded me of the old priest's threats of hellfire. All of the men who work here have small scars pitting their arms and torsos from the tiny splashes of red hot metal being swung along the gantries in tubs. The crucible itself is like some ancient monster belching out its running death. I felt my heart pounding as I watched, praying I wouldn't have to stay in that section. I spent my day keeping well back cleaning the cooler areas, where women worked at benches smoothing and sanding small cast pieces. The next day I was moved to the machine shop where Olha works. I've been there ever since.

So I walk and sweep, stoop and scoop all day but no one yells at me to hurry up. Or not often. When the bins on my barrow are full I head outside to empty them into even larger containers. I'm not sure how I'm supposed to manage this on my own but there are usually some men around to help. For the price of a bit of teasing. I'm tempted to tell them that I might only be eighteen but I'm an old married woman, not the innocent girl they seem to think I am. Olha asks me which of them I like most but none of them matter to me. The important one with the dark curls, the blue eyes and the dimpled chin is lying dead on a mountain path at home. Where I left him. Lying on his back, his bloodied chest exposed to the world, the crows pecking out his eyes…

I shudder, startled. Where did that thought come from? I push my barrow hard across the yard, the rumbling of its wheels rattling up through my hands and arms. I focus on the dirt making myself be as thorough as my German *Hausfrau* has taught me to be.

'*Gut, gut,*' nods Manfred, the fat, hairy foreman on our section.

I duck my head and do my work. I'm not interested in him either.

Walking back to the camp in the early evening, the scent of spring surprises me on the greenest part of our journey between the factory's metallic stink and the stale smell of the camp. I lift my head like an animal to sniff the lovely air. The hedges and trees are full of leaves shaking out their creases and I'm filled with hope. It's irrational I know, but we can't be crawling between the bombers and the rubble forever. We all feel a change coming and it's not just Nature's change. There are moments of cheerfulness in the foreign labourers, while the expressions on the faces of our German masters are anxious. I pray to God that the handover won't harm us and that the Germans don't kill us before the Americans arrive. Because they're on their way.

I turn to Olha grinning.

175

'What's cheered you up?' she asks.

I shrug. '*Vesna.*' Spring.

She sniffs the air too and then takes my arm grinning herself. We pick up the pace.

A few days later I get some proof that the end of the war is truly coming. We're walking back from the factory. Just before the corner of the road where we turn into the camp a young soldier stands talking to three other German infantrymen. My eyes pass over him noticing only his uniform and his dusty boots, but when he bows his head to his chest I can see his shoulders shaking. Is he laughing or crying? I see the other three glance behind them and close ranks around him, one of them patting him on the shoulder. So he's crying. My spirits soar. It may not quite be over yet but the end of the war is coming and they have lost. Those highly polished Nazis have been ground into the dirt and they have lost. We can go home. I pick up my feet almost dancing my way towards the camp. We can go home.

Every day after that I walk with an air of expectation watching for any changes. The days pass and we wait. Each morning as I wake I think maybe it'll be today. Then the factory boss reverses everyone's clock. Suddenly we work all night and hide all day as the bombing becomes fiercer than ever. There are no shelters provided for us at the camp. We have to shift for ourselves. Returning as the dark sky breaks with a crack of dawn I say to Olha, 'Where can we go? We can't stay in the barracks.'

'There are some old water pipes we could hide in.'

'How big are they?'

'About a metre across.'

'They stink though,' says a voice behind us.

I turn to see Marichka, a tall, well-shaped girl. 'You come with me,' she says. 'I'll show you a good spot.'

Olha and I follow her from the gate to the furthest corner of the camp where the ground falls away and is overgrown with hawthorn trees.

'You can barely see this area from the barracks,' I say and am rewarded with gales of laughter from several girls who have followed us. It seems that this has been a useful spot for lovers' meetings.

'Aha!' I say. 'Thank you, Marichka.'

She doesn't even blush. Just tosses her long black curls over her shoulder and says, 'Well, it was certainly more fun than today promises to be.'

Although there are dozens of us, each girl finds a place to lie under the dappled light of the leaves with the heady scent of blossom in our nostrils. We doze like holiday-makers until we hear the first engine approaching then we huddle down trying to imprint ourselves into the ground. I pray that the planes will only target buildings. That I won't be blown to shreds, to be scattered among the branches of the trees. Or that the trees will splinter and impale us with their wooden shards. The noise is tremendous. The earth trembles. I lie with my face pressed against the grass waiting the booming torrent out.

This pattern of laborious nights and terrifying days is barely set when we're targeted by a different bomb. As this one explodes it pours fire into the forest. It pours and pours, as if the whole forest is not big enough to hold it. It whooshes crackling like a mad monster as it storms towards the factory. All day we lie low clutching our fear to ourselves. As night begins to fall, we hear the *Appel* whistle. We climb out of our precious hollow to make our way towards the *ploscha* to be counted again.

The *Führenlager* stands, legs spread wide, hands behind his back, rocking slightly on his heels. He is as clean and shiny as a new pin. We on the other hand are covered in grime and oily smuts.

'*Meine Damen und Herren…*'

We try not to look at one another in astonishment. We have never in all our years in German camps been addressed with this level of civility.

He continues, 'In a moment, you will dismiss to your barracks to collect your belongings. We reassemble here in five minutes. *Fünf Minuten*,' he repeats, as if we haven't understood his instruction. 'Dismiss!'

I run with the others to gather what few things I own. I lift the thin straw mattress to pull out my *rushnyk* with the photo hidden in its folds. I roll my things into the thin camp blanket and strap it across my body. I hurry back out to the *ploscha*, Olha close behind me. We stand together in line as we're counted off.

The *Führenlager* bellows, 'Right turn! Quick march!' so we head for the camp gates and the open road. Olha's fingers reach for mine. She gives my hand a quick squeeze as we're marched away.

This time there's no *Werkschutz* to harry us along the road to work, just the German foremen from the factory.

'That's funny,' begins Marichka.

'*Halt's Maul!*' barks one of the foremen.

We raise our eyebrows at each other. The little men are being allowed to grow bigger. I glance at Manfred, my old foreman, wondering where his bravery has come from. He has no weapon except a long piece of iron tubing from the factory but perhaps he'll be willing to use that to keep us in line. We are after all a valuable asset. All these pairs of hands to churn out the means of destruction. I wonder how far we'll have to march. Manfred doesn't look as if he could keep going for many kilometres. But we're told nothing. We simply keep our eyes front and walk. Hundreds of us. Visible to any passing planes.

At a crossroads our captors stop to discuss the route. We watch as they consult maps and point in various directions appearing to argue. We're in safe hands then. We stand waiting for further orders, which come eventually and we set off again. Walking till night begins to fall. We seem to have reached the correct destination for we're hurried along the last kilometre or so until we come to an enormous house in unkempt grounds. They wave us inside.

The rooms are large with high ceilings. While we stare at our surroundings, the foremen try to separate the men from the women. We're housed in what looks like a ballroom. Then they close the door leaving us in blackness.

'Well, thank you kindly,' mutters Marichka to my left.

'We might as well make ourselves comfortable,' I say feeling for the knots in my bundle. I separate the blanket from the rest of my possessions and kneeling down, sweep the floor with my hand around my feet in the lightening gloom. There are no curtains at the tall windows and a little starlight has begun to help us.

I wrap myself in my blanket using the rest of my bundle as a pillow. Olha stretches out on my right. All around the room I hear hundreds of us trying to make ourselves comfortable on the hard wooden floor. But at least we're dry. Although whether we're safe is another matter.

In the morning the room seems less full than it felt the night before. Marichka is nowhere to be seen. I unroll myself from my blanket and stand up. I nudge Olha.

'Are you awake? Take a look.'

She sits up rubbing her eyes. 'Have some people gone?'

'Looks like it. Let's go and see what's happening.'

She stands up. 'I'm really hungry.'

'Me too. Let's see what we can find.'

We cross the room stepping over the prone bodies. I open the door and peer out. Beyond us lies a circular hallway which opens right up to the roof of the house. I look around. There are other closed doors but no people. We step into the hall. Beyond us lies what appears to be a partly glazed door to the outside. We tiptoe across the hall, peer through the door and then walk outside onto the stone step. We can see no one.

'Where are the guards?' asks Olha.

We find no guards at all and follow an echoing staircase down to a huge kitchen which contains not one scrap of food, although we search every cupboard and drawer. As other people waken, they come in ones and twos to cover the same ground with no greater reward.

I watch Olha checking another empty drawer and tug her sleeve. We wander away from the kitchen into the garden which also contains nothing edible. 'We have to get away from here,' I mutter to her.

She looks around the once-grand formal beds. 'We can't eat flowers.'

'The guards might have gone but there are a lot of people here who need feeding.'

She nods. 'Let's get our things.'

As I roll my bundle up I glance around the ballroom and wonder about safety in numbers. Just then Marichka strides into the room. 'Where is everyone?' she asks as she climbs over others who are dozing or, like us, packing.

'Should I ask where you've been?' I say.

'No, don't bother. Nowhere memorable.'

'You're as bad as my sister,' Olha says.

'So little sister, give me a hand with my packing.'

Three then. That's better than two.

'Can we come with you?' asks a voice.

I turn to look at two young women.

They're both tall and big-boned but the years of poor rations have pared them back from the healthy village girls they must have been. The one who spoke to us still has her neat plaits braided in two. She watches us intently. The other girl looks as if she has had her hair hacked off just below the ears. She has scraped the top back and pushed in a hairgrip or two. She doesn't look at us. She stares at the floor while I wonder if she's all there.

'We don't know where to go,' says the girl with the plaits.

'Neither do we,' I say. 'But we need to find food.' I glance at Olha and Marichka.

Olha pauses. She's noticed the other girl too but she nods.

Marichka ignores both of them.

'Yes, you can come with us. We can look after each other,' I say. 'I'm Natalya. This is Olha and Marichka.'

'I'm Irina.' She gestures to her silent friend. 'This is Slava.'

So we are five. Enough to defend one another perhaps and not too many mouths to feed.

As we walk towards the gates of the grounds Marichka glances at the overgrown pond. 'It's a pity there's no water to drink.'

That will be our first priority, to find water, since the taps in the house were dry.

We reach the road then look left and right.

'I didn't see anywhere useful like a farm last night did you?' I ask the others.

'No,' says Marichka. 'So let's go the other way.'

'Is it a main road though?' asks Olha. 'Maybe we should get off it as soon as we can.'

'Alright,' I say. 'Let's see where it takes us.'

We set off in the brightness of a perfect spring morning. The birds are busy in the hedgerows and the blossom is sweet.

As soon as we can we take a quieter lane and meander through the German countryside. But we come across no stream. As the morning becomes hotter I begin to suspect we would drink from a trough if necessary.

We're tramping automatically when Marichka wails, 'I can't go much further.'

'Don't sit down,' says Olha sharply.

'No, Marichka, you'll never get up again. We must keep going.'

'See over there,' says Irina.

'What?' asks Olha.

'There. It's a chimney.'

She's right. We stop to peer down into a bit of a hollow and see where the rest of the building must be. Without discussion we set off across the field heading directly for the chimney. Our beacon of hope. After several minutes we come to a bare farmyard surrounded by silent buildings. No people. No animals. No dog. But there's a pump. We rush towards it and take turns at wielding the handle dipping our heads and hands under the flow. We're laughing at the sparkling bounty when we hear a gruff, '*Guten Morgen*.'

There's an old man standing in the doorway of the farmhouse. He's leaning heavily against the jamb. I can hear his breath crackling even from the pump.

'*Guten Morgen*,' we reply.

'*Haben Sie Brot?*' asks Marichka walking towards him.

'*Nichts*,' he says and shakes his head.

'Do you think he's lying?' mutters Olha.

'Definitely,' says Irina. 'It's a farm. There must be some food.'

'Even if it's hidden,' I say as I glance round. I notice Slava is standing behind Irina.

The man's pale blue rheumy eyes watch us. He repeats, '*Nichts*,' as if that will convince us.

'Nothing in the barn?' asks Marichka pointing.

'*Nichts*,' he says again.

We look at one another deciding whether to be polite or to

182

take matters into our own hands. We're all country girls. We've all lived with the terror of the NKVD and we've all hidden food from German soldiers so we head for the barn.

We split up to search inside the outhouses as well as the barn, kicking up dusty floors and piles of straw. We stamp our feet listening for echoes and call encouragement to each other.

I stand still in the yard – where would I hide my store of food? Where there's an animal with hooves or teeth. But there are no animals here. So where would they have been? My feet take me towards an old pig pen deep in stale, dry muck.

'Olha!' I shout. 'Bring a spade.' I look at the pen. I'll just have to shift some of the muck and see what happens. I reach for the spade but jump back as if stung when my fingers meet not Olha's hand but a man's.

I turn to look at the owner of the hand and find myself being silently mocked by his grin.

'Come on, *divchyno*,' he says. Ukrainian, then.

'You do it!'

'Alright. Out of my way.' He strides past me into the pen and begins to fling spadeloads of muck over its walls into the yard beyond. He's joined by another man with a spade. I look around to see a couple more men coming out of the barn. My heart thumps in my throat but Marichka follows the men out. 'Where've you come from?' she demands but smiles to draw the sting.

'The same place as you.'

'The big house?' asks Irina. Again I can't help noticing Slava. She's gripping Irina's hand, her knuckles white.

'Yes. Haven't you found anything to eat yet?' one of them asks.

'Not yet.'

The old man is looking agitated, changing his weight from one leg to another and he's beginning to whimper.

'We have now,' I say.

One of the diggers shouts, 'Find some wood for a fire.' He waves a potato. There's a scramble as the earth falls away and we see the lovely round shapes of the farmer's stockpile.

It doesn't take long for nine hungry people to gather enough wood to make a good fire. While we work we ignore the old man's whimpering.

'You'll get your share, old fella,' shouts one of the diggers.

'He should consider himself lucky to get that,' says one of the men building the fire.

It's not until we sit down to eat the baked potatoes around the fire that I look at the men again. Vlodko, the cheeky digger, has seated himself beside Marichka. The other digger sits between myself and Olha.

'I'm Oleksa from Halychyna,' he says.

I don't look at him. I just nod.

But Olha gives him an answer. 'I'm Olha, also from Halychyna.'

'And you?' he turns to me.

'From there too.'

'We're from Zakersonya,' says Irina but he's not interested. He just gives them a nod.

The other two men are sitting quietly. When I glance up to see if they're going to take part in the introductions, one of them is looking straight at me. This gives me a moment's shock. He doesn't smile, just looks at me. I look away.

'I'm Taras,' he says.

'Dmitro,' says the fourth man.

Each time I glance up to check him, the one called Taras is looking at me.

After we've eaten, it begins to get dark.

'We should find ourselves a comfortable place to sleep,' says Vlodko with a smile at Marichka.

Irina and Slava make for the barn so I go with them. Irina chooses the furthest corner for them, then she places herself diagonally across that corner hemming Slava into the tight triangle. I begin to unroll my bed beside Irina when Olha comes in.

'Are we girls going to sleep in the barn?'

'People can sleep where they like,' I say.

Olha looks at me. 'Are you alright?'

'Of course. We should sleep while we can.'

She glances back at the men still seated around the fire. 'Are we safe?'

'I think so,' but I touch the blade nestled inside my coat.

'Then why are you being so unfriendly?'

'I don't want any confusion.'

Olha slowly prepares to lie down too. I wonder briefly which of the men she has been attracted to, then I turn on my side and close my eyes.

Chapter 22
Germany 1945

We wake to the sound of artillery fire and peer out of the barn. The men are already in the yard so we go out.

'How far away is it?' asks Olha.

'A couple of kilometres,' says Vlodko going beyond the farmhouse to look across the fields. Oleksa joins him and they gaze at the horizon.

'What should we do?' asks Olha turning to me.

'Wait to see which direction it moves in. If it doesn't come any nearer to us we should stay here and let them get on with it.'

I look up. The quiet man is watching me again.

'But what if…'

'Olha, we have some food, a shelter, so there's no need to put ourselves in danger. This isn't our fight. I plan to wait here till they've gone past.'

'Alright,' she says but I can see she's torn. Her decision will depend on what the men decide to do.

We explore the farm buildings but find no more food. However we can live on potatoes and water for a while. The old man stays in his house where Vlodko and Oleksa submit him to a search. They find precious little.

Then we're forced to take cover. The sky fills with the roar of bombers flying north to the next town. We hear their load of bombs being dropped and wonder at the distance as we feel the earth shuddering beneath us.

It doesn't stop at night either. When the darkness falls we hear the warning rumble of approaching bombers. It's a good night for them with some help from the half-moon shining on a half-mad world.

'Olha, get up. We need to go into the field.'

'Natalya, we should hide in here.'

'We shouldn't. When those bombers come back, if they have any bombs left, what are they going to drop them on? Roofs or an empty field?' I look around and see that all of the others are listening, even the men. I rise to go out tugging Olha by the hand. 'Come on, I'm not leaving you in here.'

She rises reluctantly but when the men get up too she joins me. Marichka gets to her feet with a yawn but Irina kneels beside Slava who is huddled in the corner.

'We're better here,' says Irina with a glance at her friend.

'Alright but we won't have gone far if you change your mind,' I say.

Vlodko now takes charge leading us out of the barn, across the yard and into the first of the fields. I turn to follow the darker line of its border. Olha comes with me but hisses, 'The others have gone the opposite way.'

'I know.'

We reach a bit of cover under some young plum trees bordering the field and we lie down on the damp grass facing the dark outlines of the farm. As my eyes grow accustomed to the surroundings I can see the horizon where the flat darkness of the fields ends and the stars begin. But their twinkling is soon put out by the flashes of red and yellow to the north of us.

I feel the earth trembling as the bombs are dropped and I smell, even here, smoke and burning. It's as if dawn has come early in a chaotic world in which the sun has forgotten where east is and time has been destroyed. I lie in the half-dark, my body buffeted by explosions which are destroying other people's lives. But if I press my face into the shuddering earth I can still smell the grass.

Olha whimpers pushing herself against me. I put my arm

187

over her back and we lie close together, her hair tickling my face as I tell her, 'We'll be alright. They're not bombing us. We're safe.' For now...

The bombing continues all day and all night. Then there's a lull. We still hear the planes going over but we don't hear the bombing. So the Americans must be advancing into Germany leaving us becalmed.

At nightfall as we settle down in the barn to try to sleep, Vlodko says to the other men, 'Maybe we should take turns to stand guard. There are four of us. We could do a couple of hours each.'

'There are nine of us,' I say.

He looks at me with pity.

'I know how to stand guard.'

'And where did you learn that?' he asks. 'As a German lady's maid?'

I shrug. He doesn't need to know.

Taras says, 'Take the first shift if you want to.'

'I will,' I say.

'And wake me when you think two hours have passed.'

I nod.

I take my coat, leave the barn and look around. There's a good spot in the lee of the building which has a clear view of the yard. I make my way there and see Vlodko nod to Taras.

'Good spot,' he says grudgingly.

'For a lady's maid,' I mutter. Vasyl, who trained me, probably forgot more than Vlodko has ever known. I lean back into the corner and reach into the pocket inside my coat. I decide on the large, visible knife rather than Herr Kuhn's cut-throat razor. I hold it lightly in my right hand while I start to count. Taras won't have to begin his shift early.

The sky is clear and the stars get brighter as the canopy behind them darkens. I hear the hoot of an owl on the breeze.

Vasyl wouldn't allow Roman to accompany me on my guard shifts. He was right not to. Thinking about my lover kept me awake then and thinking about my husband keeps me awake now. I miss him with the sharpness of the blade I'm holding. A change is coming. We could have looked forward to a new world together… But there's no point in longing for it. Roman is dead and I must make my way alone.

Just as I prepare to go in to fetch him Taras crosses the yard.

'All quiet?' he asks looking at the blade of my knife glinting in the moonlight.

'Yes, all quiet,' I say. 'Goodnight.'

'Goodnight, Natalya. Sleep well.'

I don't put the knife away until I reach the safety of my bedroll in the straw.

***

The days pass in this limbo. We eat and sleep, rest in the sunshine and as the sounds of war leave us behind we forage in the hedgerows. There are plenty of young greens so Olha and I gather sorrel, young nettles and dandelion leaves. Marichka's happy to eat whatever we gather while Irina and Slava stay in the barn. The men remain around the yard since foraging is woman's work.

But one morning as we're about to set off Taras says to me, 'We're beginning to run out of kindling. Have you seen any small dry wood on your trips?'

'I suppose there might be some. I haven't looked.'

'Then I'll come with you and see what I can find,' he says. He goes into the barn returning with an old grain sack.

'Why don't you like him?' mutters Olha.

'I don't dislike him,' I say. There's nothing to dislike. Taras is taller than me, fair-haired with blue eyes. He's always got himself under control.

'Are we ready?' he smiles at us both.

We set off out of the yard.

'Wait for me,' shouts Dmitro. 'I might as well come and guard you all,' he laughs.

We laugh too. Dmitro is more often seen reading one of the two precious books he carries in his pack, turning the pages with his long, thin fingers.

Olha smiles into his face and I wonder if I've missed something. Dmitro isn't handsome. His face is too bony for that. But with his dark wavy hair and his brown eyes, I can see Olha warming to him.

We set off along the lane and take the path to the woods. There's wild garlic in flower on the banks. As we stoop to pluck their pungent leaves and blossoms the men continue into the wood. It's curiously peaceful. Not even the distant thunder of the guns, just the blackbirds embroidering their summer songs.

It doesn't last. Suddenly one morning, we hear rumbling on the road behind us. I turn around to see what's causing the sound which becomes a roar. The tears catch in my throat as I see an American tank slowly moving forward between the verges. The Stars and Stripes flutter in the turret. Shiny young faces grin down at us as we wave and yell at one another.

I wave too and shout, '*Slava Bohu!*' although these boys from across the ocean will have no idea that God has been thanked. I step back as the first tank trundles past and I meet the eyes of a laughing soldier who says something to me. I can't hear him over the din and probably wouldn't understand him even if I could. The dust rises making me sneeze but still I'm grinning as the column goes on and on, driving past us towards the town beyond. I don't try to count how many tanks there are nor do I feel any fear of their mighty tracks passing so close before my eyes. I feel only joy at the white star on their backs. I join hands with Olha and we dance in the road as the last of the tanks moves away from us. We're like children yelling and grasping one another, jumping up and down. I don't know what to do with myself, with the wild energy I feel and the glorious happiness which threatens to burst me apart. We dance and dance.

Breathless I pause and look around to see Vlodko, Oleksa and Marichka heading for the town.

'Shall we go?' asks Olha.

We link hands and hurry along behind the others, Taras and Dmitro bringing up the rear.

As we follow the high tanks, other former slaves join us on the road appearing from their hiding places and soon a whooping crowd dances towards the ruins of the town. As the excitement grips us we run along the verge to catch up with the first tank. On the outskirts of the town we see the *Volkssturm* waiting in the middle of the road, their ancient leader at their head leaning on his stick while beside him another old man holds a dingy white flag. We see thin crowds of German women and children beside the road, some still pulling and tugging at the logs which had formed a makeshift tank barrier. They look relieved to be able to surrender while they're still alive although some eye the soldiers with anxiety.

The first tank grinds to a halt and a GI drops to the ground. He turns calling out, 'Captain, Captain!' The rest of what he says is lost to us in a blur of words we don't understand but a soldier strides forward to salute the old man.

The old man returns the salute. Behind him, the ranks of boys are scattered with a few old men, all unwilling to meet anybody's eye. Their shoulders sag as they face the end of their dreams. It doesn't matter to them that they won't be uselessly killed now because they know they've betrayed the Fatherland. The American Captain receives their weapons one by one and the motley assortment creates a growing pile. More GIs drop from the tanks to frisk the rows of defeated men and boys. One of the boys hesitates to step forward and be searched. He hasn't reached his full height yet. I can see his thin chest beneath his crumpled uniform. He has a wide face with a thick fall of blond hair but his features are distorted by grief and shame. Instead of raising his hands he slams his pistol onto the heap and stumbles away trying not to sob aloud as he wipes his eyes angrily on the sleeve of his jacket. When he disappears into the ruins no one calls him back.

The surrender seems to be a signal to head for any *Bierkeller* still open for business among the ruins. Both men and women stream towards these places where only the foreigners are celebrating. The tanks move on to *Adolf Hitler Platz* and Olha clutches my hand to run towards the one which has halted. The GI's are sitting on top of the tank passing packets of cigarettes and chocolate to the foreign girls gathered below. Olha pulls me toward another tank where the soldiers have only just started to share out their gifts.

She reaches to grab a packet of cigarettes. 'Come on, Natalya. Get what you can.'

'But I don't smoke.'

She pauses for a moment almost incredulous. 'For trading!'

I grab what I can.

We come away with our booty, our hands full. As we pause to look around us we see that there are no Germans here. Even the *Volkssturm* have melted away. They must all be hiding in what remains of their homes or in the cellars beneath them wondering whether these big GI's will treat them as the SS would have done. Many families must already have left the bombed-out ruins for there are chalked notices written on the pillars of doorways: '*Familie Ehrle...*' with a new address, often only the name of a village. Sometimes the vital information, '*Leben Alle*' has been added to give hope to the man returning from the defeated Front. Although there is also a putrid stench coming from some of the piles of rubble. I wonder whose job it will be to remove the corpses.

Olha and I link arms to walk around the square where already there are men swaying and waving bottles, sometimes singing, sometimes shouting invitations.

'This could turn nasty,' I mutter to Olha as one of them staggers towards us hissing, 'Girls, girls!'

'You're right,' she says.

So we turn our backs on the noisy celebrations and head for the ruined avenue with its decapitated trees through which the tanks passed earlier. As we leave the noisy crowds behind the road broadens out with the fields and woods on either side and I breathe more easily. It's sunny and green, there's birdsong from the hedges and the Americans are here. I allow myself to hope…Then I hear the clear call of the cuckoo from the wood on our left.

Olha says, 'I think we're being followed.'

As I turn around, she hisses, 'Don't look!'

'It's alright. It's only Taras and Dmitro.'

'Oh, thank goodness.' She turns to wave to them.

'Wait for us, girls,' calls Dmitro.

We pause to let them to catch up.

'Couldn't stomach it either?' says Dmitro as they reach us.

'It was getting out of hand,' says Olha.

He shakes his head. 'They need to be able to forget.'

'To forget?'

'Yes. The Germans may have been defeated but the Russians haven't.'

'They've been back in my village since last year,' I say.

'Yes. Long enough to have killed and deported plenty of people. They'll shoot any of us who go back or deport us to Siberia. Stalin says we're all traitors, although he has kindly announced we'll only be punished with a five.'

Why does he have to be such a Jeremiah? I look at him with distaste. He may be intelligent and clear-eyed but why spoil this day when we're more free than we've ever been? When we could set off east with some hope of seeing our loved ones again in our own country? But Dmitro, with his dreary realism of a mere five year prison sentence in Siberia has just torn the fabric of our dreams in two.

A moment ago I wasn't walking along this paved German road, I was kicking up the dust in the ruts beneath the cherry trees. Our little whitewashed house was just visible, Mama's irises lining the fence with their purples and golds. I would push open the little gate with its creaking hinge and call out, 'Mama, I'm home!'

She'd come out wiping her hands on her apron, her cheeks pink from the stove looking so surprised. 'Natalya, is that you?' she'd call. 'Lyubka, Verochka, she's home. Our Natalya's home!' They'd run out and we'd hug and hug...

But then the Russians would shoot me. Or deport me. I swallow my tears and I look at Dmitro with disgust. Does that mean that the American tanks don't really bring the gift of freedom for us? They will liberate Europe but Ukraine won't have part of that blessing?

'Take no notice,' says Taras. 'None of us knows what's happening at home nor what will happen to us here.' He looks at me. 'Were you going back to the farm?'

I nod though I don't tell him which one.

'It'll be safer than the town for the moment. It's a lovely day for a walk. We can at least enjoy the sunshine.'

So we set off together. I want to tell him not to misunderstand the fact that I'm walking beside him. It means nothing and can mean nothing. I know he's been watching me so I wonder about his decision to leave the fun in the town behind. I'm touched by his kindness but that's all. However, if I say any of this, it will make it all the more important. To him. Not to me.

I can hear Olha and Dmitro chattering behind us. I hear her laugh at a long speech he's just made. She's not taking him seriously then. That's good too.

When we get back to the farm, I see Irina peer out of the barn then wave her hand to someone behind her. She turns to speak to whoever it is so I approach warily. But it's only Slava huddled in the darkest corner of the barn.

'Hello,' I call out.

Irina smiles apologetically. 'We didn't know who it might be.'

'Well, there's nothing to worry about. It's only us.' I go into the darkness of the barn and decide it's time to approach Slava. 'You could have come with us. The war is over. The Americans are here.'

Irina kneels beside her friend but looks up at me. 'The Americans?'

'Yes, they've liberated the town. We're free.'

'You hear that, Slava? The Americans have saved us.'

Slava doesn't look up, just hunches herself further into the corner.

'We can go home,' Irina says as she strokes her friend's cruelly cut hair.

Slava lets out a moan burying her head in Irina's side. Irina puts her arms around her and rocks her back and forth as if she were a baby.

'Can I do something to help?' I ask.

She looks up and shakes her head, so I reach into the top of my dress bringing out a bar of chocolate which a smile has won me.

'Look, Slava. Look what an American soldier gave me.'

She peeps up at me as I crack the chocolate bar into pieces.

'Here try some.' I offer her a piece of chocolate.

She looks at it suspiciously.

'It's delicious,' I say giving a piece to Irina. We both put the squares of chocolate into our mouths and begin to make genuine noises of satisfaction.

'Eat it, Slava,' says Irina. 'It's good.'

Slava raises the piece of chocolate to her face to smell it. Then she bites off a tiny corner. As it melts in her mouth her eyes widen and she takes another tiny bite. She repeats the action until the whole square is gone.

'It's good isn't it?' I ask.

She nods. There's no smile but her face looks a little lighter.

'Thank you, Natalya,' says Irina.

'You're welcome,' I say but I wonder how Irina plans to get Slava home.

We women have been using the old farmer's earth toilet and later when Irina and Slava head off in that direction, I follow a short distance behind them.

When they reach the toilet Slava goes in. I hear Irina say, 'I'll wait here. Don't worry.'

I approach quietly.

When Irina sees me she shrugs her shoulders at me as if to ask, what can I do?

So I mouth to her, 'Is she...' and I point a finger at my temple.

Irina shakes her head, mouthing back at me, 'She was raped.'

'How terrible!' What can you say? I thought I'd killed the man who tried to attack me.

Irina jerks her head and we move several steps away from the privy. 'It was a gang of German boys. They threw dice to see who'd go first,' she whispers.

I try to swallow my nausea. I can't imagine how terrified Slava must have been. Nor how afraid she still is. 'How many of them were there?'

'Five.'

'Poor Slava. Has she seen a doctor?'

Irina shakes her head. 'No. I helped her after it happened. Washing her you know.' After a moment, she says, 'She's had a period since, thank goodness.'

My heart sinks for her. Whoever Slava was when she left home she's not that girl now.

'What happened to her hair?'

'She had a long plait like the rest of us. They caught her and held her by it.' Irina paused. 'She chopped it off afterwards.'

'My God!' I reach out to touch Irina's arm. Her face crumples into tears and I hold her tight and rock her just as she has rocked Slava.

'Irina,' calls Slava, 'who are you talking to?'

'Only Natalya.'

'I thought you'd gone.'

Irina wipes her eyes on her sleeve. 'Never.'

'Are you alright?'

Irina swallows again. 'Yes, I'm alright.'

I'm going, I signal to Irina and she nods at me. So I withdraw as Slava comes out. I walk towards the barn and go past it to look across the field which hasn't been ploughed or planted this spring. In the distance the wooded hills stand before the mountains and I think of all the obstacles in our way before we can reach home.

Olha comes to stand beside me. 'I wondered where you were. Are you alright?'

I surprise her by putting my arm around her. 'We have to stick together to get to the end of this safely.'

'We will,' she says and I love her for her simplicity.

'What's upset you?' she asks.

'Irina just told me Slava was raped.'

She stares at me. 'When?'

'I don't know. But that explains her behaviour.'

'You're right,' she says, after several moments' thought. 'We girls must stick together. Even today in town…' she shudders.

'We have to be ready,' I say. 'For anything.'

The following day we decide to venture into the town again but I tell Olha to give me a few minutes before we leave. I cross the yard and knock on the farmhouse door. There's no answer but I know the old farmer must still be inside. I knock again.

'*Entschuldigung*,' I say as I open the door. I look inside and see him standing at the far end of the gloomy corridor, framed by the light from the kitchen window behind him. 'Excuse me,' I say again. 'I saw you had a walking stick…'

He has one which he's leaning on now but I've seen another one which I'm going to take. There's no handle at the top but a smooth rounded paler knob which would fit into the palm of my hand very neatly.

I peer around the door to the wooden cage beneath the coat pegs. He has a battered umbrella in there but the chestnut coloured head of the walking stick is still there.

'*Darf ich?*' I say as I lean forward to take it. I am going to take it but I don't mind being polite to him.

He watches me without moving.

I pull the cane from the holder and run my hand down its knobbled length. It's perfect. '*Danke schön*,' I say as I withdraw from the house, loot in hand. I close the door behind me and go back across the yard where Olha is waiting with Taras and Dmitro.

'What do you want that for?' she asks.

'To smash some heads, eh, Natalya?' laughs Taras.

'And anything else which gets in the way.'

Dmitro smiles. These men. For them it's a joke.

'I'll be back in a minute,' I say going back into the barn. When I come out, hands empty, Dmitro says, 'What have you done with the stick?'

I smile at Olha who nods and says, 'Let's get going.' We link arms and direct our feet to the main road into the town.

When we arrive at the shattered buildings of the central square there are bodies lying on the pavements, in the gutters and even in the roads.

'What…' begins Olha.

'Drunks,' says Dmitro.

Other bodies are being taken from the ruins and piled like logs on wagons by the Americans soldiers. But not all of their work is dirty. A team of GI's are working on stand pipes. As we pass, the water gushes up to '*Gott sei dank*!' from a couple of *Hausfrauen*.

We skirt the square to take an avenue where once there were shops. The face of the *Führer* is now in shreds as posters have been ripped from the walls. Remnants of red banners lie in the gutters. We hear hammering then the shattering of glass, but rather than take flight we make our way slowly towards the source of the noise.

As we approach we see a small group of men and women ripping back the boards which have been nailed over the doors of what was once a grocery store. Taras tries to wave Olha and I back but we're going to see what might be left. The little crowd surges forward into the doorway so we follow.

'Grab anything,' mutters Olha.

I hope to be more careful than that but the press of people is too great. In the end I have little choice so take hold of anything I can reach. I pull up the gathers of my skirt using it to hold the slippery jars and tins I manage to reach. Clutching the folds of the fabric to my chest, I manage to force my way back onto the pavement against the crowds who are still pushing in. Outside I'm in danger from those who would loot from the looters. I clutch the bundle to me like a child.

Taras pushes his way out of the shop, his straight blond hair in his eyes. I see him looking around for me. He hurries over. 'Good, you're safe.'

'Not for long,' I say glancing around at the people who keep coming.

He takes my elbow. 'Come on, let's go.'

'I can't. Olha hasn't come out yet.'

'Then at least let's move down the street until she does.'

We walk fifty metres or so and stand well back in a doorway while we try to stow our booty less obviously.

There are shouts coming from the store and I wish Olha would come out. A very dirty man with a thick black moustache, wearing only a grubby vest over filthy trousers staggers out of the shop with a couple of bottles tucked under his left arm, an open bottle of *Schnapps* in his right hand.

'Fuck the Nazis!' he shouts. 'Take it all! Take it all, my friends.'

'We should go,' says Taras again.

'No. I won't leave Olha.'

'Wait here then,' he says and begins to cross the road just as I see Dmitro pushing his way out of the shop clutching Olha by the hand.

'Come on,' calls Taras. He hurries back to me. 'Now let's go!'

We walk quickly down the broken avenue. I turn around to check for Olha but she and Dmitro soon catch us up.

'What did you manage to get?' asks Dmitro.

'Let's get clear of here,' says Taras, 'before we start looking at our stuff. There are plenty of people to take it off us.'

Groups of people keep passing us as we make our way out of

the town back to the sanctuary of our barn.

When we take stock we find we have quite a haul. There's butter, sugar, salamis, but best of all two jars of jam. None of us has tasted jam in a long time, although I probably had the most recent taste of the hedgerow jam I made with Frau Kuhn's children. We are like children now dipping our fingers into the fruity sweetness and licking it off in delight.

We let a few days pass before we go into the town again to see what's happening. There seem to be more homeless Germans. I see women in small groups clustered around fires of salvaged wood with metal sheets or grilles to serve as their cooking plates, an odd assortment of pans holding whatever food they've scavenged. Everyone is hungry. Everyone is searching for food except the smooth-faced Americans who have their own supplies which are being cooked up for them in requisitioned German homes in the kitchens of these very women making do in the rubble. They know now what it is to be defeated.

On the roads we have passed French voices, large groups walking west as if setting out on holiday. They lift their feet energetically hurrying towards the homes these Americans have liberated. They expect to find their families and pick up their lives again. We wait, cautious and suspicious, for who rules in our villages now? Not these calm and confident men from across the ocean. Doubt traps us.

But we don't have to wait long. On the day we decide we must all move on we make our way up to the main road. Or at least Vlodko, Oleksa and Marichka set off ahead of us.

'What are we waiting for?' grumbles Dmitro.

I hear Taras reply, 'I don't know but we have to wait for the girls.'

Olha and I are on our knees in the barn.

'Slava, we must go with Natalya and Olha,' says Irina.

'We're not safe on our own.'

Slava shakes her head and won't meet anybody's eye.

'Slava, you know there's no food left,' says Olha. 'We'll starve if we stay here.' She pauses. 'Those Americans have delicious chocolate.'

Slava looks like a cornered child. Tempted but not much.

'Come on, Slava,' says Irina. 'We'll find somewhere nicer to stay, where we'll be safe and they'll feed us.'

Slava shakes her head. I'm reminded of little Verochka when she was three or four, wanting to join in but not wanting to, and Mama trying to persuade her.

'Well, you must stay here on your own then,' I say. 'Irina and Olha and I have had enough of this dirty barn. We're going to a place where we can wash in warm water and eat *varenyki*. Bye!' I get up to go, gesturing to the other two to join me.

Olha rises but Irina hesitates, so Olha gives her hand a tug.

We make for the door of the barn. Slowly. We reach the door and, as we step out into the sunlight, there's a cry of 'No!' Slava runs out barging into the three of us. She blinks in the sunshine and Irina takes her hand. As Olha and I walk ahead of them they follow.

When we reach Taras and Dmitro Olha flaps her hand at them to shoo them on. Dmitro looks as if he would speak but Taras takes his arm and shakes his head at him. They set off at a good pace. From time to time Olha and I look behind us to check that Irina and Slava are still with us. They are. They're carrying their own bundles now and Irina has a firm grip on the old man's walking stick.

We reach the main road and begin to walk towards the town. Before we get there we're rounded up and invited to climb into the lorries which will take us to holding camps where we're told we'll be fed. These vehicles manned by American soldiers are tidying up the flotsam and jetsam off what they consider to be their roads.

It's the promise of food more than anything else which entices us, and everyone else, to take up their offer so eagerly. Olha and I stand opposite Taras and Dmitro on the back of a crowded lorry, while beside us Slava holds firmly onto Irina's arm. Not all of the voices around us speak our language so rumour and speculation take on an added mystery as we try to imagine what the Americans have in store.

'Don't get your hopes up,' warns Dmitro. 'They need people like us out of their way while they mop up Europe.'

I turn my face away from him.

'Perhaps they'll help us to get home,' says Olha.

'Perhaps,' I reply and we look into each other's eyes and smile.

When our lorry is full the driver sets off in a northerly direction and after about an hour or so we enter the gates of a camp. I read 'UNRRA Displaced Persons Camp Bavaria' and wonder what UNRRA means. But whatever delights we were hoping for they surprise us by the welcoming rituals with which we are already familiar.

As we climb down from the back of the lorry we're divided into two groups according to gender. I catch sight of Taras's worried face. He calls out, 'I'll come and look for you later.'

I shake my head at him. 'We'll be alright.'

Olha links her arm in mine. 'Yes, come and find us,' she calls.

We're herded towards a large brick building and enter an open space furnished with benches around the walls and in rows along the centre. We're told to strip then to queue to go into the showers.

I can't look at Olha. The disappointment is too great.

But my heart pounds at the thought of the photo in my bundle. 'My things!' I shout as a grey uniformed woman scoops my possessions into a basket.

'You'll get them back later,' she says as I'm told to hurry up.

I bow my head under the water in the shower and take the opportunity to wash myself thoroughly. I won't cry this time though. I am going home. Somehow. I think of Slava. How on earth is she coping?

When I leave the shower I'm given a thin towel and we're all funnelled through an area made narrow by long tables covered in clothing. It's not new but looks and smells clean. We're given some choice and I pick out a dark green dress which reminds me of Frau Kuhn. I'm also given a pair of leather shoes which are a bit too long, but sturdy, so I pretend they're a good fit. Perhaps they're not all bad these UNRRA people, I think.

We're guided through a closed door to another area where we queue again, only this time we can see what awaits us and I change my opinion of our liberators once more. There are chairs scattered across the room, each one attended by a young woman clad in white and armed with a hand pump. I look around me but I can't see any of my friends. I wait until directed to a free chair. Once there I'm told to sit while my head and hair are sprayed with a foul-smelling white dust. I close my eyes and mouth. The woman taps me on the shoulder so I open my eyes and get up.

I leave the room to go through another narrow area where I rescue my photo and *rushnyk*. I insist on having my coat but am only given it to empty the pockets. I slip Dieter's razor into the pocket of what could be his wife's dress but they don't let me keep Frau Kuhn's kitchen knife.

We're given a ration pack with some pills which we're told are vitamins then we're given a barrack number. As the names for my barrack are called I notice that they're all Ukrainian.

It's not just the Germans who care about race and nationality.

Chapter 23
England October 1991

'Are you sure you've got everything?' asked Lyuba.

Valeria and Adrian flicked their eyes at one another.

'Yes, Mum,' said Val.

'Anyway, there's no more room in the car,' said Adrian.

'Well, I suppose if you've forgotten anything we can bring it when we come to visit,' said Lyuba, as if no one else had spoken.

They went out to the car and as Val approached the rear passenger door, Lyuba said, 'Sit in the front, Val. With your Dad.'

'Are you sure?'

'Yes, it's your adventure.'

Val grinned and got in, leaning forward like a child in her excitement.

Lyuba was glad to sit where neither her husband nor her daughter could see her face. She intended to keep herself firmly under control until Val was safely stowed at her university and only then would she allow herself to think of her only child, alone in a strange city surrounded by strangers.

They set off for the motorway, the bright blue sky a perfect backcloth for the russet trees.

'What a beautiful day,' said Adrian, turning towards the ring road.

'Specially for me,' said Val, with a broad grin.

'Of course,' said her father.

They eventually reached the university campus and followed the signposts to the Student Accommodation Offices, finding a small square brick building which resembled a public lavatory.

205

Adrian drew up in a parking space.

'Is this OK?' he asked Val.

Val consulted one of the typed sheets of paper which she was holding. 'Yes, I pick up my key here and then we have to find my flat.'

'Shall I come in with you?' Lyuba couldn't help asking.

Adrian shot her a glance.

'No, Mum, I'll be fine.'

They watched her walk up the path and disappear through the office door.

'Lyuba…'

'I know. I'm trying.'

Adrian turned to look at her. 'She'll be fine.'

'I know she will,' said Lyuba, not believing a word of it.

They waited in silence until their girl reappeared in the doorway, then they sat up straighter and smiled simultaneously.

Val got into the car. 'Got them. And a map.'

'Will you direct me then?' asked Adrian.

'Yes. You'll need to go out the way we came in…' Val directed her father without hesitation, even when they drove up a narrow service road beside a supermarket.

'Is this right?'

'Yes,' said Val, although she'd never been there before either.

They emerged into a leafy area with lawns stretching between several modern high-rise buildings.

'Mine's on the left here,' said Val.

'There'll be lots of students about,' said Adrian. 'I don't think you'll be lonely.'

'No, and I'll have three flatmates.'

They approached the outer door of Val's block. It was metal-framed with reinforced glass and an intercom unit beside it on the wall. Val selected a key and unlocked the door. She let her parents in then they obeyed the security notice telling students that the outer door must never be left open.

'That's good,' said Lyuba. 'Only residents can get in.'

'Yes, though there's an intercom so you can buzz people in.'

Lyuba hoped that all the students in her daughter's building would be responsible and keep the door securely locked at all times.

'How far up are you?' asked Adrian as they mounted the concrete stairs.

'Second floor.'

As they climbed Lyuba wondered why no one had bothered to remove the posters for last year's gigs from the walls where they hung in unkempt shreds.

When they reached the second floor they followed Val down a corridor away from the stairwell. She stopped before a wooden door which looked like all the others apart from its number. Putting her key in the lock, she pushed it open and called, 'Anyone here yet?'

A mouse-like girl emerged from the kitchen. 'Hello, I'm Sammy.'

'Hi, I'm Val.'

Lyuba watched her daughter give the strange girl a hug and was amused at Sammy's surprise. She would soon get used to Val's enthusiasm, she thought.

'I suppose you've picked your room?' said Val.

'Yes, I'm next door if you don't mind.'

'Of course not. First come and all that.' Val went along the corridor and looked at the other three bedrooms. 'I think I'll have this one in the corner next to yours.'

Sammy smiled.

'Come and look,' said Val, waving to Adrian and Lyuba who were still standing in the doorway. 'Oh, this is my Mum and Dad,' said Val.

Val's room was a narrow cell with built-in bed, desk and

wardrobe. Lyuba didn't care that it wasn't spacious. It would be safer for Val to live on campus, surrounded by other students.

As the three of them set off to fetch more luggage from the car, Sammy said, 'Can I help you?'

'You can guard the door,' said Val, 'then we won't have to unlock it every time we come up.'

'OK,' said Sammy.

They clattered up and down the echoing flights of stairs several times, laden with all the things Val could not live without. But they didn't unpack.

'I'd like to do that myself,' said Val.

'Of course you would,' said Adrian. 'Give your Dad a hug,' and he took his daughter in his arms.

Lyuba watched them and then it was her turn. She kissed Val's cheek holding her close for a moment. 'Ring us. If there's anything you need…'

'Don't worry, Mum. I won't disappear.'

'I know. Take care of yourself.' She made herself walk away down the path. She got into the car without looking round and, as Adrian reversed out of the parking space, she smiled and waved at her only child standing alone outside an ugly building.

She didn't allow herself to turn to wave as they drove away, but concentrated on not sobbing aloud. When they drew up at the junction with the main road, Adrian waited for a gap in the traffic. He reached for her hand. 'Are you alright?'

Lyuba managed a nod. That was all she managed until she reached home an hour and a half later. She went straight upstairs to her bedroom and lay down to cry into her pillow as she hadn't cried since her mother had died.

Later Vera rang her. 'Did she get off alright?'

'Yes, she was fine.'

'How are you?'

'I'm managing.'

'Want to go for lunch on Saturday?'

'Yes, let's.'

'OK. Don't brood in the meantime.'

'I won't.'

But she did.

Lyuba tried to go into Val's room the following day, but found herself choked with grief as she looked at the tidy bed and the gaps on the walls where Val had taken down her favourite posters. She emptied the few items from the linen basket to put them in with her own washing, then left the room, closing the door, clutching her child's clothes to her chest.

On the first Sunday of Val's absence, there was only herself and Adrian for dinner. No friends of Val's, no cousins or sisters. As Lyuba and Adrian prepared their small meal, Lyuba went into the pantry to fetch some carrots. But instead of bending to get them out of the rack she stood holding onto the shelf of table sauces and let her tears come. She closed the door so Adrian wouldn't hear her crying for the tiny family they had become.

'Where are those carrots?' he called and after a few moments he opened the pantry door. 'Oh, Lyuba! What are you doing?'

She turned and sobbed in his arms.

'She'll be back at Christmas and we'll go and see her in a few weeks' time. She's only up the road.'

Lyuba couldn't speak.

He rubbed her back. 'She hasn't gone forever.'

But Lyuba knew she had.

Chapter 24
Germany Summer 1945

I sit in the sunshine with the other girls hardly able to believe that our life of slavery is over. But the chairs beneath us speak of a different camp life. This is the first assembly I've been to where chairs have been put out in rows for us. I notice too that I can understand all of the conversations around me. We are all Ukrainian.

I peer around the gathered thousands. The men are at the back, rows and rows of them; some bare-headed, some have found caps, a few have found trilbies. As I look towards the front rows I see the occasional headscarf, but mostly bare heads. The girls have recovered from their spraying with DDT and have been trying to create flattering hairstyles with the front of their hair primped and pinned, the ends curled. No one will recognise them in the villages. I still have my plaits. I'm not sure why except I have no one to impress. Olha still has her *kosi* too wound around her head. She's scanning the back rows for Dmitro and Taras but before she can find them we're all called to attention.

An American lieutenant and a couple of corporals stand in front of us. We're invited to stand while the Stars and Stripes is run up the flagpole to a lone musician's rendering of what I assume to be the American national anthem. When their salute is over, a single Ukrainian voice begins, '*Shche ne vmerla Ukraina…*'

Before he finishes the first phrase we all join in to sing our own national anthem. No, Ukraine hasn't died yet and I feel my chest fill with pride. We are not broken.

The Americans wait until we're finished and then the lieutenant gestures we are to sit. We resume our seats and wait to be told what is to happen to us now. The lieutenant is joined by a man in civilian clothes who interprets.

'Good morning, ladies and gentlemen…'

Whatever he says next is drowned by a wave of '*Dobroho dnya!*'

He smiles and nods. 'As you know, this is an UNRRA camp. That is the United Nations Relief and Rehabilitation Administration.' There's a slight hesitation as the translator explains this title to us. The lieutenant continues. 'Our task is to feed you and give you medical attention where necessary. Then we will help you to return to your homes.'

There's a swelling murmur at this last intention. That's exactly what we want as long as we're not given over to the Russians. We know that Stalin will see us as traitors to the Soviet State because we worked for the enemy. He won't see that most of us did it at gunpoint. But the lieutenant focusses only on meal times and medical check-ups. He tells us that over the next few days we'll all be registered and given ration cards and that we'll be called to do this one barrack at a time. Then we're dismissed.

When it's my barrack's turn, we line up to wait. I'm issued with another card bearing my name, date and place of birth, but my marital status is no longer required. The pass gets a couple of American signatures, my own and three UNRRA stamps. I also get a number, which I can tolerate because it corresponds with my meal card. This is a simple beige card with space for my name and this week's date. The card has seven columns across, one for each day of the week, and three down for breakfast, lunch and supper. So we'll be fed regularly.

Each day we're assembled and checked. We're not prisoners, but we're expected to stay until sent home.

211

'Natalya,' I hear a male voice shouting as I make my way from the canteen. I look around and see Taras hurrying over. 'Are you alright?' he asks, looking at me closely.

'Of course. Why?'

'Are you settled in alright?'

'We're in a barrack with the other girls,' I say, meaning Marichka, Irina and Slava. 'What about you?'

'Yes, we're in a barrack as well. It's very noisy.'

'The women can be noisy too.'

'But you're alright?'

'Yes. There's nothing to worry about.'

'Natalya,' he looks over his shoulder. 'Make sure the last person in at night shuts the door carefully.'

I look at him properly. 'What are you suggesting?'

He shrugs looking embarrassed. 'It might just be showing off but some of the men were talking last night about raiding the women's barracks.'

I shake my head. We've all been through so much and might yet have even more suffering to deal with but here we are, having to protect ourselves against our own.

'I know,' says Taras. 'It's terrible. But lock your door, Natalya.'

'Has anyone spoken to these men?'

Taras shakes his head.

'I don't even know if there is a lock on our door.'

He hesitates and then says, 'I've heard there are rooms for couples.' He blushes.

I wait.

'They're not just for two people but for four. You know, two couples sharing.'

'But they're couples,' I say.

'Well, yes. But there's no reason why two men and two women couldn't share a room and claim to be couples.'

'It's something to think about.'

He looks hopeful so I add, 'But it's not something we need to do at the moment.'

'Perhaps not,' he says.

The opportunity to escape the barracks is shelved when we're moved on the following day with no explanation. After the morning *Appel* we're given thirty minutes to pack our things, including the bedding we've been given and are crammed into US army lorries again. We're driven about fifty kilometres to another camp. This one consists of half a kilometre of four-storey green buildings. Not only are there rooms upon rooms, we're to sleep in bunk beds.

We're not showered this time, but we are sprayed with DDT again. The men line up on one side of a wide hall, we women on the other. They spray our hair and this time they spray up our skirts. I don't want to look across at the men and hope they're not seeing this. But I can't help peeping. They're being sprayed down their trousers.

There is little conversation as we head for our dormitories.

***

As summer moves towards autumn we're questioned by American soldiers and UNRRA volunteers. The politicians have agreed that those of us from Western Ukraine can't be forcibly repatriated to live under Soviet rule. Because we were living under Polish rule until 1939 we are not Soviet citizens, so should not be repatriated to Stalin's USSR. The Americans will have to repatriate those displaced from the rest of Ukraine because that's what Truman agreed to at Yalta. But we're safe for now. We wait to see what the next stage of our journey will be. Rumours fly as those from further east go about the business of changing their places of origin.

Olha and I both boarded the cattle truck in Ternopil so

213

we're the genuine Galician article. Marichka sits opposite me on the grass. She's managed to find a red lipstick somewhere. Heaven knows what she traded for it but it suits her. She flashes a glance at the young men who are passing and laughs.

'Marichka!' I say.

'Yes, but the tall one's handsome.'

'They're all handsome…and all trouble,' I reply.

'Wait and see,' says Olha. 'We don't know what's going to happen to us yet.'

'What's there to wait for?' asks Marichka. 'I can have some fun in the meantime.'

'What would your mother say to such behaviour?' I ask.

'My mother's not here so I can act as I please.' After a moment's thought she adds, 'Besides, I might be sent back.' She leans forward. 'I'm not from Halychyna,' she whispers.

'What?' I ask, startled.

'I'm not from Halychyna.'

'I thought you were.'

'You assumed I was because you two are. But I'm not.'

'So where are you from?' asks Olha.

'Odessa.'

'Did you tell them that when you were registered?'

'No,' she says. 'I told them I was from your village.'

'Mine?' I say.

'Yes.'

Then I remember. 'You asked me where I came from when we were queueing to be registered.'

Marichka smiles, delighted with her own cleverness. 'Yes, I did.'

'You've never been to my village so you won't be able to answer questions on it.'

'I will because you'll tell me all about it.'

My stomach turns over. How much will I have to tell her

for it to be convincing?

She sees the anxiety in my face. 'It's alright. You'll go in first and then you'll be able to tell me what to say.'

'Yes.' I know I'm caught. If I don't help Marichka I might be sentencing her to a term in Siberia, or even worse to be shot. If I do help her, I could be endangering myself.

'Other girls come from the same village,' she says. 'Look at Irina and Slava.'

'I know,' I say. 'I'm just trying to anticipate problems.'

'Always careful, eh, Natalya?'

That's why she asked me which village I come from. Because I'm the careful one. I sigh. 'Alright, I'll help you.'

She smiles at me. 'Of course you will, Natalka!'

I feel the slap of the use of the affectionate version of my name. 'Natalya,' I say. 'No one calls me Natalka.'

I turn my face away from her, refusing to let her see any sign of my old grief. I hear Roman's voice as he stroked my face, my neck… 'Natalka, my Natalka.' I close my eyes. How am I going to manage every day left to me without him? I lift my face as if I'm sunbathing and hope neither Olha nor Marichka see the tears gathering in the corners of my eyes. Roman…Roman…

But I'm not the only one suffering loss. One morning, it's announced at the *Appel* that some mail has caught up with us. We're told it will be issued at our barracks later. The excitement while we wait is intense. When one of the brown uniformed volunteers arrives at our barrack with a small sheaf of letters, we close around her in a tight silent group. The list of names called is short. It has become too dangerous for our loved ones at home to admit to having contacts abroad. I hear Olha's name called, but mine isn't. When the UNRRA volunteer passes over the last letter I have to swallow my disappointment. It takes several efforts.

I sit on my bed and tell myself that Mama, Lyubka and

Verochka are well despite the cold winter. They will have planted the garden and be tending the vegetables as the weather warms up. I slap down a black creeping doubt that they haven't written because they've been deported, or worse still because they're dead. There's a hole in my heart where they should be but it's only because I miss them. I know they can't be dead.

Olha breaks into my loneliness with a sharp gasp. I look up. She has one hand over her mouth while the other grips the thin paper. Her eyes are wide and fill with tears as I watch her.

'What is it?' I ask moving across to sit beside her on her bed.

'I can't believe it.' She looks at me as if somehow I can deny the facts of her letter. Then she goes back to reading it but now her spare hand grips my sleeve.

I wait for her to finish reading. She drops the letter into her lap shaking her head.

'It's not possible,' she says.

There's nothing I can say because I don't know her news, so I continue to sit beside her. She shakes her head again and takes up the letter.

'Can I read it to you?'

'Of course, if you want to.'

She begins, '*Dorohenka moya donechka…*' It's from her mother then. I bow my head and try to concentrate on Olha's mother's words, longing for them to be my own Mama's.

'*I don't know where to begin with all of the news I have to tell you. So I will begin with your sister. Sofia has gone who knows where. She left the baby with me. Levko and I are managing. Thank God Sofia took my savings to help her on the road. I feel sure she must have gone to look for Ivan who hasn't been heard of since Brody…*'

Olha pauses and looks at me. 'That's my sister, Sofia. She'll do anything that suits her – abandon her baby, leave my mother and brother penniless in winter.' She shakes her head. 'My mother will still make excuses for her. She hasn't gone to look for her husband. She'll be looking after herself. Like she was when she sent her younger sister off to Germany.'

I look at Olha with new eyes.

She resumes her letter. '*She is safer away from the village. There have been arrests and shootings…*'

I'm shocked into saying, 'Your mother speaks very openly.'

'Yes, she does. I wonder if she doesn't realise the danger or doesn't care. Perhaps she thinks the NKVD won't harm an old woman.'

I can't help a snort of derision.

'I know, I know,' says Olha. 'Listen, there's more… '*Anna has been taken. We think to Ternopil but no one has heard from her. Her mother died and then her Petro was killed. He was shot in the forest and brought into the village for us all to see.*'' Olha is quiet for a moment and then she says, 'He was with the partisans. He was so handsome, Natalya. All the girls liked him. But he fell for Anna.'

And Roman is there before me. My handsome partisan. Dead too.

Olha's eyes have a faraway look as she sees her village again. 'It was so romantic. Anna had had a lot of unhappiness. Her father and brother had been shot by the NKVD. It drove her mother mad. People were happy for her when she began walking out with Petro.'

'Does your mother say why she was arrested?'

'No but she must have been helping the partisans, don't you think?'

'Perhaps. Although it could have been anything,' I say with a shudder. I can't help thinking that if I'd stayed at home and managed to survive the Germans, my own actions in the forest with the insurgents might have earned me the same fate.

I move over to my bed and lie on my back, looking up at

the whitewashed ceiling of the barrack. I must be careful when I go home. I won't be able to see who's left of the boys straight away. I'll have to see who's in charge of the village first. I can't ask Mama about Vasyl and the others so I have no way of knowing what has happened to their unit...or whether there's any disruptive action still going on.

'Are you alright?' asks Olha.

'Yes.'

'No letter?'

I shake my head.

'They're being cautious,' she says.

'I know.'

I can feel her sympathy across the gap between our beds.

'What will we go home to?' I can't help saying.

It will be a leap in the dark. Last year my mother and sisters were holding on. Now I don't know if they're dead or alive. Or, and this gives me pause, if I go home will my secrets be safe? I try to remember who knew I was helping the partisans. Are there any of those people still living? What are they doing to stay alive? And what are the NKVD doing?

But my thoughts are interrupted by Marichka. 'Come on, you two. Stop moping about. Letters are supposed to cheer you up.'

I sit up. 'Did you get a letter?'

'No, thank God! They'd have seen where it came from and that would have ruined my story.' She laughs as if she hasn't a care in the world. 'Let's go and sit in the sunshine,' she says, taking my hand to pull me up off the bed.

'Come with us, Olha,' I say. 'There's nothing we can do for now.'

We go out into the sunshine and see Irina and Slava sitting a short distance away from the other groups of young women. We go over to join them.

'Not more moping here, I hope.'

'Marichka! Did you get any letters?' I ask.

Irina nods. 'Yes, I did.'

'Are they all well?'

Irina shakes her head. 'Mama and *Tato* have been finding it very hard.'

'Are they on their own?'

'No, there's my brother but he's only ten.' She stops. 'No, he's eleven now.' Her eyes widen with the guilt of misremembering.

'They're growing up without us,' I say.

Olha looks as if she's about to speak but then looks down into her lap.

'I have to go back as soon as I can,' says Irina, as if she's just realised this.

'But the Communists…' says Olha.

'Even so. Mama and *Tato* don't say what's been happening in the village. But I do know that they're getting older and my brother can't help them yet. They're depending on me.'

'Did they ask you to come home?' I ask.

She shakes her head. 'No, but I must go. They can't manage without me.'

'And Slava?'

Slava doesn't look up. Irina strokes her friend's back. 'Her brothers are waiting for her. We'll go back together.'

Slava sits completely still.

There's a silence as we all try to make sense of the unknown future we're facing.

Olha breaks it. 'My mother's alone,' she begins. 'Well, apart from my younger brother. He's a bit older than yours,' she says to Irina. 'He'll be twelve now.' She swallows. 'My older sister has left her baby with Mama…but I'm afraid. They say we'll be sent to Siberia if we go back.'

'And that's no joke!' says Marichka suddenly.

We all look at her.

Her lovely face is serious for once. 'I know. I've been there.'

'Marichka!' I say. 'When?'

'When I was five.'

'Five?'

'Yes. My whole family was deported.' Her voice rises. 'They said my grandfather was a *kulak* so they sent all of us.'

'Don't…' I begin.

She shakes her head. 'All the family worked on *Dido*'s farm but he also employed some labourers to help him. So the Bolsheviks said he was a *kulak*. They took everything. The house, the land, the animals…We were all sent away for five years.' She shivers in the sunshine. 'When we came back there was nothing. We had no home. Nothing.'

'Oh, Marichka,' I say feeling ashamed that I hesitated to help her. No wonder she doesn't want to go home.

'I remember it all,' she says. 'Those bastards!' She gets up and walks away.

Olha runs after her. 'Marichka, wait!' I see her take Marichka's arm. They slow a little but walk on, their arms linked and their heads bent towards one another.

We three are silent until Irina says, as if there's been no pause since she last spoke, 'I know it will be hard, but what choice do I have?'

I wonder about my own choice and find myself thinking of home in June. I see ducks waddling down the rutted lane in front of our house to the muddy area around the spring. The chicks follow, cheeping. I don't know why I remember this and not the presence of the dirty green uniforms and blue caps of the NKVD, but the image brings a lump to my throat.

'What about you, Natalya? What will you do?'

'I don't know. I have family too but I don't want to go back for nothing. To be shot in the village…' But I've said too much. 'What about you, Slava? How old are your brothers?'

'They're nearly grown up, aren't they, Slava?' says Irina. 'They'll be waiting for you. They'll look after you.' She turns to me. 'There are three of them.'

'You're lucky, Slava, to have people who'll look after you,' I say.

But Slava doesn't look at all comforted by this.

Irina raises an eyebrow at me. 'We'll do what we have to do,' she says.

'That's true enough.' I get up to walk alone in an attempt to straighten out my thoughts.

But I run into Dmitro who has never been troubled by considerations of other people's feelings and who won't let me escape.

'Natalya, Natalya!' he calls.

I wave turning as if to continue walking away from him.

'Natalya,' he says, taking my arm. 'Where are you hurrying off to?'

'Oh,' I say, 'I have to go…'

'Come, sit with me. Tell me what you've been doing.'

He leads me to a bench in the outdoor canteen. I feel both foolish and captive at the same time. I have nothing to say to this man.

'What have you been doing, Natalya? Every time Taras and I try to find you, you're always busy.'

'Oh this and that,' I say. 'What have you been doing?'

'Having the great debate.'

'The great debate?'

'Yes, haven't you?'

'Haven't I what?'

'Been discussing endlessly whether to go home or not.'

'Oh, that.'

'Yes, that.' He peers into my face. 'So what are you going to do, little sister?'

Little sister! 'I don't know yet,' I say in a tone which I hope will put him off any further questioning.

But it's no use.

'What have you been thinking?' he asks.

'Oh well,' I sigh, 'none of us trusts the Russians.'

'Of course not.'

'So do I risk going back to be shot in the village. Or being deported to Siberia?'

'And will you…?'

I think of Mama and the girls. 'I don't know. My family…'

'You don't know whether they're dead or alive,' he says bluntly. 'When did you last hear from them?'

'Last year.'

'They might still be alive but they could just as easily be dead.'

'I have to find out.'

'But be shot or deported in the process.'

'I know.' I hesitate to tell him my other worry.

'What?' he asks as if he's read my mind.

'What are we if we don't stand on our own soil?'

'Natalya, look at you. With your serious face and your long plait. You couldn't be anything but Ukrainian. You don't have to live in a Ukrainian village to be Ukrainian.'

'I know that.' Although I'm not certain that I do.

'How long have you been in Germany?'

'Two years.'

'Can you speak German?'

'Of course. You know I can.'

'Have you become German?'

I look at him as if he's lost his wits. 'Of course not.'

'Of course not,' he mimics. 'And you won't become English

or American or Canadian. Or wherever they send us.'

Wherever they send us. Into the wide world. Into exile. I think of Roman and Vasyl fighting for what was ours or should have been ours. Was it for nothing? I wonder what Roman would have done… but I know. He would have stayed and fought till his last breath.

Dmitro watches me thinking. 'You would have left your family sooner or later.'

'Perhaps.' So even if I survive going home, would I rejoin the boys in the forest? Do I have the courage for that? Could I put my family into jeopardy by doing that? 'It's too much to think about. There's so much I don't know.'

Dmitro gives me a little smile. 'Just do what you've been doing. Survive each stage of this war. I know it's supposed to be over but there's a lot more to be resolved yet. Take one day at a time. You're not alone. You've made good friends,' and he pats my arm.

'I'm not just a homesick girl. If I go west now, when will I ever be able to go home?'

'As soon as the Allies intervene. They'll have to when they see how the Russians treat those returning from here.'

I shake my head. The Americans aren't cruel but they want to be rid of us. 'They won't fight for us. They want to go home too.'

'Maybe, but the world has changed. They won't put us all back into tidy boxes so easily.'

I know Dmitro is right. Everyone, and there are hundreds of thousands of us, everyone is determined to do what they choose to do, regardless of the rules. We've been thrown up into the air and we'll do our best to land where it suits us. But where do I want to land?

Before that question can be answered, another one is.

We're woken in the early morning, not by the bugler

223

sounding reveille, but by a long piercing scream. I sit up in bed, my heart pounding to see that all the other beds are similarly occupied – young women snatched from sleep looking confused. Only the bed beside Irina is empty.

'What was that?' asks Olha in a whisper.

'I don't know,' I say but I see Irina rising from her bed so I get up to join her.

She walks towards the door of our dormitory as if she can't help herself. She goes out into the yard. I follow her, hardly daring to breathe, afraid to utter a word. She opens the door and steps out into the early morning light to the sound of more cries.

'Help! Help!'

I follow her across the compound to our shower block pushing against a wave of dread. Irina enters ahead of me, pauses and crumples. I run towards her to catch her and when I'm on my knees with my arms around her, I look up.

Slava is hanging from a crossbeam by a length of rope, her head lolling on her shoulder. Beneath her an upturned stool tells us the rest.

I hold Irina tight while she sobs as if she will never stop. I stroke her hair, her back, murmuring, 'It's alright, Irina, it's alright. Slava can't be hurt or frightened anymore.'

A couple of UNRRA staff arrive and instead of ushering us out, one of the women leads Irina and me to the medical barrack. The girl who found Slava is guided there with us.

'These need to be treated for shock,' she says, and I sense rather than see her mouthing the word 'suicide'.

We're seated and given hot, sweet tea while I stay as close as I can to Irina, my arm around her. She has slumped in on herself. There are no more tears, just a shutting down. After the tea a nurse suggests she lie down.

'I'll stay with her if I may,' I say.

The nurse nods. 'Good idea.'

I lie beside Irina putting my arm over her, hoping the contact of our bodies will give her some comfort. I don't know how long we stay like that but the day brightens and an orderly brings us some soup. I sit up.

'Come, Irinochka,' I say and lead her to the table to sit down. 'Eat this nice soup. It'll make you feel better.'

She looks at me blankly so I take a spoon, fill it with liquid and lift it to her lips. She swallows it like a trusting child and after two or three more mouthfuls, she takes the spoon into her own hand and eats. I eat my soup too but am ashamed to acknowledge my hunger.

When we've eaten the nurse returns. 'You can stay here this afternoon if you'd like to,' she says.

But Irina says, 'We must go and see Slava.'

'Alright,' I say. She'll want to know what they have done with the body. And what is to be done.

Slava's body has been taken to the infirmary and is awaiting burial in the camp cemetery. The priest comes to find us. He takes Irina's hand in his and offers her his condolences.

'Thank you, Father. When will the burial service be?'

He glances at me then says, 'Tomorrow, but it will be a short service.'

Irina looks up at him. 'Why?' although she knows what the answer will be.

'The manner of her death,' he says. 'The poor unfortunate took her own life.'

'No, she didn't!' snaps Irina. 'Those German rapists took her life.'

The priest looks shocked. 'I didn't know about that.'

'She didn't want to announce it.'

'No, of course not. But I cannot give the full funeral rites to someone found hanged. I'm sorry.'

Irina bows her head. 'Then do what you can, Father.'

The following morning we gather at the outdoor chapel, Irina mourning her childhood friend, the rest of us her recent acquaintances from the barn. The men come to pay their respects to the girl who wouldn't speak to them. It is they who dug the grave and who now lower her body into the ground.

'Let this foreign soil lie gently upon her,' intones the priest.

It's hard not to shed a few tears for the girl who couldn't bear the cruelty she'd suffered. I turn away from the others after the brief service. I haven't gone far when Taras catches me up.

'Are you alright, Natalya?' he asks.

'I'll be fine in a minute,' I say.

He continues to walk with me so I turn to him. 'There's no need to stay with me. I'm alright, really.'

'I know. But it's such a sad day and it's better not to be alone at such a time.'

I shake my head. 'We're always alone.'

'We don't have to be.' He continues to walk with me but he clasps his hands behind his back. Perhaps so I won't worry that he's going to try to take my hand.

We continue to walk in silence towards the lower end of the *ploshcha* stopping at the line of trees. The fence beneath them lets us go no further but we stand under their boughs looking at the dappled light beyond the wire.

'I don't think she could face going home,' I say at last.

'Because she'd been raped?'

'That and she would have been in a house full of men. She had three brothers.'

'Surely they would have looked after her?'

'Or expected her to look after them,' I say. 'She couldn't look after herself. How would she have coped running a household for three growing boys?'

'Poor girl.'

'Yes, indeed.'

'And you, Natalya. What will you do?'

'I don't know.' I pause for a moment. 'I want to go home, to be in my own house with Mama and my sisters…but only if I'm allowed to do that.'

'The rumours aren't helpful, are they?'

'The deportations and the shootings?'

He nods. 'The Russians will treat us as traitors. That much is certain.'

'What will you do?'

'Go to England, if I can.'

'For ever?'

'Until we can go home safely,' he says.

'Safely…' Oh, if only we could. I know I have my German labourer status as a mark against me, but I also fear the discovery of my partisan past. The NKVD don't need one excuse to shoot someone, but a person with two strikes against them…that would surely be too much temptation to shoot both the perpetrator and the rest of her family. I sigh.

'Never mind, Natalya. Your job now is to be strong and to wait until you can go back. Don't be in a rush to meet death.'

'That sounds more like Dmitro,' I say.

He smiles. 'Ah, my optimistic friend. But he's right about some things. We're young enough to wait and if we go to England it's not too far from home. There's only a little channel of water to cross then we could do the rest on foot.'

'That's true,' I say, ignoring his use of 'we'. 'I can wait.'

Chapter 25
Germany Autumn 1945

The weeks pass. One day we're summoned to an additional *Appel*. There's no explanation. We were counted as usual this morning and were all present and correct. Even more ominously, we've been told to bring our belongings.

'What do they want us for?' hisses Olha as we line up. 'Are they moving us again?'

I wait in silence, Marichka and Olha on one side of me, Irina on the other.

The head of the camp comes out of the Administration barrack and there's a collective intake of breath as we recognise the green uniforms of the Red Army officers with him. The man and the woman approach our assembly to stand watching us, their eyes scanning the rows as they are introduced.

It's alright, I tell myself. There are only two of them. We could easily overpower them.

The male officer begins to speak. 'Comrades! The Fascists have been defeated. Now you must return to your homes where you will be welcomed. Comrade Stalin wants us all to benefit from our victory over German imperialism. The Great Patriotic War has ended in our complete victory. After the enormous sacrifices we have made, our country will be stronger than ever. We must all work together for the future of our Motherland. The period of war is over and we are entering the period of peace. So come with us. Be a part of the fight of the Slav people for their freedom and independence.'

Freedom and independence. Is that the freedom to rob villagers of their harvest and shoot or deport anyone who objects?

'It is true that you have had to work hard for the Fascists but now we will work together in our fields and factories so we will all benefit from the greatness of Mother Russia. *Domoy za rodynu!*' he says.

Russia is not our Motherland so why would we want to return?

There's a pause then he invites us to step into the future and go home to our loved ones.

I'm amazed that there are some who do step forward. I raise my eyebrows to Olha but we both stand still. Who would believe what even a child knows to be lies?

But Irina steps forward.

'No, Irina,' I say trying to hold her arm.

Olha grabs her other arm. 'Don't go! You know you can't trust them.'

'I must,' she says, pulling herself away from us.

We let go, afraid we're attracting the attention of the Bolsheviks. I bow my head. The jostling continues for a few more minutes. When I try to count how many 'volunteers' have gathered, there are a couple of hundred. Why? I can only assume they're so desperate to go home they're willing to believe the fantasy they're being peddled. The volunteers try not to look conscious of themselves as they're ushered away to open lorries. We watch as they climb up into the backs of the vehicles and only as they start to move away does the murmuring grow to a roar.

'Why did she go?' wails Olha.

I don't answer. I only know that I will not go home in a Red Army lorry. I understand that Irina feared for her family but how will they feel if she's shot before their eyes? Or if she's deported? My heart thumps as another thought strikes me. Those Bolshevik devils might deport her whole family with her then what will happen to her little brother and Mama and *Tato*? But I know she felt released by Slava's death. She only had herself to think of so she couldn't resist the pull of home.

Those of us who remain are dismissed by our American minders. Olha and I walk slowly back to our barrack. She puts her arm through mine.

'Home,' she sighs.

'Yes.'

We try to smile at one another.

'What will become of us?'

'I don't know. We'll go on living I suppose, waiting till all of this is over.'

It's not over yet. Some thought that a few hundred volunteers would satisfy the Red Army. They dared to hope the officers would not return but they do. A few days later another lorry appears with several of the volunteers from the previous visit. They're waving and shouting to us as the driver circles the barracks.

'Who wants to go home?' they shout.

'Come on! We can go home.'

I run with the others to see what might happen. As the lorry comes to a halt we gather around it. There are three Ukrainians on the back of the lorry passing single cigarettes into the crowd. There's a bit of pushing as people reach up for comfort or currency. The Red Army driver gets out of his cab while his companion gets down from the passenger side.

'We need more cigarettes,' calls one of the Ukrainians.

Both of the Russians lean into the cab to get more bribes.

In a flash the three Ukrainians jump down into the crowd pushing their way towards the back. Realising what their intentions are, we all turn and begin milling about and moving away in large groups towards the barracks.

I don't look to see the surprise on the faces of the Red Army officers but I hear their shouts.

'Where did they go?'

'Stop them!'

But it's too late. We wander away, camouflaging the three who thought better of their desire to return to live under Soviet rule.

The crowd don't go far. A wave of muttering begins to spread as we turn to face the Red Army lorries. The muttering changes to booing, the bass sound growing to such a crescendo that the Red Army officers hurry back into the cab. We sense we have the advantage and begin to move forward towards the lorry. A couple of UNRRA staff appear looking bewildered then shocked. One runs to open the gate while the other ushers the Red Army vehicle out as quickly as possible. The gate is closed again. We press against the fence, rows and rows of us, howling our contempt at the receding lorry.

The Red Army don't return to speak to us en masse. At a morning *Appel* our camp leader announces that later in the day we will be interviewed, one by one, by officers from the Red Army. This will be our opportunity to say we'd like to return home. He tries to ignore the rumble of complaints, telling us the interviews will be conducted outside the camp gates. We will have the chance to say if we want to go home.

We do want to go home but home is not the firing squad or the cattle truck to Siberia to which the Americans have conveniently closed their minds.

Later the lorry with red stars on its doors returns but parks beyond the wire fence of the camp. A tent is erected and we're told to line up for our interviews. We queue up in silent rows.

When it's my turn, I'm called from the sunlight into the blinding dark of a khaki canvas tent. As my eyes adjust I see with a lurch of the stomach the ugly green uniforms of the two Red Army officers. Lower ranking but still the splashes of red staining their uniforms fill me with dread.

The male is seated on the right and even in his chair I can see he would be a metre eighty or ninety tall, with square shoulders and a deep chest. He's had a good war wherever he's been. There's no sign of him having gone hungry. His large hands rest on the documents on the rickety folding table, the pen not far from his meaty fingers which look more used to the scythe than to this delicate instrument. He has the high cheekbones and deep-set eyes of the descendants of the Tartars. There's no warmth here, just a hard rock of a man. He gestures to the empty chair in front of him.

I sit and find myself on eye level with the female. She wears the same uniform but is younger. Whatever she's seen over the last six years hasn't surprised her. She expects to see depravity and weakness wherever she looks so she despises us all. She should be sympathetic with her round face and brown eyes but she's not. Her mouth is a firm line, the full lips stretched tight in scorn.

'*Imya?*'

I want to thank her for her bark. I remember who I'm dealing with.

'Natalya,' I reply, glancing at the American officer seated to the side. His smooth skin and thick hair speak of an alien world of plentiful food and freedom of speech. He's here because we're in the American sector but he's only an observer.

'Father's name?'

'*Tato.*'

She gives me a withering look. 'His name?'

I shrug. '*Tato.*'

She tries again. 'Your mother's name?'

'Mama.'

'Where are you from?' she asks changing tack.

'Over there,' I say pointing vaguely eastwards.

'When did you leave?'

'May '43.' That should tell them enough. I know they won't accept that I was forced to go. They simply see a betrayal of Stalin.

'Why?'

'I was taken as a slave labourer to Germany.'

'Why didn't you stay at home?'

'Because I would have been shot.'

'Who else do you have at home?'

Now my stomach lurches. What do they already know?

I've waited too long and the square-built female sets her jaw. 'What family do you have?'

'My mother and two sisters.'

'Where's your father?'

'Dead.'

'When?'

When you bastards shot him in our yard I think, but I say calmly enough, 'August 1940.'

They don't miss a beat.

'A traitor.'

It's not a question. If the NKVD shot him he must have betrayed Mother Russia.

'No,' I say.

The American sits oblivious to the meaning of what we're saying. He hears the words but doesn't understand the language. Still I'm grateful for his presence. While he's here they won't shoot me or drag me off.

'Did you have a boyfriend?'

'No,' I reply.

'There must have been someone. He'll be going home. Don't you want to see him again?'

If only you knew.

I sit in silence.

I get a long stare from both of them then the man says, 'You're needed at home.'

I know I'm needed by Mama and the girls but I'm not needed by anyone else. I'm not needed by a State which defines the truth by whatever the colour of that moment happens to be. I won't let them send me back. Not now. Maybe in a year or two when the West has seen what they do to us it might be safe to return, but not yet.

I keep perfectly still through the silence which follows. I wait them out. I won't fill it with explanations and excuses. I watch the canvas between their heads.

'Only traitors won't go home,' he barks eventually.

I don't reply. What would be the point? They'll twist whatever I say to suit themselves. They might even promise me a rosy future with an unmolested life in my own village. But I'm not going yet. I've received no letters from Mama and the girls for over a year which can only mean they're afraid to write or the letters are being stopped. Either way it's warning enough.

The interrogation remains unresolved. I won't agree to go and they aren't making me go…yet. A trainload has left, the cattle trucks garlanded with green branches, but we haven't heard how they were received. The Americans want us to go – we're just more mouths to feed and they want to tidy up Europe before they can go home themselves. The French and Dutch have flooded west, back to countries which have been freed of tyrants. Mine hasn't. I am no longer a slave labourer but a displaced person and there must be millions of us if our camp is anything to go by. The Americans must think it strange that we won't return to our homelands but they have little knowledge of the wilds of Siberia where so many have died. Nor of the summary shootings before the Germans came. But if we won't go home we make ourselves stateless.

'Get out,' says the male officer.

I step out into the sunshine and walk back into the camp before I let out my breath in a sigh of relief.

That night I dream of Mama again. She's not at home this time but by the stream where we used to do our laundry. She's slapping the wet linen on the rocks and singing with the other women. I can't see Lyubka or Verochka but I recognise our neighbours. Their alto voices rise in a mournful wave as they sing: '*Bula viyna strashna i zla…*' There was a terrible, evil war which brought ruin…

As I approach Mama she turns and sees me. She pushes me away with her strong bare forearms shaking her head at me. I try to get past this pushing to hug her but she won't let me. I struggle but have no strength to reach past her red hands.

I wake up with my face wet with tears. What does it mean? Is Mama angry with me for not coming back? Or doesn't she want me to come back? And where are the girls?

I turn on my side wondering when I will ever get any answers.

***

The Red Army visits seem to have unleashed some kind of devils amongst us. One night shortly after the interviews with the Bolsheviks, we're woken in our dormitory by a hammering at the door.

'Come on, girls! Open up!' yells a male voice. 'We're going to have a party!'

There's laughter as another shouts, 'We've brought the *samohon*.'

So they've been distilling some sort of alcohol and have now tasted it, which has caused a further loosening of the rules which used to bind us in our villages.

One or two girls get out of bed and Marichka heads for the door.

'No,' I call as I jump out of bed. 'Don't let them in. They're probably drunk.' I clutch Marichka's arm.

'Don't be such a spoilsport,' she says. 'It's only a bit of fun.'

'It won't be fun if they get carried away,' I say.

By now everyone is crowding towards the door. There's a muddle of shouting as we argue back and forth.

When the hammering is renewed one girl breaks free of the crowd to unlock the door. A dozen or so men almost fall into the room while some of the girls cheer. I retreat to my bed, as does Olha.

'I don't know any of these,' she says. 'Do you?'

I shake my head.

'What shall we do?'

'I don't know.' I look over at the group nearest the door. They are now sprawled over several beds, men and women alike, passing around the bottles of home-made alcohol.

'We could stay here,' I say, 'if this is all there'll be, but we can't be sure no more men will come.'

'We could go to the *medpunkt*,' says Olha.

'That's a good idea. I don't really want to wait to see if it'll get any worse.'

'No, me neither.'

I reach for my coat and check the hidden pocket, feeling for the *Sturmbannführer*'s cut-throat razor then we get up from our beds and stride towards the door.

'Not joining us, girls?' calls one of the men.

'Later,' I say. 'Call of nature first.'

There's some laughter then Olha and I are out in the scented dark. The camp is dimly lit but we can see our way across the compound to the medical barrack.

'I'll have stomach cramps,' says Olha, 'and I can't bear for you to leave me.'

'Good enough,' I say as we present ourselves to the night

orderly.

She looks doubtful of our story but there are a couple of free beds so she lets us stay. Perhaps she too has heard the shouting. We lie down pretending to sleep.

The next morning we return to the chaos of our dormitory. There are girls lying fast asleep sprawled across their beds while several men remain with their partners of the night before. Others are going about the morning's business of bathing and dressing. My own bed is empty. I check under my mattress. My *rushnyk* and photo are still there but I make up my mind. I won't live like this.

'I'm going to look for Taras today,' I say to Olha.

'I'll come, too. I want to speak to Dmitro.'

We find the men in the canteen.

There's no point in hesitating so I sit down opposite Taras. 'Those rooms…'

'Those rooms?'

'The ones for couples.'

Dmitro gives him a look I can't interpret.

'Do they have them here too?'

'Yes,' says Taras. 'Why?'

'We want one,' says Olha, 'with you two.'

Taras looks at me.

'Our barrack was invaded by drunks last night.'

He nods. 'So to be safe…'

'Yes,' I say.

'It'll be fun,' says Olha smiling at Dmitro, who also has a broad grin on his face.

'It will,' he says.

I don't smile.

Taras stands up. 'We'll go to the Administrative Office now and see what can be done. Come on, Dmitro. You can chat to your friend there.'

They leave us to our breakfast.

As Olha and I eat our porridge I can see she can't help twinkling with excitement. She catches me looking at her.

'Don't worry, Natalya. It'll be fine.'

'I'm not worried. I just want everyone to be clear I'm not going to be Taras's girlfriend.'

'You don't have to be. You just need to say you are.'

'There's not going to be any funny business,' I say and want to laugh out loud at myself. I sound such a prude.

'Funny business?'

'You know.'

'I do,' she says, 'but I like Dmitro.'

'That's alright. You can do what you like. We can share a room without having to behave in the same way as one another.'

'It'll be nice, Natalya. We'll have a bit more privacy.'

She's right. Sharing a room with three people will be preferable to sharing a room with thirty. But I still want to make my terms clear to Taras.

I do that later in the day as we move our things over to a block containing *malozhenstvo*, the smaller rooms. In ours there are two beds so we suspend one of our precious blankets on string to divide the room in half.

I make for one of the beds but realise I've missed a conversation between Olha and Dmitro as she blushes and sits down on the other bed. Dmitro sits beside her. They grin at one another like two children.

'It's alright, Natalya,' says Taras. 'I'll stretch out on the floor.'

I put my bundle on the bed saying to Taras, 'We should go for a walk.'

He puts his bag on the floor and we step outside.

It's windy and there's an autumnal chill in the air. I shiver. 'It's going to be too cold for you to sleep on the floor.'

'I'll be alright. I've done worse.'

'I know but it's not fair.' I pause. 'I'm sorry but I assumed Olha and I would be sharing a bed.'

He manages a smile. 'They like one another.'

How to say enough but not too much?

'I don't dislike you,' I say.

He pulls a face.

'It's just that we're only friends.'

'Friends is alright,' he says.

'We can sleep in one bed without…you know.'

'Yes, we can,' he says. 'But I can sleep on the floor till it gets colder.'

Chapter 26
England 1992

'Should auld acquaintance be forgot...' could be heard up and down the street as the New Year was ushered in. It was also being sung loudly in Lyuba and Adrian's house, although Taras was still not sure of the words. Flanked by his grand-daughters, Valeria and Lydia, he smiled at the nonsense of a Ukrainian exile singing a Scottish song in England. But at least his three daughters were smiling.

'Happy New Year!' shouted Simon as the song finished and the adults exchanged kisses. He waved an empty champagne glass at his sister and cousin.

'Only one more,' said Vera.

'I'm sixteen.'

'I know.'

'OK,' he said disappearing into his aunt's kitchen after Valeria and Lydia. 'Only one more,' he said to the girls.

'What? Bottle?' said Val waggling a bottle of wine at her cousins.

Lydia laughed. 'Yeah, for now. Let's take it up to your room.'

The three youngsters clattered up the stairs as Adrian entered the kitchen with an empty champagne bottle.

'Alright?' he called after them.

'Yeah, we're fine,' shouted Val.

He opened another bottle and went back into the sitting room.

'We could go for the first anniversary of independence,' said Nadiya. She was sharing the small sofa with her father but

240

looking across at her sisters.

'Where are we going?' asked Adrian.

'To Ukraine,' said Lyuba. 'Well, we three are.'

Adrian looked across at his brother-in-law, Tom.

'We're excess baggage apparently,' said Tom.

'No, that's unfair,' said Vera, turning to her husband. 'It's just that it'll be our first visit to Mama's village. You can come next time.'

'Oh, thank you,' said Tom. 'Well, maybe Adrian and I will go on a trip somewhere else.'

To his annoyance, Vera nodded and turned back to her sisters. 'We'll have to write to the aunties to see if it's alright for us to go in August. Or to visit them at all…'

'Of course we can visit them,' said Lyuba. 'I'm sure they'll be curious to meet us. Won't they, *Tatu*?'

Taras looked anxious. 'Yes, they would love to meet you but I'm not sure how safe it will be for you to go yet.'

'Ukraine's independent now. The Russians don't have control anymore.'

'Everything is still a bit chaotic,' insisted Taras.

'Yes, but Parliament voted for independence in August and then the referendum ratified it just a few weeks ago,' said Lyuba.

'And should there be any problems, we all have British passports,' added Nadiya.

'We'll be fine, *Tatu*. You could come too,' said Vera.

Taras shook his head. 'I can't. It's not my village but I would still be seen as a traitor.'

'What, even after all this time?' asked Lyuba.

'Yes.'

'But the NKVD, or the KGB, won't be in the village,' she persisted.

Her father gave a short laugh. 'Not in name. But the people who did their dirty work will still be there.'

'It's alright, *Tatu*,' said Nadiya, stroking her father's arm. 'We'll go first and test the water. Then you can come next year with Adrian and Tom.'

Taras sighed. 'You don't know…'

'You know what they're like once they've made their minds up,' said Adrian to Taras. 'Let them go this year and we'll have a whole family pilgrimage next year.'

'Pilgrimage?' said Lyuba. 'It's not a joke, Adrian. We've never met Mama's sisters or seen where she grew up. This means a lot to us.'

'I know it does,' he said and leaned over to kiss her cheek.

Mollified, she said, 'What about the children?'

Tom sat up suddenly. 'No. Not this first time.'

Vera looked at him in surprise.

'I mean it, Ver. They're not going this time.'

'I'd prefer Val not to go either,' said Adrian.

'Alright,' cut in Nadiya. 'That's settled then. The three of us will go and report back to the rest of you. Alright, *Tatu*?'

'Yes,' said Taras, 'but you'll find things very different.'

'You mean from what Mama told us?' asked Nadiya.

'Yes. Your mother left the village in '43 when it was under the Germans. The Bolsheviks will have done terrible damage to it after that.'

'I want to see if it's as beautiful as Mama said, the river and the forests.' Lyuba paused. 'It'll be strange to think of her there as a girl.'

No one said, 'And as a young wife and a partisan…' but all thought it.

Nadiya took her father's hand. 'It's alright, *Tatu*. We just want to find a little of Mama.'

'Me too,' he muttered and rose stiffly from the sofa. He walked out of the room.

Nadiya glanced at her sisters. 'He must miss her all the

time.'

'He does,' said Vera. 'When I went round the other day he was in the kitchen with the back door open as if he was expecting her to walk in from the garden at any moment even though it's almost two years since she died.'

'How long were they together?' asked Tom.

'They met in 1945 in Germany,' said Vera.

'And they came here in '47,' said Lyuba.

'So Mama was away from home all that time,' said Nadiya.

'But they made a home here,' said Tom, as Taras came back into the room.

'Ah, Tom,' he said, 'you see this lovely family but it's still a foreign country. Natalya wanted to go home from the moment she left. We all did.'

Lyuba swallowed. 'Well, at least we can go home for her.'

'Yes, she'll like that,' said Taras.

Chapter 27
Germany Winter 1945-6

I wake with a shudder and try to pull more warmth out of my two thin blankets. I pull them up to my ears but expose my feet. With a groan, I lift myself up to flick the blanket downwards then I remember why there's a dark silhouette beside me on the floor. I lean over to whisper, 'Taras!' There's no reply so I lean over further and shake his shoulder. 'Taras!'

He moans a little stretching out a hand. I grasp it pulling him up towards me.

'Wait,' he says, as he untangles himself from the blankets he has had to wind around his body to soften the floorboards. He stands up, throws his blankets over me and climbs into my bed. I wriggle over as near the wall as I can while he tries to lie with his back to me.

But the bed's too narrow.

'Sorry,' he mutters as he spoons me. Then he sighs. 'You're so warm.'

'Not so warm,' I say. 'The cold just woke me.'

He leans into me and I can't help myself. I relax into his warmth. Soon we're both asleep.

We wake to a peculiarly quiet world. I turn towards the window and recognise the wintry light. 'It's snowed.'

We kneel up on the bed gazing out entranced by the whiteness which has bewitched the camp.

'Olha, get up. It's snowed.'

There's a grunt from the other side of the blanket curtain which separates us.

'Go back to sleep,' says Dmitro. 'There's no point going

outside into the cold.'

Taras and I grin at one another. We dress quickly leaving our friends to sleep.

They're not the only ones who've decided to hibernate. When we open the outer door no one is stirring. We smile at the glistening expanse of snow and set off, making giant strides across the compound to the canteen. The thin plume of smoke from its chimney assures us of a warm welcome. When we reach its door, we look back at two sets of footprints side by side in the pristine snow. Hot porridge revives us and we drink tea by the pot-bellied stove as other inmates are forced out of their beds by hunger.

We'll be able to light the little stove in our room later. We just need to eke out our share of the wood Taras and Dmitro helped to cut last October as the UNRRA officers began to panic about how they would get us through the winter. They want us to go home quietly but they don't want us to die of cold.

Little post arrives at the camp as we continue to hibernate. Outside the snow remains deep and I can only imagine that my family are hibernating too around the brown tiled stove. But one letter does reach us.

When the mail is distributed one morning in the canteen, my name is called. With a thudding heart I step forward to take the envelope. I look down at the address. It's not Mama's beloved hand I see but a stranger's. It can only be bad news so I hurry away to our room to open it away from prying eyes.

I rip open the envelope to remove the single piece of cheap, grey paper then look for the signature.

'Olha, it's from Irina.'

Olha comes around the blanket curtain leaving the men on the other side. She sits on the bed with me and we begin to read.

'Dorohenka Natalya,

I have little time to write because I must be ready for the transport this morning. All the younger people in my village have been ordered to be ready to depart for the Chelyabinsk region. They are taking us to work there. So I must leave Mama and Tato after all. I will not be able to look after them as I had hoped.

When I left you I thought we might never meet again but now I am certain that we won't. They say few people survive the work camps.

Do not come home to Ukraine, dear Natalya. Tell the others, Olha, Marichka and anyone who will listen. The Russians have lied to us again. We won't be allowed to stay in our villages but will be sent into exile in Russia. If you must be in exile, go somewhere kinder.

I send you my love, my dear friend, and I thank you for all that you did, and tried to do, for me.

Irina

Olha puts her arm around my shoulders. We don't try to hold back our tears. We cry not only for Irina's terrible fate but for ourselves. Alone and adrift. We thought it might be dangerous to go home but now we know it cannot be done.

As if from a long way away, we hear shouting across the compound. It sounds like, '*Paketi! Paketi!*'

I hear the door of our little room opening then closing. A few minutes later Dmitro returns. 'Come on, quickly. They're giving out Red Cross parcels.'

We hurry across to the canteen to join the chaos. UNRRA officers are trying to establish some sort of order but they have little chance against hundreds of hungry adults. Dmitro and Taras lead the way while Olha and I do our own determined pushing to reach the front of the crowd. We're packed in shoulder to shoulder, all trying to wriggle forward.

'There's no need to push. There are parcels for everyone,' shouts one of the UNRRA officers but no one pays any attention to that. We've been lied to by those in authority all our lives.

At last I manage to reach out to take a parcel. I clutch it to my chest with both arms and drive my way back out of the crowd. I find Taras waiting for me at the back of the canteen. We hurry across the snow-filled yard to indulge ourselves with the sweetness of our parcels.

And there is sweetness in abundance. We find tins of cocoa and condensed milk, sugar and biscuits, a bar of chocolate, a packet of tea. There are also savoury treats – tins of fish, ham, cheese, dried eggs and margarine. Things to supplement our diet but also things we can trade, especially the cigarettes. I allow myself a mouthful of chocolate while I consider how I will ration the rest.

Olha and Dmitro join us clutching their own parcels. They too exclaim over the riches we've been given.

'There's soap,' says Olha.

I smile at her. 'A real treat.' The sliver I took from the Kuhn's house has long gone.

'Hmm. What to eat first?' says Dmitro when Olha suddenly turns on him.

'What can we trade?' she says.

He looks blank.

'You know …for clothes.'

He continues to look blank for a moment then recognition dawns. 'Oh yes.'

But we all hear his disappointment.

Olha blushes. I'm not sure whether it's with anger or embarrassment.

'What's the matter?' I ask.

Olha looks at me and then at Dmitro. He looks up at us

both smiling now. 'You might as well tell her.'

I look at Olha.

'We're going to get married.'

'Oh, congratulations!' I say. 'When? In spring?'

Olha blushes again. 'No, sooner than that.'

So that's it. I hug my friend and kiss her cheek. 'Congratulations.'

She smiles. 'It's a bit soon, but…'

She's right, it is. I'm torn between anxiety for her and envy. She will have her husband by her side and their baby in her lap.

I get up.

'Where are you going?' asks Taras.

'I want to ask those Red Cross people something,' I say.

'Want me to come with you?'

I shake my head. I take Irina's letter from the bed and put it in my coat pocket. Then I cross the yard again.

The canteen's almost empty. The camp inmates have all received their parcels and have retired to their beds to look at the riches they now own. Only a few UNRRA volunteers and a couple of grey-uniformed Red Cross staff are tidying up the larger cartons.

I approach one of the women, her curly hair billowing out beneath her cap, the red cross visible on its white background high on her left arm.

'*Pereproshuyu*,' I say. She looks at me blankly so I try again. '*Entschuldigung.*'

She smiles so I continue in German.

'I wonder if you can help me?'

'I will if I can,' she says.

'I'm troubled by a letter I've had from Ukraine and I wondered if you have any further information.'

'Go on.'

'My friend returned to her village in Ukraine from this

camp with the Red Army. But now she says that the Russians are taking all of the younger people and sending them to Russia to work.' I look into the Red Cross woman's face. My heart sinks as I see no surprise there. 'Do you know about this?'

She nods. 'We've received some troubling reports but like your information, so far it's only been anecdotal – people telling us about their own, or their friends' experiences.'

'I see.'

There's a pause, then she says, 'The Red Cross can't go wading into a country uninvited.'

'I know,' I say. 'So if we go back there won't be any protection.'

She shakes her head. 'I'm afraid not.'

So we're on our own. I knew we were really but the generosity of strangers with the parcels we've just received fooled me for a moment. There can be no going back. Yet.

***

As if to hand us all of our troubles at once, a few days later an anxious rumour ripples its way through the camp. It's Marichka who brings it to us.

'Natalya,' she calls as she raps on our door.

I open it to her. She looks rosy – her cheeks red from the cold, her lipstick bright.

'Marichka, come in.'

When she enters our room I detect a sweetness. So she has found some perfume too. My glamorous friend.

'What can I do for you?'

She glances at the men.

Taras sighs. 'Dmitro, let's go and top up our firewood shall we?'

Dmitro is about to object when Olha nudges him none too gently.

'Oh yes, alright,' he says, and the two of them pull on their coats and scarves to leave us alone with Marichka.

'What is it?' I ask as the door closes.

'There's going to be another round of screening,' says Marichka in a low voice.

'What kind of screening?'

'Where we're from…What kind of work we can do…'

'Who's going to do it?' asks Olha.

'The UNRRA officers.'

'How do you know?'

Marichka looks at her with what could be pity. 'I have a friend…'

'Of course you do,' says Olha.

'If the Americans are doing the screening what do we have to fear?' I ask her.

'The high-ups don't want us. They want us to go home so they're going to comb through us again. Anyone not from Western Ukraine must be sent back whether they like it or not.'

'Can't your 'friend' save you?' asks Olha.

Marichka barely glances at her. 'Natalya, can we do some studying again?'

'Yes, of course. When will this screening begin?'

'Soon. I'm not sure when. But we can't give them any excuses to send us back.' She tries to pin me with her eyes. 'You said they sent Irina to a work camp. What do you think they'd do to me if I go back now? They'd know I avoided that first sweep.'

'It's alright,' I say. 'You don't need to worry, Marichka. I'll help you.'

She breathes out a long breath as I put on my boots.

'Let's go for a walk.'

'Thank you, Natalya.'

We pace up and down the access lane to the camp, while I

test Marichka on what she can remember from the first screening. Then I give her more facts about my village which I make her repeat to me.

'Would it help to see a map?' I ask her.

'Where would you get one?'

'I'd draw it for you.'

'Oh, I see. Yes, it would.'

As we head back to my room we pass a volunteer who gives us a curious glance.

'Man trouble,' I mouth to her.

She nods sympathetically.

When we reach my room I hunt out Irina's letter which was written on only one side of the paper. On the blank side I begin with the church almost in the centre of my village as Olha watches us in silence. I ask Marichka to try to place her supposed house and my real one, the school, the little shop and then further afield the kolhoz barns. Then we sketch in the road to the town, the river and the woods.

Taras and Dmitro return, their arms full of cut logs, as our map becomes more dense with detail. Taras closes the door then asks me in a low tone what I'm doing.

'Marichka comes from the east,' I whisper. 'She's going to say she comes from my village when they screen us again.'

For a moment he looks shocked then he looks at Marichka. 'If you put Natalya in any danger I will expose you to the authorities. And you will be sent back.'

'Taras, don't.'

'She needs to know she isn't the only one who wants to survive,' he says to me. He looks at her again. 'Don't be under any illusions. If you endanger Natalya, I will betray you.'

'Yes, I can see that.' She rises to go putting the map in her pocket.

Taras rises too. 'Give me the map.'

251

'But I need to study it.'

'Do it here. Now.'

She sits again and looks at the map we have drawn. 'Alright,' she says after a few moments.

Taras holds out his hand and she gives him the flimsy piece of paper. He lifts the hot lid of the stove dropping the paper into it, where it curls red, then grey and is gone.

Marichka says, 'Thank you, Natalya. If I hear when they're going to begin I'll let you know.'

'Thank you, Marichka.' I stand and we kiss one another on the cheek. 'Be careful,' I say.

'You too.' She gives a little smile. 'Bye, Olha, boys,' she says and is gone.

I sit on my bed unsure how to begin with Taras. Olha and Dmitro sit on their bed so I pull the blanket curtain closed between us.

'What?' he says.

'You know what.'

'I know she's your friend but there's another word for the kind of woman she is.'

'Be careful.'

'She's the type who will look after herself first.'

'We all will.'

'Yes, but would you betray your friends?'

Before I can answer, he says, 'Of course, you wouldn't. You're a decent human being. Not everyone is.'

I try to flick his compliment away with a gesture but he's not finished.

'Why your village? Because she knows as well as I do who you are.'

'I'm no saint.'

'No one's saying that, but you are good. I've seen it. More than once.'

I shake my head. If only he knew…

'Anyway, I'm not letting her save herself on your back.'

'You're not letting her? We're only friends, you and I.'

'I know that. I accept it. I see that's what you want. But I care enough about you to want to protect you. That's what friends do.'

I feel my eyes prickle with tears, but I won't cry here for all I've lost…and all I could have. So I get up from the bed, take my coat and leave our little room.

'Natalya,' I hear him say, but I need to get myself under control.

I go back out into the cold and march up the service lane to the road. I walk until it begins to darken then I turn back towards the camp. As I draw near the camp's entrance I see a figure smoking a cigarette.

'Natalya,' calls Taras.

'Yes, it's me.'

He begins to walk towards me. 'Are you alright? I didn't mean to drive you out into the cold.'

'I'm alright. Taras, there's so much about me you don't know.'

'That's true of all of us. We've all been through a lot.' He takes my hand and puts it through his arm. 'I don't want you to slip,' he says.

I let my fingers rest on his sleeve as we make our way back to our temporary home.

***

Marichka joins me in the laundry room a couple of days later. The facilities are basic after the Kuhn's efficient washing machine, but for girls who are used to the stream in the centre of the village the sinks and cold water aren't so bad.

Marichka has some small pieces of lacy underwear to wash

while I hold up my once white knickers.

'I could get you some nicer ones,' she says. Then with a sly smile, 'For Taras.'

'It's not like that.'

'He was very protective the other day.'

'Yes, he was. He's my friend.'

Marichka raises her eyebrows.

'He is.'

'There are only two beds in your room.'

'We sleep like brother and sister,' I say.

'For how long? He's a man after all.'

'Marichka, we're not all the same.'

'I know, I know.' She draws her fancy knickers out of the water. 'But I want nice things. Don't you?'

'Not for myself. But for Olha. She and Dmitro are getting married.'

'So she needs something nice to wear.'

'Yes. Do you think we could get her something as a surprise? I'll give you some of my Red Cross rations.'

'No need,' says Marichka. 'I'll see what I can find.'

I know she won't have to look far. She has her American contacts but she has also made herself close to our black market dealers in the camp.

She comes by our room a couple of days later when the men have just gone out to what they're calling a meeting, but will be DP's huddled around a stove somewhere discussing our foggy future. Her timing is so good I wonder if she's been waiting for them to leave.

She taps on the door then opens it and peeps at us. 'Can I come in?'

'Of course,' I say.

'Hello, Olha,' she says.

Olha gets up to leave.

Marichka puts a hand on her arm. 'Don't go. I want to show you something.' She opens her coat and pulls out a small bundle. She unrolls a maroon tailored dress with cream flecks. She holds it up against Olha. 'It's a bit long but we can soon take up the hem.'

Olha looks astonished. 'What are you doing?'

'I thought you might want a smart dress for a special occasion. I know the colour's a bit dark but it's the best I could get.'

Olha blushes. 'There was no need.'

'There was. Every girl wants to look nice…' Marichka trails off while Olha looks at me.

'I told her, Olha. I wanted you to have something nice to wear. It's not a secret, is it?'

Olha shakes her head. 'No, but…'

'And I got these shoes,' says Marichka. She offers a pair of brown leather shoes, flat with an ankle strap.

Olha takes them in her hands then looks at us in turn.

'Try them on,' I say.

She sits on the bed. I help her put the first one on.

'They're a bit too big,' she says.

'Well, you can tighten the strap and perhaps put some newspaper in to line them,' says Marichka. 'Try the dress too.'

Olha lifts the dress from the bed and fingers the fabric of the grosgrain. I realise that she might never have had such a good dress before, either in her village or in the German factory.

'It's very fine,' she says.

'So it should be,' says Marichka. 'Every girl deserves one good dress.'

Olha takes off her sweaters and thick skirt. We help her slip the dress over her head. It was made for a petite *Hausfrau* so it almost fits Olha perfectly.

'Hmm, the waist could be tightened,' says Marichka.

'There's no point,' says Olha. Then she looks at Marichka with a little smile.

'Well, you're a dark horse,' says Marichka leaning forward to kiss Olha on the cheek. 'Congratulations!'

'Thank you, and thank you for my outfit.'

'You're welcome.'

As Olha changes back into her winter layers I ask Marichka, 'Do I owe you anything?'

'Of course not,' she says.

***

The wedding itself is a makeshift affair in comparison to the weeks of preparation and the days of celebration there would have been at a village wedding. But Olha seems happy. The camp priest, our own Ukrainian Father Andriy marries Olha and Dmitro at one end of the canteen while our camp colleagues are delighted to help the couple celebrate at the other end of the same room. The men have set up a bar with beer, plum wine and the inevitable *samohon*. The camp's musicians gather with their looted accordions, guitars and drums and settle to play for the dancing for as long as is required.

But before the dancing begins, in the absence of their parents, Taras and I formally welcome Olha and Dmitro to their wedding reception with bread and salt. Olha didn't have time to embroider her own *rushnyk* so I have lent her mine – the *rushnyk* which should have served Roman and I. Laid on top of it is a round loaf of bread and a small glass of salt has been inserted into a dip in the centre of the loaf.

'*Vitayemo*,' says Taras as we greet our friends with symbols of love and lasting friendship.

Dmitro bows his head and takes the loaf of bread from Taras. Olha breaks off a small piece, dips it into the salt and eats it. She passes a portion to Dmitro to do the same then he hands the loaf back.

We smile at one another, no doubt all of us remembering more lavish weddings at home in our villages.

Later I watch Olha take to the floor with Dmitro. Their first dance is a rather shy affair. I feel as if someone has taken my heart in their fist and is squeezing it tight. Roman and I had no dancing, just the UPA chaplain and Roman's *kurin*. But it was enough. As I watch Olha's sweet face pink with happiness, I know that this wedding in a bare hall in a strange land is enough too.

Taras says, 'Would you like to dance?'

'I can't,' I say.

'I'll teach you.'

'No, I know how to dance.' I just don't know how to explain.

'Do you know if he's still alive?' asks Taras.

I stare at him.

He goes on. 'Well, it's obvious, Natalya. You're young and beautiful. You're not interested in taking a lover. So there must be someone at home.'

I look and look at him, but can't speak. Has it been so obvious? I shake my head and go out of the canteen. The cold helps to cool my burning cheeks as I take deep breaths. In and out. Just keep breathing.

'Natalya,' says Taras quietly. I realise he's standing behind me. 'I'm sorry if I upset you.'

I shake my head.

He comes to stand beside me. 'I shouldn't have said anything. You're entitled to your secrets.'

I'm horrified by the wail which erupts from my mouth. It keeps pouring out of me. I can't stop it. I can only hear its shocking noise.

Taras takes me in his arms and holds me tight. As the

wailing subsides, it's followed by sobbing. He rocks me but doesn't let go. We stand there long enough to get cold then he leads me across the compound to our room. He helps me take my boots off before I climb into bed and face the wall. Taras lies down beside me on top of the blankets and puts his arm across me.

Chapter 28
Germany 1946

I walk across the compound to our little room hugging a pencil and notebook to my chest. I can now say, 'Good morning. My name is Natalya,' in English. The class is being held in a meeting room where one of the UNRRA volunteers is teaching about twenty of us. She's a Ukrainian Canadian, her family having emigrated after the First World War so she's the perfect teacher for us since she speaks both Ukrainian and English. I plan to surprise Olha with my skill and grin to myself as I approach our door. I fling it open saying, 'Good morning…' when the rest of my speech is torn from me. I revert to Ukrainian. 'What have you done to your hair?'

She's sitting on the bed simpering but she can't help blushing. She pats the short curls at the back of her head. 'It was getting to be such a nuisance, Natalya, and it was getting thin, with me being pregnant.'

'It'll get even thinner if you keep curling it.'

'I won't need to. This is what they call a permanent wave.'

'Permanent?'

'Until it grows out. Don't you like it?'

'Yes, I do.' I sit down beside her on the bed. 'Can I touch it?'

'Yes. Feel how soft it is.'

It is soft…but short.

'What did you do with your plaits?'

'Oh, they threw them away.'

I gasp. My lovely Ukrainian princess now looks like all the other girls in the camp.

'You look very pretty,' I say.

She smiles. 'You could have yours cut.'

I shake my head. 'No.'

'No?'

'No.'

'Alright, then. What have you got there?' She points at my notebook.

It's a soft exercise book like the ones we had at school in the village but this one is unlined. I have written in my smallest handwriting to make the pages last as long as possible.

'I'm learning English. Listen. *Good morning. My name is Natalya.*'

'Why?'

'Why what?'

'Why are you learning English?'

'Do you think they'll let us go home to live in peace with our families?'

'No, they won't.'

'So where can we go?'

'To England?'

'Yes.'

'Is that where you're going, Natalya?'

'If I can't go home, yes.'

'Why not America or Canada?'

'Too far. When things improve, we'll only have to cross a little sea and then we could even walk home to Halychyna. If we go to America, we'll have to cross an ocean.'

She looks down at her abdomen. 'What will I do?'

'You'll come, too.'

'And the baby?'

'The baby too. Why wouldn't the baby come?'

Her eyes fill with tears.

'It'll be fine,' I say. I put my arm around her shoulders.

'Dmitro will look after you. And you'll have me.'

She leans against me like a tired child. 'I want Mama.'

'I know. I do, too. But we're all there is. We'll look after each other.' I rock her as we contemplate our shadowy future.

***

Towards the end of March the Red Army officers return. We see them going into the offices but they don't come out for more than an hour. The news ripples through the camp and, despite the cold, we stand in groups at a safe distance watching the door of the Administrative block. Eventually they come out again and get into their jeep. They drive out of the camp gates to wholesale jeering and booing. There's safety in numbers.

But at our next *Appel* an announcement is made. The camp commander tells us:

'You may have heard of Resolution 92. It states that you must all be registered. My staff will be interviewing each of you so that we can compile information about your past histories and your employment skills.'

There's a muttering among the gathered thousands but he's not to be put off.

'You have nothing to fear. We would like to know how and where you could be employed in the future. Of course, if you want to return to your homes we will be glad to facilitate that.'

After we're dismissed I walk back with Taras to our room. Olha and Dmitro are already there.

'What are we going to do?' asks Olha.

'Tell them how much they need us,' says Dmitro.

Olha looks doubtful.

'Look,' I say to her, 'you may be pregnant now but you won't be forever. You need to tell them about your work in the factory. You were a skilled worker so that means you can be trained. You're a quick learner and can work with dangerous

261

machinery accurately. You're young and healthy…' I don't add and still only seventeen.

She looks at me in surprise. 'Well, if you put it like that…'

Taras smiles. 'And Natalya will be a diplomat.'

'My history's worse. I was a housemaid and I swept up at the factory.'

'Ah,' says Olha, 'you cooked and cleaned. You looked after three children. You were trusted in the household. Then you had industrial experience in the factory. Now you're learning English.'

'There you are,' says Taras. 'Me, I worked machinery while Dmitro hid in the store cupboard and read.'

Dmitro laughs. 'Yes, tell them that if they need lazy intellectuals then I'm their man.'

There's a knock at our door and Dmitro, still laughing, gets up to open it. Marichka is standing on the corridor, the fur collar on her coat turned up against her soft cheek.

'Aha, you,' he says. 'You'd better come in.'

She flicks a glance at Taras as she enters but he's polite to her. 'Good morning, Marichka.'

'Good morning,' she says. 'I hope I'm not disturbing you.'

'No,' says Dmitro. 'Taras and I were just saying we'd like a walk in the cold.'

The men pull on their coats and shuffle around Marichka, who's still standing in the doorway.

I pat my hand on my bed. She sits beside me. As the door closes, I say, 'What is it?'

'What do you think?'

'Marichka, you're the one who can charm the birds from the trees.' I stroke her collar with my forefinger. 'Do it now when it matters most.'

She nods. 'I managed to get this for you,' she says to Olha reaching into the folds of her woollen coat. Some Nazi's wife is colder somewhere, I think to myself. She pulls out a large ball of soft cream wool. Then like a magician, she removes a crochet hook from the sleeve of her coat.

'Oh, Marichka,' says Olha, squeezing the ball of wool. 'It's so soft. Where did you get it?'

Marichka shakes her head. 'I know it's not a lot. I might be able to get more but heaven knows what colour it'll be.'

'That doesn't matter,' says Olha. 'I've been worrying about clothes for the baby.' She strokes the ball of wool.

I look at the unforgiving crochet hook. 'Do you know what to do with this?'

'Yes, Mama taught me how.'

I turn to Marichka. 'Want to take a walk to talk over old times while Olha practices her crochet?'

'Yes, please.'

We leave Olha unravelling the end of the wool. We go out into the compound and down the lane.

'Who was the *starosta* when you left home?' I begin.

We trade questions and answers for the length of our walk.

Eventually I say, 'There, you've remembered it all. If you don't know an answer, make it up. They won't know everything.'

'We hope.'

'Remember to emphasise the skills that you can take into a new life.'

Marichka smiles at me.

'Well, perhaps you won't have to mention them all.'

But as I return alone to my room, I wonder how many of us have skills and experience we'll lie about or not mention. How useful will my knowledge of forest craft be?

'Well, Officer, I know better than to skyline and I can walk silently in a wood. I can track a clumsy walker. Oh, and I know the best way to attack a man if I'm unarmed.'

263

The UPA training didn't include lessons on how to handle interrogation. We were told to avoid it at all costs and were shown how to kill ourselves rather than be taken alive. So I'm on my own again.

When my turn comes to be screened I walk over to the offices alone, but as I cross the compound I feel Mama at my back. She catches up with me and is just behind my right shoulder. I don't look round for fear she'll disappear. But she's there. I put my shoulders back, raise my chin in an echo of Lyubochka. Mama knows I can't come home so she wants me to be safe even if it's across the sea. I know it as clearly as if she had shouted it across the compound to me.

I knock on the office door and enter.

***

'So how did it go?' asks Taras.

'Alright. I told them I'm preparing myself by learning English. But they know so little. They asked me if I would be able to cope with the alphabet. I had to remind them that under the Poles we all learned their alphabet as well as the Cyrillic alphabet. So I shouldn't have much difficulty in learning to type before I go to England.'

'Were they impressed?'

'Not really. 'Your country needs workers, too,' they said. So I said I would only work for Ukraine. That's my country. Russia isn't.'

'I shouldn't think they wanted to know that.'

'No, they didn't. But they can't send those of us from Halychyna back. We just have to be stubborn.'

He smiles. 'You're good at that.'

'I've had to be.'

So the Americans make lists of our skills, real and imaginary, while every one of us prepares to wait them out.

As the weather improves Taras gathers some of our precious Red Cross tins.

'What are you going to do with those?' I ask.

'I'll show you later,' he says leaving the room on his mysterious errand.

I meet him returning as I'm coming back from my English lesson.

'What have you got?' I ask in English.

'*Shcho*?'

I repeat the question in Ukrainian.

He shakes his head and I follow him into our room. He removes a dirty piece of fabric from his pocket and opens it out on our bed. In the hollow of his parcel lie some brown wrinkled seeds. I grin up at him.

'Where…'

'German farmers can't buy evaporated milk. We're going to have a garden, Natalya.'

I trace my finger through the seeds. 'Beans, peas and,' I hold up a small, pale brown, wrinkled ball, 'beetroot?'

'Yes. I wanted some potatoes but couldn't get any.'

'We could check what the kitchen throws away. There might be some small ones we could plant. Just think…we could make our own *borshch* and *varenyki* instead of those endless lentils. Where will we plant these?'

'At the back of this building. The men have been talking about digging it over, each of us having a section for ourselves.'

'Can I help?'

'Of course.'

We smile at one another in anticipation of a bit of earth of our own. Or at least borrowed by us.

But even the borrowing might prove to be short-term. A few days later, Dmitro strides into our room and slams the door.

'Mother of God!'

'What? What is it?' asks Olha.

'Those stupid boys…' He throws his coat onto the floor.

'Which boys?' asks Olha.

I mouth to her, 'Should I go?'

She gives a quick shake of the head and then Taras comes in anyway.

'It's alright,' he says to Dmitro. 'I've talked to them.'

Olha and I wait.

'And they won't go?'

'They won't go,' says Taras.

Dmitro breathes out loudly.

'Don't worry. It's all been sorted out.'

'What has?' I ask.

He glances at Dmitro who nods.

'Two boys from the next village to Dmitro,' he says. 'They told him they'd decided to go home. They were going to volunteer when they were next screened.'

'Bloody fools!' says Dmitro beginning to roll a cigarette.

'And?' I nudge Taras.

'They had no idea that they'd be interrogated at home. None at all.'

'Interrogated?' asks Olha.

'Yes. The NKVD would want to know which camp they'd been in and most important who else was there. You know, 'Did you have neighbours from home? Who were they?' Then they'd go round to Dmitro's and start terrorising his family until Dmitro went home.'

I stare at Taras. I hadn't thought of that one. 'Those Bolshevik devils!'

'Devils is right,' says Dmitro. 'Those stupid boys thought they could go home and live happily ever after with no consequences for themselves or anyone else.'

'And you explained to them?' I ask Taras.

'Yes. They understand now.' He pauses looking at his hands.

'Taras?' I say putting my hand on his arm.

He looks up at me. 'They cried.'

The four of us sit in silence. There's no going back into that tight trap. We can only move forward into the unknown.

**

By the time we harvest our peas and beans, another kind of harvest has come. I'm sitting on the doorstep of our building shelling peas when I hear a cry indoors. I pick up my bowl and run into our room where Olha is standing, looking at the puddle around her feet.

'It's alright,' I say. 'Can you walk?'

She looks at me as if from far away. 'Mama?'

'It's me. Natalya. I'm going to walk you over to the infirmary. Alright?'

She doesn't nod but keeps looking at her soaked feet.

I put one arm around her shoulders, the other where her waist should be and propel her through the door. We pass the rooms where our neighbours are also squashed in cosy foursomes. No one is to be seen. The corridor seems to have stretched although Olha is compliant enough, walking slowly towards the outer door. When we reach its sunlit rectangle we take two steps down and then I point Olha diagonally across the compound. It seems like a huge expanse to cross but I keep her moving. After several steps she pauses and grips my hand. I see her abdomen ripple. I try to keep calm. I've never seen a baby delivered but when Olha begins to pant I sense the crisis is over. We set off again, one foot in front of the other.

There are a group of women gossiping in front of the other married quarters. They look up as we pass and I call out, 'Do any of you know Dmitro?'

One of them calls back, 'I do.'

'Can you go and find him? He's probably playing chess. Tell him the baby's started.'

'Alright,' and she sets off towards the tables outside the canteen.

Olha and I keep putting one foot in front of the other.

As we reach the infirmary, a nurse comes out of the door. 'Oh,' she says, 'you'd better come in.' She takes Olha's other arm and guides us up the steps. 'I was just going to fetch some tea but it'll have to wait. You're more important,' she says to Olha, who barely glances at her.

We lead Olha into the ward and the nurse guides her to a bed. She helps her to sit down. 'I'll go and get my colleague and then we'll examine you. What's your name?'

Olha just looks at her knees.

'She's called Olha.'

'Don't worry, Olha,' says the nurse. 'We'll soon have you comfortable.'

As she walks away, I kneel beside my friend and rub her hand. 'Alright, my lovely?'

She seems to wake up. 'Natalya, don't leave me.'

'I don't know whether I'll be allowed to stay.'

'Don't go.'

'I'll stay if I can,' I say but I can see she's not listening as she's gripped by another contraction.

Two nurses clatter towards us, one carrying a bowl of warm water, the other pushing a trolley of instruments.

Olha flinches.

'It's alright,' I tell her. 'They know what they're doing.'

The taller nurse parks her trolley and wheels over a couple of screens, creating a barricade around Olha's bed.

'You'll have to go now,' she says to me.

I get up to leave but Olha lets out a piercing shriek. 'Nooo!'

'Olha, I'll just be outside.'

'Don't leave me!'

We hear loud footsteps thumping across the floor then the screen is torn back. Dmitro's head appears but both nurses shout, 'Out!' in unison. The stockier one charges towards him. I hear her forcing him from her domain. 'Out, out, out!'

'She's my wife.'

'She's my patient. You can wait outside.'

All goes quiet. The nurse returns alone to Olha's bedside. 'You can stay,' she says to me, 'but don't faint or make a fuss.'

I don't…

***

A few weeks later on a Sunday after Mass I hold Olha's baby close. His head is warm against my chest and I'm enjoying the weight of him in my arms. At the moment he looks like an angel because he's asleep. His eyelashes lie against his rosy cheek, his mouth is partly open. I know he'll fly awake when Father Andriy pours the holy water over him.

This baby will be my godson so I will be able to borrow him from Olha from time to time. It will be a joy to watch this small creature grow. I'm glad Olha has tied me to her with her request that I watch over him. It means we must cling to one another until Levko is safely stowed in manhood.

'What are you going to call him?' I had asked her when she sat up in bed nursing him in the infirmary.

'Levko. For my little brother.' Her lip had trembled.

'Who will one day meet his nephew and be proud of him.'

She had tried to smile.

'He will. You'll take Levko home to meet his uncle and *baba*.'

'But not his aunty. God knows where Sofia is.'

269

So I stand as the baby is baptised with Taras beside me as the boy's godfather. I know Olha and Dmitro want to tie the two of us together. They want us to marry almost as much as Taras does. I'm not ready.

But I'm called back to Levko to renounce Satan and all his works. The devil would want the soul of this four week old child apparently. Well, he can't have him. This baby is ours. And he is. He wakes us all at night. We hear him sucking with gusto and smell his other activities. He has come to dominate our room although Taras and I escape often into the fresh air.

After the priest has made the baby cry by pouring cold water over his head, I wrap him up again in his *kryzhma* – the white cloth which will protect him from all evil. He's red in the face and as he stuffs his clenched fist into his mouth I try to rock him out of his misery. He needs Olha's breast to have his faith in the world restored.

I hand him to her as soon as I can and she sits in a corner of the canteen, where she opens her blouse to feed her angry son. Dmitro and Taras pour drinks for the sudden onslaught of friends come to wish the baby well. But they'll leave a gift of silver for luck. I see Marichka among the crowd and Olha raises her eyebrows at me.

'I don't know how she does it but she's kitted Levko out single-handedly.'

'Let her. She wanted to give something back for passing the screening.'

'Yes, but it was you who helped her with that.'

I lean over and kiss her pink cheek. 'We're *kumi* now. We're family.' We have entered the special relationship of parents and godparents who, in the absence of our blood relatives, will make up our extended family in exile.

Chapter 29
Germany 1946

Taras comes into our room grinning from ear to ear.

'What's happened?' I ask.

'I've found a master tailor,' he replies.

I look at him unsure why this is such good news.

'I began to train as a tailor in my village, or at least in the next village along. Mine was too small.'

This is the first time he has told me about his home.

'Someone told me there was an older man here, a Ukrainian from Vienna. He's prepared to teach the younger men some of his tailoring skills.'

'That's good.'

He must hear the doubt in my voice because he goes on. 'First of all, Natalya, it might impress the English. They need us as farm labourers but they also need clothes to wear. It must be similar there to the rest of Europe – clothing shortages after the war. Secondly, I can make some money for myself by sewing for other people. It's good to be able to work. I don't want to depend on Red Cross parcels and handouts.'

'Me neither,' I say and wish it was as easy for me to find work. 'Will he train women?'

'I don't know. But there's talk of some sewing machines being delivered. You could see if they're teaching people how to use them.'

'I will,' I say.

The sewing machines aren't the only things to arrive in the camp. People have been coming and going recently. A group of Lithuanians moved from our camp to one further north where

271

they'd heard there were more of their own and we've had an influx of Ukrainian men. Like all of us, it's not clear what they've been doing for the last three or four years. Their arrival causes some ripples in the pond of rumours.

Taras and I see them one evening not long after their arrival. It's not being called a meeting but lots of us gather after supper. The talk is all about how we should fight back against the Russians to see if we can't carve out our own country. There are about thirty new faces in the crowded canteen. They're mostly young, in their twenties, but one or two are a bit older. I listen as they talk about how an independent state might be achieved. I shift in my seat to examine each of them carefully. There's one who talks of training us while we're at a loose end in the camp. I watch him closely. He's saying the same sort of things Vasyl used to say…but it's not him. I feel oddly disappointed. The atmosphere of excitement and hope they've created reminds me of the days spent tramping the forests to deliver leaflets to other villages, the days of seeing Roman set off with his *kurin* on secret missions. I feel taken back to my younger self. There's a man with black curls and a dimple in his chin… but he's not my man. Stupidly, I look to check and then stare at my hands in my lap. These are the hands which held his lifeless body. There's voting for a committee before we begin to disperse, but some remain to talk in excited groups. I just want to get out of there. I hurry out into the starry evening.

'Did you know any of them?' asks Taras.

He makes me jump. 'Know who?'

'Any of those new men?'

'No. Why would I?'

'No reason. You seemed interested to see who they were.'

'I was interested in what they were saying. Weren't you?'

'Yes, but even if we form self-help groups here, I don't see how that'll help us get our country back.'

'It might not. There's nothing wrong with wanting your own country.'

'No, of course there isn't. It's what everybody wants.'

'Yes, they do. Enough to die for it.'

'Natalya, are you alright?'

'Yes. I've got a bit of a headache. I'm going to walk for a while. The fresh air might clear it.'

'Want me to come with you?'

'No.' I see his disappointment but I can't deal with it now. 'I'll see you later.'

***

I don't join this political group, but I do join the women's group that grows out of all this talk of our country. We can't go home yet but we can preserve what we still have of our own culture. Olha and I go to the meetings and help organise activities, including a dance.

On a lovely summer evening, the compound is strung with blue and yellow bunting and the musicians gather. A bar is set up on trestle tables. Some of the UNRRA volunteers look in but are clearly confused by the wild dancing of the Hutsuls from the mountains. The high-pitched pipes and whirling reels are beyond American experience. After smiling politely they withdraw.

The dancing settles later to waltzes and quicksteps. Olha and Dmitro take to the floor, Olha pink-cheeked despite being married to her partner. Taras looks at me and holds out his arms. My feet itch to dance, so I smile and move into his hold. We whirl around and around to the waltz. I let myself lean back against his arm knowing that he won't let me fall.

Waltz follows waltz and, although the band have a singer, all the dancers sing along too.

'Nich yaka misyachna…'

273

'The night is so bright with moonlight…'

My head spins. As the music pauses, I say to Taras, 'I'm so hot!'

'Do you want a drink?'

I shake my head. 'Maybe later. I just want to cool off first.'

We move away from the dancing and walk towards the hedge where a tall chestnut tree provides shade in the daytime and cool shelter in the evening. I lean against its friendly trunk and Taras leans towards me. He kisses my cheek and when I don't object, he tries to kiss my lips.

I move my head away.

Taras sighs.

'I've been thinking,' I say.

He waits.

'You've been so good to me. You are so good…'

'But…'

'There's a lot you don't know about me.'

'You've said that before.'

'I know I have. But I want you to know.'

'Know what?'

'I was married before,' I say in a rush.

'And you were a partisan.'

'How did you know?'

'I've known from the beginning.'

'How?'

'You knew how to stand guard.' He pauses. 'Then when those nationalists came you were looking for someone.'

'Not my husband.'

'No?'

'No.'

There's a silence while he waits for my story.

'He died in my arms,' I say at last.

'Oh, Natalya,' and he hugs me. He hugs me. 'Natalya,

Natalya,' he murmurs.

I can't help myself. I cry and cry. He seems not to mind. He just holds me, rocking me while I mourn Roman. I think I won't ever stop crying but I do. He gives me a scrap of handkerchief.

'Better?' he asks.

I nod. I do feel better. I blow my nose. 'Yes, I am. Thank you.'

He keeps his arms around me.

'No one else knows.'

'No, I didn't think so.'

'Not even Olha.'

'No.'

'I only told Mama and my sisters the night before I left…' Then I tell Taras the whole story.

When I've finished I feel hollowed out.

Taras looks into my face. 'I think you should sleep now. You need to rest.'

I nod and he leads me back to our room. We go to sleep spooned together, but when I wake up the sun is high and I'm alone in bed. I can hear Olha crooning to Levko on the other side of the curtain. I get up and after kissing my *kuma* and my godson I go to wash myself. Then I walk over to our strip of garden where Taras is bending over to weed between our precious crop of beans.

He looks up as I approach and I feel flooded with relief when he smiles at me.

'Good morning. Have you caught up on your sleep?'

'Yes,' I say.

Chapter 30
England August 1992

The two cars headed for the higher level of the car park in the hope that they would be able to park side by side. They didn't quite achieve this but managed to park opposite one another. The cousins, Val, Lydia and Simon, tumbled out of Tom's car and hurried across to their mothers emerging more sedately from Adrian's car. Taras climbed out of the front seat stiffly.

'Are you alright, *Tatu*?' asked Lyuba.

'*Tak, donechko.*'

Tom and Adrian exchanged 'We made good time' comments and then helped Lyuba, Vera and Nadiya unload their luggage. Taras watched as the large hand luggage and larger suitcases were assembled. The men locked the cars and the whole party turned towards the lifts, spreading out across the width of driving space between the parked cars.

For the moment the sisters did not have the burden of their luggage as the others played their supporting role in the adventure. Adrian, Tom and Simon shouldered the hand luggage while Taras and his grand-daughters pulled the heavy cases lightly on their wheels, the shiny exteriors hiding weeks of discussion.

There had been the creation of an inventory of immediate relatives: the two aunties, Lyubochka and Verochka, their sons and daughters and their children. What to take?

'Assume they have nothing,' Taras had said.

'What will the Communists have allowed them to have?'

'Nothing, you can be sure.'

So English toys and sweets were bought for the children, sweaters and cardigans for the cousins and two beautiful woollen coats for the aunties. They had also created an album of photographs charting Natalya's life in England and had included pictures of the nieces and nephew as they approached adulthood. Their own clothing and toiletries for the fortnight's visit were crammed into their hand luggage along with the precious cameras. However, Nadiya had secreted an extra pair of shoes in her suitcase. Now they trundled along the concrete floor to the lift for Departures.

Lyuba, Vera and Nadiya were having to break their journey in Amsterdam. They would then fly on to Kyiv but once the heavy luggage was checked in they would feel freer. The three sisters queued at the busy KLM desk and were about to shuffle forward into the space created ahead of them when they were barged aside by four middle-aged women speaking in Russian.

'Excuse me,' said Vera. 'There's a queue.'

The Russian women continued talking to one another, taking no notice of Vera and her sisters.

Lyuba leaned forward into the face of the nearest woman. 'There is a queue here and we were in front of you. You need to be behind us.' She pointed to the space behind.

The woman gave her a lizard stare then turned away to talk to her companions again.

Nadiya leaned towards her sisters saying in loud Ukrainian, 'Never mind, let the old whores go first.'

The Russian women did pause then to look the sisters over but returned to their conversation with barely a blink.

'Thank God for independence,' said Nadiya. 'Can you imagine being ruled by the likes of them?'

Vera turned away from the women to look at her family across the concourse. 'Look at *Tato*.'

'He's getting to look old,' said Lyuba.

'Of course he is,' replied Vera. 'He's lost Mama and he's worried about us.'

'He'll still be here when we get back,' said Nadiya, voicing Lyuba's fear. 'He'll want to hear all about it.'

Finally, they stepped forward across the privacy line to the check-in desk.

'Are you travelling together?'

Across the shiny Departures hall, Taras, his sons-in-law and grandchildren waited.

'I'm definitely going next year,' said Val to her cousins but looking at her father.

'So am I,' said Lydia.

'It'll be different next year,' said Tom. 'Once we know how your mothers got on.'

'They'll be fine,' said Adrian. 'They've all got British passports.'

Taras remained silent. Simon put his arm around his grandfather's shoulders. 'Don't worry, *Dido*. Can you imagine anyone taking on those three?'

The sisters left the check-in desk and returned to their family clutching their boarding passes inside their passports.

'You should go through security now,' said Tom, 'in case it's busy.'

The farewells began.

Lyuba held Valeria to her hardly able to believe that they would be separated by thousands of miles and half a dozen borders.

Lydia hugged her mother and then Vera turned to Simon.

'OK then, just a quick one,' he said.

Nadiya embraced her father. 'Don't worry, *Tatu*. We'll have a great time looking at Mama's village.'

As Adrian held Lyuba tight, she returned her husband's embrace but said, 'Please keep an eye on him.'

278

'I've said I will. Don't worry. One of us will call in on him every day. You go and find your Mama,' and he kissed the top of her head.

Lyuba turned to Taras and kissed his cheek. 'Bye, *Tatu*. Try not to worry.'

He nodded and she held him for a moment longer.

Then Vera hugged her father. 'If you need anything call Tom.'

'I'll be alright,' he muttered.

There was a moment's pause when they all seemed to look at one another unwilling to break the contact. Then Nadiya turned away saying, 'Let's get through security then we can have a coffee.'

They turned towards the escalator and the sisters stepped onto the moving stairs. As they rose up into the Departure lounge they looked back at the group below. The youngsters smiled and waved, while the husbands tried not to look anxious. Taras stood a little apart from the others and, as his girls looked towards him, he raised his hand in farewell.

***

Germany 1947

I wave to Olha from the bus. She's clutching Levko while Dmitro has one arm around her shoulders and is waving to us with the other. Taras leans across me to wave.

'We'll see you soon,' I mouth to Olha.

She nods trying to hold back her tears. I make a writing gesture and she nods back. We will keep in contact with one another even as the sea separates us.

Dmitro and Olha have decided not to leave the camp yet.

279

They wouldn't be allowed to take Levko to England, where the authorities are only interested in those of us who are free enough and strong enough to work. Dmitro was willing to discuss the possibility of leaving the baby with foster parents, but Olha wouldn't hear of it. There are couples who have gone on to England, leaving their babies and toddlers behind in the paid care of other Ukrainian DPs. But Olha has seen those children's treatment vary and she doesn't want to be parted from her baby. I think she's right. Who would care for him as she would? Although we stateless people are beginning to be resettled, life is still unpredictable. So Taras and I will go on ahead and try to prepare the way for our *kumi* to join us later.

We are ready. The door to the east is closed so for now we will travel west to make a life. I can't tell Mama and my sisters that this is only temporary but I send my thoughts to them. There have been no letters for more than two years. I don't think they're dead. I miss them but I don't feel their absence, so I comfort myself that they must be alive and that I will see them again. I wonder if Mama knows I dream of her. I saw her again last night. I went to tell her I couldn't find my travel pass, but the door to our house was shut. I rattled the handle and knocked on the door but no one answered. I looked in through the window. Mama was at the stove cooking. She was stirring something in a pot then she looked up and spoke to someone. I couldn't see who she was talking to. I knocked on the window but she didn't look up. She turned back to her cooking. 'Mama, Mama,' I wanted to say, 'I can't find my papers.' But she didn't hear me.

I reach into my pocket and feel the card cover of my precious pass enabling me to travel to England. Taras looks at me.

'Is it still there?' he asks with a smile.

'Yes, I've still got it.'

The bus driver starts the engine and as we pull away from the camp we all wave and shout '*Dopobachenya!*' through the windows. I turn in my seat to see Olha for as long as possible. She's waving too, but as we turn out of the camp I see Dmitro leading her away to our little room which they will now have to themselves. I turn to look at the road ahead.

***

It is two days before we board the ship. The bus deposits us at the station and we get on the train to cross Austria. The mountains make us gasp. There's more excitement as we run along the flat plain to the Adriatic coast. I feel like a child as I look at the expanse of water. Our river Dniester was wide and strong, but this calm blue stretches away to the horizon where the sky and sea slide into one another.

However, there's no time to gaze at this strange beauty. We're marched from the train to the ship. I tremble as we approach its bulk. It's bigger than almost any building I've ever seen yet, somehow, it will take us across the sea to England.

Taras reaches for my hand and we walk towards the gangplank like children. We have to walk in single file up into the ship so Taras lets me go ahead of him. I struggle with the weight of my bundle which is tied with string. My worldly goods have somehow accumulated over the last two years. I still have my *rushnyk* but I now have two wedding photographs.

I step onto the deck and as I'm directed by a crew member, I reach for Taras and say in my best English, 'Married quarters, please?'

He pauses then says, 'Oh yes…' The rest of what he says is lost, but I gather he's re-directing us. We find we're to share a cabin for ten with two towers of five bunks. So we claim our bunks, one on top of the other and wait to see who our travelling companions will be and whether we can safely leave our luggage. Four other couples eventually appear and there's no choice about our worldly goods as we're called to an *Appel* on deck. We line up, are issued with life vests and instructed what to do in case of emergency.

The engines rumble then the tone changes slightly as we see the land begin to withdraw. There's a cheer and Taras and I reach for each other's hands. The ship pulls out to sea, but instead of turning south it continues to travel east. There's a grumbling of voices as we turn to one another.

'Why aren't we going south?' I ask Taras.

'I don't know.'

I can see he's worried too.

There's no one to ask. We're surrounded by other DPs, all looking from the direction we're taking to the direction we'd rather take.

Someone whistles and others take it up.

'Have they lied to us?' I ask Taras, a ripple of fear running through me.

'Perhaps.'

The shout goes up, 'They're taking us back to Russia!' It's followed by a loud booing. My heart is thumping in my chest. Is this it then? After all my soul-searching is my decision to be taken from me?

I feel the crowd's anxiety throbbing as loudly as the ship's engines when there's a lull in the mechanical sound, a pause in the ship's movement and the huge vessel begins to turn. It travels through ninety degrees, the engines thrumming loudly, and then we set off again. South.

The cheer which goes up could power us all the way to England as we sail south through the Adriatic to meet the Mediterranean.

Taras and I make for the railing and lean on it. We're not sure where we are or where this ship is going but we look

282

towards the hazy horizon and grip one another's hands tightly.

To be continued...

Historical Note

Natalya's story begins in 1943 when the Germans occupied the whole of Ukraine. Hitler's plan was to use the country for *Lebensraum*, living space for the German population. The Ukrainian population, therefore, would have no rights to their land but could serve another of Hitler's purposes, that of slave labourers. The *Ostarbeiter* programme, overseen by Goering, took approximately two million young men and women from Ukraine to work in factories, on farms and as domestic servants in Germany. There were quotas to be filled and retribution was harsh for those who did not comply.

Throughout the Nazi Occupation the Ukrainian Insurgent Army harried and harassed the German troops. However, after the Red Army success at Stalingrad, the tide turned. The Germans were driven west by Stalin's hordes and the *Ukrainska Povstanska Armiya* had two enemies to fight in its bid for independence.

The effects of the repeated defeats in the east were also felt in Germany where there were not only increasing shortages but the Allied bombing programme became more and more intense. Even before Germany surrendered, Churchill, Roosevelt and Stalin met at Yalta to discuss the re-establishment of nations. Stalin was adamant that he wanted the return of any former citizens of the USSR at the end of the war. Churchill and Roosevelt complied in part to protect their own prisoners of war. However, for Natalya and others like her from Western Ukraine, there was a loophole. They had not been citizens of the USSR in 1939 as Poland had been in control of Western Ukraine, so they could not be returned to face Stalin's wrath. He treated any returnees as traitors who were either summarily executed on returning home or deported to Siberia, often to be worked to death in the gulags.

After Germany had surrendered, there was a hiatus as the Allies advanced at speed to cover as much of the country as possible before the Red Army advance. They were then faced with millions of displaced persons whom they wanted to tidy away as quickly as possible. Many nationalities who had been imprisoned by the Germans were delighted to be helped home but for those who might have to face Stalin's NKVD the prospect was grim.

The United Nations Relief and Rehabilitation Administration was responsible for caring for those who could not return home. They created camps, often on previously military sites, where they provided food, shelter and medical support. Millions of Ukrainians were returned to their homeland by the Allies until September 1945 when Eisenhower decreed that there would be no more forcible repatriation. However, Red Army officers were still allowed to enter the US zone and interview those defined as stateless to put pressure on them to return. Some buckled under the repeated screening but most remained convinced of the dangers of returning.

A solution eventually presented itself as the Allied countries suffered a shortage of labour. The hundreds of thousands of displaced persons languishing in camps in Europe could be relocated to Britain, Australia, America and Canada to be used as cheap labour. Thus people like Natalya and Taras found themselves on board ships bound for the west.

The ensuing Cold War destroyed any hope of returning to Ukraine and for many even letters to their families were prohibited. Their lives were lived on opposite sides of the Iron Curtain until an easing began in the 1980's with perestroika under Gorbachev. For Ukrainians, this culminated in the declaration of Independence on 24 August 1991 and the freedom to travel in and out of the country.

The history of this period is complex but some of the texts which I found useful and full of fascinating detail are listed below. All very readable, they gave me an unfailingly horrific picture of the nightmare that Europe was for Natalya and the millions like her.

Under the Bombs: The German Home Front 1942-1945 by Earl R. Beck

Berlin: The Downfall 1945 by Antony Beevor

The Long Road Home: The Aftermath of the Second World War by Ben Shephard

The Bitter Road to Freedom: The Human Cost of Allied Victory in World War II Europe by William I. Hitchcock

DPs: Europe's Displaced Persons, 1945-51 by Mark Wyman

***

For a complete bibliography, go to my website:
www.mariadziedzanauthor.com

Author Biography

MARIA DZIEDZAN was born in Grimsby in 1951. She studied Philosophy at Nottingham University before becoming an English teacher. She taught for several decades in Nottinghamshire and then retired from teaching to focus on her writing. *When Sorrows Come* was her first novel. It won The Big Bingham Book Read in 2015 and was one of the finalists for the Historical Novel Society Indie Award 2016. *Driven Into Exile* is the second book in Maria's *My Lost Country* series. She is married with two children and lives in north Nottinghamshire.

You can visit Maria's author page on Amazon where you can find out more about her other books and where you can follow her so you receive updates when she publishes a new novel automatically.

The award winning first book in the *My Lost Country* series, mentioned earlier, *When Sorrows Come* can be found on all the Amazon sites.

Also if you enjoyed reading this book and would like to share that enjoyment with others, then please take the time to write a review.

Reviews are a great way to spread the word about worthy authors and will help them be rewarded for their hard work.

Acknowledgements

As ever, many of the details in this story came from my father, Ivan Semak, in our seemingly endless conversations about the war years and I am grateful for his approval of the final product as being honest. I am also deeply indebted to Katarina Zacharko for sharing painful memories of the DP camps so generously with me.

I would like to thank the readers of the early drafts for their thoughtful consideration of the writing and the time they took to give me such helpful and detailed feedback. I am especially grateful to Sonia Iwanczuk, Steve Taylor and Dr Joy Sullivan. I am also grateful to Larissa Dziedzan, Alex Dziedzan and Zig Dziedzan for their constant support and encouragement and their frank thoughts on the work in progress. I would like to express my thanks to the readers of *When Sorrows Come* who also kept encouraging me by asking when the next novel would be completed.

This novel would not be the finished article without the invaluable help of Jonathan Veale at *www.Writeaway.co.uk*. Nor would it have appeared at all without the expertise of Brian Stephens at *www.moulinwebsitedesign.com*.

I would like to thank Julia Marriott for the thorough proof-reading she gave the manuscript towards its completion, but especially for the inspiration she gave me in the first place. I also really appreciated the linguistic expertise of Linda Retberg and Eva Kampichler who corrected my many German errors. Any mistakes which remain are my own.

Made in the USA
Middletown, DE
24 July 2017